Map of Gaia

For Robert
I love how one can get involved in conversation
Hope you keep training with your coding

CALUM

(BOOK ONE OF GAIA)
By

Matthew Hamilton

with kindness

Argus Enterprises International
North Carolina***New Jersey
www.a-argusbooks.com

08/10/10

CALUM
All Rights Reserved © 2009
by Matthew Hamilton

A-Argus Better Book Publishers, LLC

For information:
A-Argus Better Book Publishers, LLC
Post Office Box 914
Kernersville, North Carolina 27285
www.a-argusbooks.com

ISBN: 978-09841342-1-2
ISBN: 0-9841342-1-2

Book Cover designed by Dubya

Printed in the United States of America

Book One

CALUM

1

I AM

The sun was breaking the rise of the forest canopy. A musty smell drifted through the air and the foliage of the dark murmuring forest. Between its trees, rays of light filtered through in those angelic beams, to light the ferns in front of him.

He could hear a gentle sound of a waterfall splashing nearby, and stood just listening; he was dazed from something he couldn't remember. *'Why am I here?'* he thought, sure there was a reason at the back of his mind somewhere.

He touched his dried blood-stained hair, short and brown, and faded down to his ears. Bruises dotted his slim, bare chest, with dried blood at his shoulder, which he was certain was from his head. He searched the unfamiliar surroundings of ferns and trees that disappeared upwards into dense foliage. Nothing around him was giving him clues to how he came to stand beside the small rays of sunlight.

He began to walk towards the sound of the waterfall, the lightly cascading water mesmerizing him in its direction. The ferns were crushed between his seemingly young bare feet, as he etched his way through the woods. The sound of the water seems familiar to him, like a past memory scratching to be heard at the back of his mind. *'Where am I?'* he thought as the leaves rustled at his footsteps. *'Who am I?'* He passed through the last of the trees that hid the gorgeous small pool, surrounded by patches of small white flowers and fed by the gentle run of the steep waterfall.

He noticed the water was crystal clear, its bottom of pebbles clean through the water. He knelt down at its edge, and cupped his hands under the water and brought the handful to his mouth. He took a few gulps and splashed another handful over his face, closing his eyes to the water, then looking over his body; his hands felt into his light brown trousers pockets. He has nothing. No money and no weapon. But somehow he felt safe, and at the same time. *'Surely I should have something.'*

He ran a hand through the brown grit-filled and blooded hair. He looked into the lightly rippling water, thinking of washing the blood and dirt from his hair; he went wading into the water. Its coolness made him shudder as it caressed his body; enjoying the feel as it touched him. It soothed his skin as he floated in its center, deep enough for him not to be able to touch the stony surface. He stared upwards, while the pools water went down the stream, and the birds sung to the air and the earth. He knew nothing, but somehow in the tranquil pool and the cascade of the waterfall, he felt safe.

He swam to the falling water and found a ledge just behind the waterfall that he felt with his hands. While his head was splashed with cool water that begun to clear the dried blood away, his head twinged with pain as he soaked, and he knew that the blood was his. He lolled backwards against the sloping and stepped rock, letting his head rest against it, and his hairless body relaxed, releasing its tension.

Σ

The birds began to brave the water's edge while his head was hidden behind the cascade, the birds beating their wings and throwing over clean water. The water fell upon his chest, and he looked wonderingly at the roof of the cave and the walls around him; strange; and patterned with swirls that had been carved into the rock. He rolled onto his front; the waterfall smashed his back, and he could see clearly to the back of the cave, cobbled stone placed there by someone. And on both sides were a total of four torches, placed into sconces, resting unlit for unknown decades. Below each of them, in a small inlet, were two flint stones that he knew he could use to light them. What took his eyes most was the iron door, crossed with wood struts that supported an emblem in its center, a protective hand around a globe of the world.

He pushed himself up onto his feet and walked the few feet to the door. *'Who would live here?'* He rapped upon the door. Nothing. Just the sound of his hand meeting iron.

Still, the moments passed, and no one answered. He stretched out his hand and took hold of the large bronze handle, turning the bronze loop and pushed. It opened easily, the hinges creaking as the metals rubbed. The door clanged against the wall of a corridor. A dark passage lay ahead.

He went over to a torch, and picked out the flints beneath, and held them just over its head. A bright spark flashed from the flints as they were struck against each other, landing onto the torch and burning instantly. A flame soon rose and spread, turning the dark grey rock bright with amber from the flickering light. He lifted the torch from its sconce and walked into the stone passageway, stopping briefly to peer down the length, staring into the eerie darkness. He felt no fear just intrigue.

He carried on, the torch brightening the way. The walls were stone slabs placed on top of each other. The tunnel went deeper, sloping downwards at first, until it turned with stairs spiraling downwards. His bare feet were making no tapping, only a faint slap of flesh against stone that echoed harmlessly.

He had an instinctive feeling that no matter what he could handle anything. And yet memories did not come. He still could not remember who he was, except a boy without much fear.

The stairwell was narrow and went down quite a way. An adrenaline-pushed feeling kept him moving downwards. The light easily and brightly was clearing the darkness, and showing that there was nothing there. He liked the strange place, and its harmonized echoes.

"Another!" His soft voice called, on sighting another door. The same emblem was upon the face of this door as well."What's behind you, another passage?" he asked into the air. He pushed the door, leaving it to swing with ease.

He gasped at the sight before him and was frozen in place by a huge painting hanging above a second level and, behind a dais that was reached by two parallel, inwardly-curved stairs.

'*Is that me?*'

Having seen his face in the water's reflection of the pool, his green eyes now recognized himself in the huge cathedral-sized painting that was centered on the back wall of the temple. The second tier's painting overlooked two lines of statues, beasts, dragons and two- legged people, some taller than him, and some massive beast-like men, all lining the wall's edge, glowing from the flickering flames that were lighting his face. He was breathless, the air seemingly lost to him. His heart pumping faster at the sight of himself upon the canvass, of five separate pictures blended into each other. The center one of him, spread-eagle like a star, white lights pouring off of him. The white blended up into the top right picture of him, converting into black, then as lit, until bright with him walking bare-chested with fire coming off his finger tips. He began to walk across the stone floor beside the statues along the right towards the painting.

The first of the statues was of *Eden*; goddess of the darkened touch. A beautiful woman, clearly a witch of some sort; her whole body was covered tightly and was, in a sense, just as revealing.

The bottom picture was of him attacking with lightning, the painting covered in strikes of electrified energy struck out by his hands.

He walked pass a reptilian dragon, wingless and surrounded by flames. *Castelli*; *dios del fuego*, god of fire. He looked next to a bird of prey. *Quetzalcoatl*; god of the white lightning. Then as he stepped on, he looked back to the painting. The bottom left was of him sliding down ice, balancing on his feet upon ice that was smooth and like a slide. His eyes returned to the statues. One of *Shiva*; lady of Ice. Dressed in tight shorts and her flat stomach left revealed, her hair fell down around her shoulders, and her eyes were closed, her head down like someone in prayer.

It was the top left painting that took most of his attention, and he had glanced at it from the start. It was of him moments before, within the gentle pool and its serene background. It shocked him that it could be so exact, and it could not have been put there after he had waded into the water. He moved on to the next statue believing what he was seeing was real.

An old frail-looking man, with a beard that reached past his stomach, and hair that had never been brushed. And even the black statue was sculpted so immaculately, that he could see each wrinkle upon the god's arms and face: *Thor*; storm god. His eyes were frowning in anger.

A man with wings as large as from his feet to head length, and a chest bulkier and wider to accommodate powerful bone and ligaments, so he could take himself up in flight: *Wowan*; god of speed. And a few steps to one side was a dragon. And he stood before it, with the torch keeping the chill away; he could feel the monster trying to break through the heat coming from his fire. He was sure this dragon was larger than those gods before. Although the statue was the same size, it gave an appearance of greater height and strength. *Bahamant*; god of flare.

The next black statue made him smile. Surrounded by cakes, sweets, biscuits and cookies, pies, fish and steaks, and standing proudly amongst it all, was *Osiris*; god of food; his bare chest skinny and showing his ribs. His mouth was wide open to take a chuck of a cake that he was placing greedily into his mouth. The god was the last statue along the side he was on, so he climbed the stairs up to the painting, the torch changing hands as he walked between the dais and painting. Nothing sat around, or looked like anything could be hidden there or behind the dais. He looked back at the painting.

"What is the point?"

The temple rumbled as his voice echoed, and dust trickled down from the ceiling. He sharply looked upwards as a beam of white wavy light shot down upon him. He was unable to dodge; too fast, the beam engulfed and surrounded him, pulling him upwards into the air before the painting. His arms and legs were drawn out, and a power begun to fill him. A perfect mirror image of the temples painting that he had just looked at. His eyes wide open and fixated upon the source above him.

"You have come," a strong voice rang out, as he winced at the ache of his limbs being forcefully stretched. "We have searched for you, Calum; searched for someone who has the ability."

"Why! I couldn't even remember who I am," he called through blinding light, understanding Calum was clearly he.

"You must save Gaia from the evil that comes for her. You may not understand now, but before the end you will. She gives you access to her power."

He felt himself stronger as the energy filled him, so much more that his head no longer ached.

"Why can't you do it?" He shouted out. The feeling of power surging through him had ceased.

"I am just a voice. These gods; find them, for they are the greatest power Gaia can offer."

The light vanished, and he fell to slap on the ground, the stone breaking his fall and forcing his breath away. He winced in pain. "You could have lowered me," he moaned.

He waited a moment as the pain subsided, and he felt something strange behind him, running furry along his back.

6

He sat up quickly grabbing around at it, grasping it within his hands. His eyes turned wide, surprised. "A tail!" he sat there confused, ignoring the cold biting at his bare skin. "What did you give me that for?" He asked into the cold darkness, his eyes could not even see the painting or dais.

Calum stood up, gently feeling the soft fine fur, and shivered at the cold. "Thanks for letting the torch go out," he said. Then thoughts of the painting flickered into his mind. *'Fire!'* he thought; he knew he could do it, he had felt the power, the strength fill him. He thought of the way the flames in the painting had shaped around his fingers, and he raised his hand, barely seen through the darkness. Shivering, he stared at his hand and focused on fire. Immediately flames ripped around the skin and over his fingers. Impervious to the fire, his hands remained undamaged, as the flames wrapped around, lighting the temple once more. He grinned at the new power.

He headed towards the first statue, along the line he hadn't walked yet. A mass for a body and without legs, and a face stern with a deep lowered brow, its arms folded over the mass: *Seth*; god of destruction.

He watched his breath cloud out into the air, and the cold was still sweeping over him. He looked at his hand again and the flame burned brighter covering his entire hand, the coldness easing away.

"Cool!" He exclaimed to the air, and his tail wagged ever so slightly. He stood beside a horned man, a face of scars, he rode an armoured stallion. *Odin*; god of death.

Calum pondered what he could do with the fire burning brightly. He took the flame, cupping it in both hands. From the closeness of his slightly showing ribs, he pushed out and thrust his open palms outwards away from his body. The ball of fire shot out and flew straight into the wall, dissipating at the inflammable stone. He ignored the cold snap that hit him to a shiver, as he smiled out in awe.

"Whoa! What else?" A noise clicked behind him, alerting him to something's presence. Above the dais, a circle opening had formed, at least that's what he thought. He wasn't sure whether it was something he needed to worry about, so he continued on, creating flames around both hands, and not even looking this time. The warmth of he fire was taking that icy feeling away from his skin.

Anubis; god of wind. A distorted figure, he knelt on one knee, one hand drooped over his raised knee, the other feeling the grass on the ground. Next to him was a faceless woman, draped with cloth that covered every inch of her, with the only exception of her featureless face. Calum momentarily stopped, as he wondered on her sculptor's reason. The face ugly, maybe forgotten, maybe never seen, or maybe the sculptor never wanted anyone to see.

Another set of clicks echoed throughout. He stayed quiet, listened for just a moment. He walked on with a glance over his shoulder as he moved on from *Alexander*; god of protection. Next, a muscle-bound man with two maces held in his grip: *Horus*; god of strength.

He jumped to the shock of his new tail rubbing against his back, he shook his head as he looked at it, disbelieving that it could have given him a start. He run a hand over his tail, liking the soft fur's comfort but still unable to see the need.

A three-headed dog was the next statue. *Cerberus*; the god-guardian. Each head was of a different type. Even the tails that hung behind were different, hairy, rough, and coated, matching to the heads. None matched the slimness and furriness of Calum's. The last in the line was *Adina*; The goddess of pain. Encased within chains of jagged spikes that dug into her big boned body, leaving her with searing pain.

In the area where he had come in, three more stood. The entrance was guarded either side by *Leviathon*; the god of water, and a sea-serpent. And another was *Diablos*; the god of the underworld. Above the sleek and stark surface of Diablos's dragon body, was *Baal*: God of suffering, standing upon a mountain of skeletons piled up like a pyramid. With a form like *Seth*, this creature's face was leering evilly to thoughts of murder and chaos, death and destruction, and a reign of hatred and suffering.

The clicking sounds echoed again, accompanied by the screech of an unseen creature, restless and agitated, perhaps trapped or injured. Either way, he was going up. He moved back across the temple with a hurried step, eager to see what was making the tapping and clicking. He looked up through the upside-down well. Certainly it hadn't been hollow before. Yet now it was, and the noises were definitely from up there. He bent his knees as if to jump, and pushed the air down with his hands and leapt off of his feet. Twenty feet flew by as he went up through the shaft, just managing to grasp the ledge of the circle, his momentum dying just as he reached the height. The creature stirred. He pulled himself up quickly to black snake-like eyes, and threw himself up on to the ledge and kicked away from a six-legged creature. It stabbed out the point of its leg at him, just late as Calum fled backwards and landed safely on the opposite side of the well. The strange leg returned back to the floor with its customary click.

With the well shaft separating them from combat, Calum scanned calmly around at the circled attic, his eyes studying the various paintings of gods and their respective gems upon the walls. The jewels of the gods were beneath each colored work, from *Bahamant's Garnet*, to *Quetzalcoatl's Diamond*, each clearly emblazed with the colors and shine intact.

The creature had no arms, just the points for legs, and a face of jagged metallic bark that created a resemblance to a tree's trunk. It moved to the right, and Calum moved parallel with it, calmly watching its face, and glad he didn't look like it did. His sight was distracted by a sword resting on two patterned corbels. A double-edged katana with emeralds adorn at the hilt, and a slight curve along the blade, perched under a painting of Castelli.

"For me, huh?' He moved back, as the creature moved in reverse. The sword hidden, its route blocked. "Fine! We'll fight." He took both of the well's edges quickly and launched over the creature, his body far from the creatures reach, its forward legs swiping the air behind him. In the air, he began creating lightning, striking down around him and into the creature, forcing it to squeal long and high, the pain shooting through its body, the lightning wrapping around the creature, and burning and melting the skin.

As Calum landed behind the creature he grabbed the emerald sword's hilt and took it from its perch, and faced the antagonized six legs. He leapt back over and brought the sword down straight through its head. The creature's body collapsed, finished, its barked head rested by its side.

Calum picked up the sheath that had rested beside the sword, placing the sword within, he looked around for a way in for the large six legs to get through.

'Nothing!' He thought. Just a wall of paintings, and jewels, a room with no way in, and hidden from everything but bugs and insects. A feeling of a test for him crossed his mind. And now with all this, the gems were glowing brightly to give him light. Even light came up from the well, he knew these were not the gems of gods; he hoped they were not.

He leaned over the side of the hole. "Can't just drop, the fall will give me broken legs," he said, sending over a leg and holding on to the sheath with one hand, he sat, and stared down in thought. "Could try ice, and slide down. Be bloody cold though," he said staring a moment longer, and then sending over another leg. He finished deciding on what to do, what was needed. He didn't even point his hands. He let the ice fall through the well and on to the floor. It begun to build up, but he felt he could better than this slow process. *'Come on,'* he told himself.

He aimed a hand towards the new pile. Ice appeared and formed, quickly rising until a few feet remained between the well and the pillar. He dropped off the ledge and landed on his new pillar of ice. "Yay!" He ignored the freeze and once again aimed his hand, and a slide of ice was created, heading for the front door, and filling the room with dazzling flecks of snow. The ice was sparkling white, and smooth on top. Clutching his new sword he threw himself down the slide path. He yelped in high pitch at the freezing cold against his bum, as he slid down the path. The end came too quickly and he flew off crashing into the door. At a halt, he groaned as aches took over his arms and legs, and he leaned against the door to allow himself some time to recover, he pondered on the light, and its voice that had spoke and given him the tail, that was now aching as much as the rest of him. He watched the statues glow, giving light to the temple, and got up from the chilling floor, when his aches were soft enough.

Looking back he asked the air one last time. "Why me?" *'These beasts surely would be enough. What could be worse or more powerful than them?'*

Σ

He left the temple, walking back up the spiral stairwell, and through the cave with its bouncing sounds. Its waterfall pouring down on him, his body clenched at the sudden coolness. And he jumped into the pool and waded to where the pool left through the forest as a small steam. The pebbles were imprinting into his feet, and dusting up into a mist around them. He walked out on to the bank of ferns and small flowers. The small stream that ran off lost the little flowers along its sides, becoming rough edges of grass and eroded soil. The stream, for some reason, became more foreboding to him, more dangerous.

With his fingers he felt the wetness of his trousers. "Suppose I can try to dry them," he said to the birds. He stepped out from the water and onto the opposite bank to where he had come. Placing down his new sword, he pulled down his trousers, held them in his left hand, and created fire, directing it streaming towards the water. A haze of misty steam poured off the trousers and from the stream, filling the air, and his face lifted with a smile. In a short while his trousers were dry, and so too was he. He put them on and wrapped the sheath's leather belt around his waist, feeling somewhat safer and tougher at the same time with the belt on his left side.

Σ

Calum walked aimlessly into the forest, immediately coming into dense foliage that hid any sense of direction and gave him a feeling of being completely lost. He was certain he should have followed the stream.

He was given direction as shouts from someone nearby echoed through the forest, someone who was clearly having a problem. He ran towards the voice.

"Come on! You pesky fangs." The voice of another boy sounded. As he ran he could see numerous brown skin critters running on their paws towards the grunting boy, with sharp teeth bared and snarling. Dodging the trees and taking the ferns brushing at his feet with indifference, he focused on and targeted the boy's voice.

"Is that it?" Whoever was there was still able to handle his situation. He leapt through the last ferns and between the trees, and out into a clearing. Two brown skin critters had come out just ahead, moving straight towards a blond-haired and tailed boy, who with two twelve-inch daggers was in the act of swiping one critter through.

Calum caught up to one and swung down into the critter, the sword cutting through with ease. The second struggled to turn and before it could complete the rotation Calum's emerald sword chopped it in half, to a splatter of dark blood. Another charged at him, leaping up to rip off his face. He skewered the animal and pushed it off with his foot. He moved quickly across the clearing.

The blond boy gutted one, dodged, and slashed another. The critter squealed, unable to move, and simply sounded its pain. As the boy thrust his daggers into another, Calum just reached his side to punch a critter in the face as it leapt up to the blond boy. Dark red blood splattered out over his arm, and on to the clearing floor. The critters ceased their attacks, withdrawing to the borders of the trees, their eyes watching the two boys.

The boy smiled at him, amused. "Nice punch." He said, grinning at Calum. He wore a blue shirt with black short sleeves stitched to the shoulders. Sheaths for his daggers were at his belt and at his lower ribs. The hilts were sparkling silver, and he placed the daggers back into the sheaths.

"Thanks! You didn't seem to need it, though," Calum said, smiling back and sheathing his sword.

"Name's Zidaini. I'm an acquirer of expensive goods." He run a hand through his spiky hair, waiting for a response.

"I'm Calum. Guess you could say I fight for those that need it."

The remark brought a smile to Zidaini's face.

"Where are you heading?" Calum asked, looking for a path.

"To the Liberian Empire; home." The boy answered, turning his head to face northwest over his shoulder. "I could do with a guard, if you're interested. Looks like you need the job," he said, smiling at Calum's lack of clothes.

"Sure!" Calum answered "What are you going to the Liberian Empire for?"

"To deliver this," he pulled out a small Sunstone. "A gemstone."

Calum's eyes opened wide.

"So where were you heading?" Zidaini questioned, his arms folded.

Calum stared at him a moment. "Em! I don't know, I just woke up in the forest, with blood on my hair."

Zidaini looked in shock at him. "Wow! You should be dead. I'm impressed." He smiled at him. "We follow that path." He pointed in a brief wave, at a worn-out road that had overgrown and went south and north.

They began walking together to the north along the path.

"So, are you from the Liberian Empire?"

Zidaini laughed at him. "What!?" The boy's laughing simmered as he realized Calum was serious. "You must have hit your head hard, eh? I'm Gaian, like you. And it's very rare to meet a Gaian who isn't from the Empire." He rubbed his hand over Calum's shoulder. "Don't worry if you need to ask anything, just ask," he said, understanding the possibility of a lost memory.

"Thanks!"

Growls distracted them, the noise coming from hidden critters.

"They were called frilixs, by the way; pesky things."

"Where are you from exactly?"

"I live in Angus Dei, which is way up north. We won't be going there. Redroa is my childhood home, in the west. We ain't gonna go there either. We are going to the Royal palace of Libernian, to deliver the Sunstone. Now that there's two of us, we'll be alright."

"Just alright?" Calum asked.

Zidaini smiled as they walked along under the canopy.

The frilixs continued following, stalking them from behind the trees and amongst the ferns, waiting for the moment to strike again.

"You know why that stone is so important?" he asked, trying to understand whether he was the only one who knew about the relevance of the gems. Calum waited on an answer as Zidaini looked off at the noises source.

"According to our history books, the stones somehow enable you to hear the gods. Those that can hear the voice of the god can call it... A lot of wars have been fought with gods. A lot of death. But I haven't seen these gods. And the last one was, so the history books say, decades upon decades ago. The stories were probably exaggerated, usually are when it comes to the gods."

"How many years are you?" Calum questioned.

"I'm eighteen. Suppose you can't remember." He smiled as Calum shrugged. "Never mind, you'll remember."

The road got narrower, and the undergrowth had grown over and torn and lifted the trail into a bumpy and cracked surface. Weeds had found home within the cracks, rising tall in places. Even new trees had started to reclaim the track that had once been used regularly.

Zidaini plucked off one of the rusty yellow colored fruit from the new and young trees. The older tree's fruit was too high up in the canopy for them to reach.

He gave one to Calum. "It's not the greatest. But you won't eat too often." He said.

The two ate greedily, breaking open the rough shell, and scoffing the soft yellow mush inside, while holding the fruit out away from their bodies as the liquidized substance squirted out on to the ground to feed the unthankful ants.

Zidaini grinned at him. "Not too messy, huh?"

Calum smiled, throwing the skin away and began looking around for some large leaves to wipe his hands.

"Can you remember anything?"

Calum shrugged as he rubbed his hands on some large soft leaves in a vain attempt to clean his hands. "I don't have a clue to where I am. Or where I've been.. Or going." He wiped his hands on his already dirty trousers.

"Really! Well, I guess I can fill you in," he said, looking around; wary of unknown dangers. "This is Foresta Nero. In our language, that's Black Forest. We are in the Adinan Empire, the allies of the Liberian Empire and Elseni." The frilixs had vanished, and to Zidaini this was more of a bad thing then a good thing, and he kept glancing out at the deep foliage.

"The track's getting way overgrown," Calum said, crunching weeds beneath his feet.

Zidaini nodded, looking concerned. "And the frilixs are gone."

The two stopped in their tracks, searching between the trees for an inclination of an explanation. Maroon eyes peered back at them, and Calum drew his sword. An enemy was out there.

"That's a nice sword, maybe I'll get one," Zidaini said, trying to alleviate his tension. "It's also the sword of the Liberian soldier, except without gems."

Calum looked at him, as he held his sword in two hands. The thoughts entered his mind; he knew how to fight, perhaps that's the path he walked. "Come on, show me out of this forest. I'll cover your back." The flies no longer buzzed and grasshoppers were silent. Only the gurgling sounds of what Calum was sure were signals of their new enemy's entrapment.

"What the hell's out there?" Zidaini said, causing a look of horror upon Calum's face.

"You don't know!" His voice showing his concern. "Why not?"

Zidaini shrugged. "Can't know everything. You seem nervous, not worried. Are you?"

Calum remained silent as Foresta Nero darkened. The sun setting behind the horizon. And the birds were tweeting with restless calls, sending the word of the two intruders and their following enemies' maroon eyes.

"Those maroon eyes have multiplied. I suggest pulling those daggers out, I'm absolutely sure you'll need them."

Zidaini listened, and unsheathed the silver hilt daggers, holding them in an ever-practiced grip. "Ahh frel! The forest's getting worse. It doesn't sound happy."

"You hear that as well?" Calum checked.

Zidaini nodded. And frowned, then rolled his eyes.

A creature carrying a scimitar shot in and out of view, the trees and ferns taking it back.

"They have swords!" Calum told his new ally. Dark maroon eyes stared out at them, giving the creatures' locations away. He noticed Zidaini deep in thought, not quite distant, but still distracted. "What is it?"

"It's been said that a green people have taken refuge here in Nero. There have been attacks against anyone entering the forest. Those that have survived have told of an army," Zidaini said.

"We're surrounded." Calum started counting the eyes and then gave up. "By a lot." The two stood back to back.

"That's a lot of maroon eyes." Zidaini stood ready to receive, watching the closest one.

16

Foresta Nero was covered in maroon eyes, silently moving through the darkness. The silence was broken only by the rustle of leaves. The forest could sense the danger, and it wouldn't take sides.

"Intruders kill!" A call sounded. Neither boy could see where it originated from as it came through the trees. A roar of goblins shook the air, and they charged forward towards the boys, their swords wielded.

"Damn it! An army!" Zidaini was shocked and almost shaking. Calum forced himself to remain calm. It wasn't just a few, or dozens, hundreds packed the forest, like ants on an ant hill. A swarm came toward them, pointy ears and angry eyes. Calum was sure even as the goblins ran at them, that the anger was forced to lift them into a rage.

The two had weapons ready, braced for the impact to greet the goblins with sharp edges. Zidaini clashed a dagger against a goblin's scimitar and plunged a dagger in the creature, and made short work of the next.

"We have to run" He said, cutting through another. Behind him, Calum lopped off a head. Zidaini struck with two daggers into another, and in a smooth motion took hold of both daggers in one hand and pilfered the money bag hung at the side of the falling goblin, its long ears rigid as death was brought to it.

"Go now! I'll follow." Calum blasted. He killed two in succession, then slashed across the neck of another, blood gushed out, and he thrust his sword into the chest of the next. Then he ran, following Zidaini who had cut a path out, and was heading rapidly north.

Calum sliced left into one and right into another who had blocked his path. The emerald sword, perfect in its sharpness, left them behind on the floor, their blood leaving as did their lives.

Zidaini glanced behind as he ran, dodging the trees and ignoring the path. He knew where north was. He glanced again, wishing he hadn't as he just missed crashing into a tree after sighting hundreds of goblins racing through the trees after them. Their eyes bursting with hate. "Stupid goblins!" He cried.

As they ran, goblins would come and intercept them, jumping out of the trees, only to end up on the blades of Calum and Zidaini.

Calum ran past a fallen goblin. Then as he went by another tree, a goblin launched down from the branches towards him, and Calum leapt off the ground. He spun round, avoiding contact, and shot out a ball of white plasma which tore and burrowed into the writhing goblin, sending the goblin flying into the trunk of a tree. As Calum landed, and the light dissipated, he brought his sword down and through the green skin of another, slicing through while the olive blood looked for somewhere else to go. Calum stepped around the goblin and sped on through the trees and lengthy ferns that brushed his face.

It seem like only seconds had passed when he caught up with Zidaini. When the spiky blond boy stopped abruptly in front of him, Calum crashed into him. The two went bowling over and landed outside Foresta Nero.

Calum lay on his back, his sword pointing towards the forest.

"They ain't coming, you scared em. And they never even got to scratch us," Zidaini was grinning. "Fun, eh?"

Calum returned the laugh. "I saw you take a pouch," he said, still smiling and panting. "You shouldn't steal."

"Only from the scum of this world... And people who try to kill us. Didn't think you'd see that?" They lay on their backs in the grass, catching their breath.

"So where do we go now?" Calum asked, looking over at Zidaini, who wiped a bead of perspiration off his forehead.

"The town of Dinero. We need to get a boat to Libera. You can see the town from here." Calum sat up and looked behind him along the fields to the small coastal town. "That stream runs to her, and out into the ocean. So all we do is walk along it," Zidaini added.

Calum looked back at the forest, not a sound came from it.

"Hey! Come on," Zidaini called, walking off. Calum jogged up to him and pushed him away, and the two jostled with each other, walking towards Dinero across the stubble of grass. The stream trickling soundly by.

2

I AM A GENERAL NOT A CAPTAIN.

The human, General Nortedes marched stern-faced, and with a well-drilled posture as he moved, draped in a black cloak, undone and hanging down to his knees. The six-feet five general wore the dark grey and black uniform of the Imperium's army. His hand pushed down on the hilt of his long sword that had to be kept from scraping along the marbled floor of the senate hall. His walk purposeful, he moved through the colonnaded lobby of the senate. The granite walls and grey pillars, and black marbled floor made those that walked beneath its roof feel so strong and powerful, so that they walked with heads held aloof. A depressing look for the Gaians who preferred the brightness of their own blues. Black and grey had long been the choice of the humans of the Imperium, colours that adorned every human home.

He walked directly towards the guarded entrance of the senate chamber. Four armoured guards watched his approach, and without a word, and without stopping the general, heaved open the doors before him. Nortedes walked straight through, into the senate chamber, with rows of concrete steps with cushions for seats, that ran opposite each other, splitting the senators in half. At its end was the chair of the Tucari, inappropriately sat in by a single fat man, dressed in the white toga of a senator, with fading hair, thin and balding. He looked at Nortedes with a contempt that he didn't hide. Around the chamber were the paintings of past battles and great leaders and heroic moments from the history of the Imperium. Adorning one was the general himself, with his great sword at his side overlooking from a hill-top. "My grand knight! General Nortedes. I have a task for you. One I believe only you are suited for." Nortedes stopped short of the Tucari's seat, hiding his repulsive feelings for the senator, whose election was dubious; and he was certain deaths had been ordered by the senator. He did not like the man sitting in the Tucari's seat either.

"What do you wish, Senator Bushia?"

"There is a Colonel Samiaraita of the Liberian Empire, a rising star amongst his people." Bushia rubbed his belly with podgy fingers.

"He is a hero, and has even been as heroic as their General Leeron," Nortedes answered, and was angered as Bushia waved a hand at him.

"Yes, yes, hero indeed." He took a breath to fill his over-size flab. "You will head to Londinium, where I have been informed he will be." Nortedes looked angrily, knowing what was coming. "And, Nortedes, you will kill him."

"Kill him in cold blood? Who do you think I am? We are not at war. What madness has led to this order?"

"You will do your duty!" Bushia shouted. "We must provoke their hand," he fumed.

"You will start a war! I will not be a part of it," Nortedes barked back.

Bushia charged up to him, with wrath seizing the fat man's face. "You dare to disobey me and the senate, General?" A major moved over with a signed paper. The general stared at the senator's face, as thoughts of Bushia's assassins came to mind. He was far from his own loyal regiments and did not have their protection, and was certain he had seen those same hooded men that his rival employed as assassins following on his way to the senate chamber.

A servant walked in with a full chicken upon the plate and a goblet of the most expensive rum, brimming inside its decorated pottery.

"The Liberian Empire is amassing an army near Cara-coa."

Nortedes looked incredulously.

"We must make them attack, and forfeit their alliance treaty with the Adinan Empire. The Adinans will not side with the aggressor," Bushia said as a matter of fact, taking a gulp of rum from his goblet and still standing before the general.

"I have received no such reports, and yet my army is at Eastania, the nearest port to Caracoa. Yours do not seem reliable," he said, the distaste reaching his lips.

"Do you not accept this duty?" He leered.

"I am second general to the Grand General. I have got here because I have always completed my orders. But I am not a captain or a meagre assassin," he fumed.

The senator spat a lump of chicken at the general's feet, whose face cringed in disdain; Bushia was pushing it.

"If you do not do your duty to your senate, you will be denounced as general. Maybe even assassins will come for you." A silence filled the air.

"I have always served the senate, always served the people. Your reports had better be true, for if they perceive false. I will lead my Specialli against you. And if you send the people into an unjust war, I'll kill you." He stormed away.

And Bushia shouted out after him. "Do your duty, General." He ordered.

"I will go to Londinium," he shouted back, leaving the chamber, knowing there was more to the senator's orders, more that Bushia had left out. He was sure the senator was to betray him; he would have to be vigilant. Humans would do anything for money, even go against him.

'But how did he get the senate's approval?' he questioned himself. *'Would they really accept a war, especially against the Liberian Empire?'* He walked through the senate lobby, his mind continued to question the need for the death of the colonel. No matter how tough the colonel was, he was still not a threat to him or his army. He left for Centrali, rattled and uncertain.

Σ

The senator drank from his mug as he sat in the Tucari's position. A figure entered the hall from a secret passage, man-like and demonic, with solid black skin that shined in the light, and was plated over and over. His face was bulky and lips were dark brown, and he wore malice upon his face. A purple and black robe covered him, and only his face and bony fingers, and their sharp nails were revealed. As he reached Bushia's side, the major who had been watching also came to the senator's side. Bushia and the demon met eyes briefly.

"He's an honourable one, doesn't want to kill in cold blood." The demon paused briefly pondering the senator's posture of ease. "Do you think he will find out why Sami-araita is a threat to us?"

"Not if he kills the Gaian first. Even if he doesn't, Hades, there are enough mercenaries and desperate people in that slimy city that he won't ever leave, and of course he'll be wanted for the death of the senate." Bushia smiled.

Hades stared at the fat upon him, wondering what the man was capable of. "Major Niratan and I have come up with the perfect solution. You'll like it." He laughed and his major dutifully added his own laughter. "It's going to get quite wonderful," he breathed deeply. "Marvellous!"

The senator paused and looked into his goblet. "Just keep in mind, Hades, he is loved by the senate and more so by the people and his Specialli have utmost loyalty to him. We need him gone. And he will carry out his mission; after all, he knows I'll have assassins after him before he's even got close to his own soldiers. Just make sure you have the assassins in Londinium organized. I don't want him coming back. In case he does, he won't get far, but I'd rather not take the chance."

"He'll die. I doubt he will survive what we have planned," Major Niratan said.

Hades looked to the secret passageway that he had entered through. "I will see you later. I will also have those mercenaries ready. Excuse me. I have to scout the Liberians." Hades wandered out the back, planning his next desires.

Once the black form had gone from sight, the major looked back at Bushia. "That's a strange creature. Where does he come from?" Niratan asked.

"Hades is a useful soul, a useful tool. Where he comes from, I don't know and I don't care. He has been helpful in the past; let's hope it continues in this way."

Σ

Nortedes stormed out from the senate hall, and on to the steps leading up to the entrance, fuming in agitation he went down the steps, and into the crowded plaza. Eyes watched him leave, and he could feel them following him across the plaza and towards his commandeered horse. As he walked, slaves veered quickly from him, and even the rich and those in high positions moved from his path, so as not to disrespect such an important figure in the human society, especially an angry one. Nortedes reached his horse, and glimpsed clearly a man watching him. The man had hooded eyes and throwing a daggered face toward the general, who knew within an instant that this was one of Bushia's assassins. Nor was he the only one, he sighted another nearby, watching from a market stall of vegetables and fruit, an apple tossing in his palm.

Nortedes placed his foot in the stirrup of the horse as a slave of the senate hall held it steady. Climbing on, he nodded before steering the horse into a trot. The assassin's eyes followed him as he left, then walked slowly away. More would be elsewhere watching the general's path, and he knew it.

3

THE TOWN OF DINERO

They had finally reached the gates of Dinero Town. Its iron bars stood fourteen feet tall, a remembrance of the long-gone war between the Gaians and Adinans.

Two guards in the uniform of red and orange of the Adinan Empire had obviously passed the age of one hundred years, which is when Adinans go past the look of Gaians and grow with age. They stood on either side of the gates; their swords sheathed, and within their grip were their spears, held tall above them.

Calum and Zidaini stopped before them.

"Halt!" One of them needlessly said. Calum gave a raised eyebrow at Zidaini, who looked back with a grin. They both started to walk in.

"Hey, stop, halt! Stay where you are," the guard added, trying to keep his voice straight and unwavering.

"What?" Zidaini asked.

"Watch how you speak to me, boy." He ordered. "You're armed."

"Your point?"

"Everyone's armed, Pablo," the other said, and Pablo's face turned up in agitation while his friend pulled out his collar to let some air in.

"You stupid idiot! I wanted his..." The guard tried to raise a smile. "Nothing! Just you two head on in." His smile wavered like an ocean, never keeping one image.

Calum and Zidaini strolled through, and while they walked along the cobbled street, the two guards began to argue. Calum briefly looked back to see Pablo on the floor, decked out. "What weirdoes!" he said. Zidaini hummed and nodded.

The streets they walked were narrow and covered with cobbled stone. Lanterns were sparsely placed, lighting the odd area, and adding to the already yellow building with a tangerine orange glow.

"We're going to an inn, which isn't too far. This area is the smaller housing. There are beautiful rich houses at the beach front, away from the port, of course. There are a lot of taverns and inns around, in other words, cheap places to stay."

"Seems nice here," Calum said. "You've been here before, I take it?"

Zidaini looked at him with a smile. "I've been almost everywhere."

They turned down an alley; the narrow pathway had a sunken side to allow water to run alongside to nearby drains.

"At least it's warm. Although, with that money, you can get me a shirt and shoes," Calum suggested, with a cheeky grin.

"Don't worry. I'll get you something."

The alley joined onto a wide street and the inn was situated on the other side; a two-story building with potted flowers, lining each balcony, the pinks and whites closed for the night, and lit up by the light emanating from inside.

Outside two drunken men stood holding their beers, under a flickering light. They stared at the oncoming boys.

To Calum it was clear they were interested in fighting. Their scattered brains were already thinking of some lame excuse to attack.

One stumbled forward a few drunken steps, still with a hold on his jug of beer and swaying as he came to a stop. "Ah! Jek, they're looking at us," he blurted in a slur of words.

"I see 'em. Stupid-" He burped loudly. "Gaians. Let's stab 'em, Lance. Make fish steaks out um, eh?" Jek said, swaying up to Lance, who was moving for the boys and unsheathing his sword, struggling to take it from the sheath, and spilling his beer as he tried.

Calum and Zidaini shook their heads at each other, and then smiled at their idiotic opponents. Zidaini moved aside his shirt to reveal his second dagger, while Calum had his hand resting upon the hilt of his emerald sword. Patrons from the inn came out to watch, eager to see a spectacle, and were calling out support, for the newcomers.

The two drunks charged. Calum dodged the swipe of Lance's sword with a simple step, and took out his sword, while turning as Lance passed him; he swung the back end of his hilt into the back of his attacker's leg. Lance collapsed in pain, clutching the back of his lower leg, he then screamed with all his lungs as Calum plunged the sword through his other leg. The screams of agony echoed loudly and Calum ignored them. Turning his head, he held the sword in the wound and watched Zidaini tormenting Jek. Zidaini was dancing around the hastily swinging man, who was trying angrily in vain to make the boy bleed.

The audience jeered and laughed at the wildly swinging Jek, shouting cutting remarks and trading jokes at the expense of the two drunks.

Calum looked to the face of his friend. "Knock him out, will ya? If you leave him conscious, he'll just be an irritation."

With that, Zidaini stepped inside a lunge from Jek and cracked backhanded his dagger into Jek's face, the hilt of the dagger cracking against the bone of Jek's nose. The drunk fell to the floor, unconscious before he landed on his nose, breaking it further on impact. The crowd clapped happily.

Calum knelt down beside the writhing Lance, pulling his sword out. Lance cringed in further pain, and looked back with fear as Calum rubbed the blade along the bloodless leg, smearing the blood from his sword on to the trousers.

Calum stood up and followed Zidaini through the crowd that was returning into the inn, squeezing through the crowded door. Patted, thanked and cheered, they entered.

The bartender waltzed over in a bright white shirt, his enunciation feminine in voice. "Welcome to the Night Owl, the bar that's filled only with the good-looking." The guy smiled and guided them over to the bar, past thick wooden tables of oak, and chairs to fit the size and textured design of the wood. The bar was crowded with Adinan women and men, packed in every chair and every available space. A few Gaians were in the corner and Calum noted them immediately.

The bartender walked behind the counter as seats were given up for the boys to sit on. He poured a couple drinks and placed them on the bar. "Here 'ar. Those two had been annoying everyone, typical humans," he said, waving a hand and then moved away to serve someone else.

"Human?" Calum asked, confused.

Zidaini begun to whisper. "You really have lost it," he smiled, "I'm Gaian, like you. These are Adinan; note the many red eyes and crimson hair. They, for the first one hundred years, look just like us, but then begin to age and look like humans. Humans were the two outside," he paused. "They were probably from Londinium, as they have no manners. It's like slum central. Imperium humans don't come here, plus we consider them a threat to our empire; not a good people. The only thing that stops their invasion is their senate's fear of our alliance with the Adinans."

The bartender came back, as Zidaini called him over. "We need a room."

"Ohh! Ok, sweetie, I'll take a look. Don't go anywhere." The guy wandered off along bar to a separate room, which was surely an office, as keys covered the wall.

Zidaini leaned into Calum. "There's also Agavian, long-time rebel city that broke away from the Imperium. Niguargans, humanish people. Then there's the Elseni, they're allies with big four arms, and they are so boring. And the ones you'll probably never see are Dracians and Stralayens.

The bartender returned. "Ok, young'un. Your room will be ready in a moment. So, where are you two from?"

Calum nudged Zidaini, who was taking in the crowd of

noise, and a game of cards on one of the tables; the cards had pictures of monsters. "Hmph! Oh! From Angus Dei. He lives down the street from me." The bartender nodded and looked at the two of them.

"You seem to be missing some clothes," he said.

"Bloodied and torn, in Foresta Nero." The bartender gasped, and placed his hands covering his mouth.

"Don't go anywhere. I have something for you." He pranced off on a new mission into the reception where he spoke to someone that was hovering inside. The two of them came back, ignoring requests for drinks.

The bartender's colleague spoke excitedly. "You youngun's are so lucky. Foresta Nero isn't the safest place in the Adinan Empire. So Fabrico and I will have a shirt ready for you in the morning." He leaned over the bar and looked Calum up and down, frowning at Calum's bare feet. "And we have plenty of Gaian-size boots at our shop. Don't worry about size, I'm an expert." He looked at Fabrico with a smile, enjoying his next work. "Now what colour?" He asked expectantly while Calum shuffled in his stool.

Zidaini grinned, watching the conversation.

"Black!" Calum said. The face of Fabrico friend was stunned.

"Black?"

Calum nodded slightly, unsure whether he should change his mind for the bright colors the two men were wearing.

"Well, it'll go with your trousers." He said, a little disappointed as the black was nothing like his own liking for brightness. Calum's choice was too dark and moody for him.

The bartender had his head resting within his hands. "Don't worry, Reyes likes bright colors. And he'll do your shirt, just for dealing with those idiots... He doesn't like getting his hands dirty, it's disgusting!" He went off to serve waiting customers.

Calum looked at Zidaini, who smiled and shrugged.

"They like you. They like Gaians, Adinans usually do,"

Zidaini said. Reyes came back to them with a key in his hand.

"Here's your room key. Now that's 100 pesos." Zidaini took out some coins and passed them over. "Thanks, hun. Enjoy your room."

"Why did you choose this inn?"

"This is a safehouse," Zidaini answered.

"I take it, this gem was quite important to someone," Calum said, tapping his fingers on the bar, looking sternly at his blond friend.

"Aye... Yeah, it belongs to powerful people." Calum raised a concerned brow. "Don't worry! They'll hide us if we ask. They might not know me but this is one of my boss's hideouts," he paused as Calum shook his head with a smile. "I didn't get seen. My stupid colleagues did though."

"I've got a feeling I should stick with you, you might need me."

"Come on, I want to sleep. Let's find our room."

Calum got up from his stool and followed Zidaini across the barroom. They walked through an old doorway of worn paint, and up clonking wood steps. A few paintings of scenic land lined the stairway at their heads. They walked from the stairs into a bright orange hallway with cushioned seating around a table that was in an embrasure along the hall. Several doors led into rooms along the hall.

Zidaini led the way into theirs.

The two entered the inn suite room. The iron bath was directly inside on the left, and a bucket within a trough for a vague shower. The room was simple and a double bed was covered in a thick chestnut colored duvet.

Zidaini, more interested in sleeping as soon as possible, kicked off his boots and dived into the bed.

Calum climbed in on the other side as Zidaini drifted off to sleep as soon as he got comfortable. Calum thought back to his more recent events. In all that had happened, in all the darkness, and his clouded mind, he had bizarrely made a friend, who slept soundly beside him.

4.

A MEETING OF TROUBLES. EMPEROR & PRINCE JULIOUS LOUSOUS, AND PRINCESS ISIS.

The palace of Libernian was two stories high and per-fectly white; its centre rose higher than its corners and was fronted by a great statue of Castelli standing beneath a stee-ple roof looking out to an unseen battle. Two tall obelisks towered into the sky at each side of the palace at corners that sat beside the palace gardens, one of which had an ivy trellis that hid a pathway to a gate. This was the side en-trance for those clandestine meetings with ones that royalty shouldn't be dealing with. The other side had its own garden and pond, with a table and chairs neatly placed on the cor-ner of the lily-dotted pond, its clear waters allowing for the easy sighting of the small fish that swam around.

The palace's surrounding wall was covered in climbing ivy which had taken over every inch of the wall, hiding the gardens from the outside.

Within the mansion walls and in a bedroom, a girl sat. A hairbrush running down the length of her light brown tail, another stroke followed as she dwelled on her unhappy times, frustration evident in her manner. She gave up on her tail and let it return to droop over the chair behind her. She got up leaving her brush on the dresser, and walked across the fluffy red carpet in her white nightdress, to her window to stare out over the darkened city. Lanterns of flickering lights glowed along the streets, being lit by the many work-ers that kept the capital of Libernian clean.

Her window overlooked the palace pond and its manicured garden. She could see a statue of Castelli, the god of fire, which overlooked the main street.

For fifteen years she had never been outside the palace walls, except for a few visits directly to San Adina, the Adinan capital, and the Lulsan capital of Lulsani. She was desperate for an adventure out of the palace, and she longed to get out of the fortified city walls of Libernian and see her people, even to just go to a bar or restaurant or see the monuments and temples to the Gaian gods, or just walk the streets of the Liberian Empire's cities, and meet the people of those cities. Her father, Emperor Lousous, had so far kept her away from the world outside. She was taken away from her thoughts by a knock on the door. She called out, "Enter!" and sat at the end of her king-sized bed within the confines of crimson drapes that fell down from each corner post, her tail laying limp as the maid walked in and curtsied before the princess.

"Isis, ma'am, Emperor Lousous wishes your attendance for breakfast," she informed.

Isis did not answer the statement, she didn't want to. "Has the Emperor given me permission to explore the city?"

The maid shook her head and Isis turned away to sulk upon her covers, her eyes asking the great painting of Odin.

"Odin wouldn't have taken this," she said looking at the horned beast of Odin riding a stallion encased within more armour than its rider. Three opals rested in a triangle formation in the painting, with two at the bottom. The god carried a great sword that was the length of his horse, lifted high above his body. The god was in a charge, his face roaring at his enemies. "Fifteen years, and I haven't seen the temple to Castelli or even Odin's." The maid felt sorrow for her; she had been the girl's care giver since she was born, had listened to her woes and laughter.

"Doesn't he realize how desperate I am to see the world," she said, burying her teary eyes into her bed. "The people still joke that I don't exist, do they not?" she said, wiping away a tear. The maid did not answer. Isis left the sight of the painting and got up from her sinking bed, and stepped over again to the window, and stared out at the moon-lit city.

"Tell General Leena and Leeron that I wish to speak with them."

"Yes, ma'am. Would you care for a drink, something to start you off for the morning?" The maid was quick to leave at Isis's nod, her tail the last of her to leave, leaving Isis to return to her thoughts.

"I have to leave you, Father. I won't be trapped here forever," she said to nothing. It was something she had been considering for some time, contemplating her escape, but she had never had the courage to cross her father. There was something in his need for her to be confined to the palace that scared her, and yet when she brought it up with the officers of the Empire she trusted, they always replied she was safe here, and she had always felt they were hiding something from her. Tomorrow would bring the generals to the palace, and she would speak with them then. She was certain the generals would assist her, help her leave her prison. They had always been close with her, kept her company as friends, and she was always entertained by them.

She went to the window and looked out, wondering whether the city was as beautiful to walk along as it was to watch. The trees lined the cobbled roads and hung their deciduous branches across the stones and she imagined just walking beneath them and along the road to the distance promenade, of shops and bars, and the dozens of Gaians, and foreigners who walked around there. She had such desire to see the kingdom, to see the proud Empire. She sighed, and sat in her chair, bored of sitting within the walls of the palace.

Σ

His face cold to those that guarded his palace walls and statue-lined halls, the Gaian wore the white cloak of peace to the Liberian Empire, attached with gold clips that shone brightly off his white clothes. Adorned along the cloaks length was the Emperor's symbol, the hilt of a decorated Katana, with gold, silvers, and jewels of quartz and crystal. The same emblem was emblazed upon his personal flag and that of his Emperor's Guards, who were the infantry that guarded the leaders upon the battlefield.

His manners and kindness were the opposite of what his position entailed to Gaians. He was deep with rudeness and had forgotten the people of the Empire, openly despising the Imperium, and ignoring the advice of his advisors, and leaving the Gaians' needs.

Each guard, girl and boy, snapped to attention, keeping their eyes forward, away from contact with the Emperor's own eyes. The many guards filled the hallways, standing between each gap of the statues of ancient emperors and famous soldiers, summoners and mages that had been amongst the great history of the Liberian Empire.

The guards clasped their shields to their chests, and held the hilts of their swords, with feared respect. These soldiers were the Royals. The Libernian Royals, the most trained and strongest of the Gaians, sworn to protect the royal family; currently their hearts held for Princess Isis, while their oath kept them in line.

The Emperor didn't concern himself with the soldiers around him, and never showed a touch of acknowledgement to any that crossed his path. If the doors to the banquet hall weren't open for him, the anger and wrath would have showed in the way he would slam the doors open as he walked into the hall of diamond chandeliers and white pillared archways that crossed the roof of the banquet hall's long table. Sidewalks around the edges were decorated with duplicate standards of each regiment of the empire, the banners still, while they hanged along the walls. A dozen advisors crowded him on his entry; his face turning to infuriation at their entrapment.

General Leena, a neatly-combed brown-haired, female Gaian, sat beside General Leeron, who had blond locks that fell and stopped just above his shoulders. His blue eyes were watching the entrance of his Emperor with caution. Opposite them sat the snobbish and pompous Julious Lousous, the emperor's son, and an arrogant brat who had left those that walked his path despising him.

His father gripped his head in frustration, the voices penetrating him with calls for money to be spent on the city, from schools to architect. The sounds of so many voices were too much for him to take, too much entering his mind at one moment.

"GET OUT! NOW!" He fumed with spittle. The advisors didn't wait to object and complain, filing out at his immediate outburst. The Emperor walked around the table, while a servant rushed to his seat and another with jug in hand filled a glass at the table. The Emperor allowed himself be seated and took an immediate sip of his juice, and looked at his choice of fruit in a bowl placed in front of him.

The generals sat, uncomfortable in his presence, and they both waved the waiter away, uninterested in eating at the same table as the scoffing son and ill mannered leader.

"Julious!" His son looked up, and briefly bowed his head. "Those light blue and white uniform look good on you two," he said to the generals with a smirk. "Shame I've decided on changing those old colours. Blue is so weak." He leaned back into his large chair.

"That would be unwise," the girl said.

The Emperor stared at her. "General Leena, you and General Leeron were called here to be informed of the Imperium's intentions-" The group were interrupted by the doors. Libernian Royals had opened them from the other side, letting in Princess Isis. They watched her walk over to the table, and she sat beside Leeron. The two generals stood in respect of her, and sitting again once she had her place.

The Emperor turned his face, twisting his lip in agitation. "I'll get to the point. Imperium forces are building near Centrali, preparing to move to Eastania, and then with their countless formations, and a feign from Hastatia's Specialli towards the west of their continent, they will invade Caracoa," He said without wavering, stern, and a matter of fact.

"The Imperium would never invade, she couldn't possibly win," Leena said, looking straight at him and allowing her anger to show.

"You know nothing." The Emperor disregarded her.

Isis sat invisible to him and her brother.

"General Leeron, you will lead any defence of Caracoa, assuming we somehow lose. Julious Lousous, with Generals Ravon and Fernadez will command the first strike."

"What!?" A unison cry came from both generals. And even Isis sat aghast with them, infuriating both Lousous and the Emperor.

"I will make a great leader. And take the Guards to victory," Julious sneered.

"Adina will not side with aggressors," Leeron blasted.

"And Ravon and Fernadez are petty, useless generals." Julious tried to cut in, but Leena shouted louder, "This untrained fool will lead us to disaster against a fortified city."

"Get out! Get out now! Leave for Caracoa at once."

Leeron stormed off.

Leena stopped as she rose. "At least take guidance from Colonel Samiaraita, or take Petrovic and the Spears," she said. Julious ignored her. Then she scorned him with a look of disdain, and then stormed off after Leeron, the doors closure echoing through the hall.

With the two generals gone, father and son sat comfortable and at ease, with their glasses in hand.

"Isis," the Emperor called, without looking at her. She did not look up from her plate, or answer the parent she now hated. "I have found a suitable teacher for your studies on these useless gods of ours. T-."

"Do not insult the gods. They are well documented throughout history," she said, staring at him.

"Ha, ha! Yet we have summoners control them. That is not a god."

"They help us. When we call, that is."

The Emperor waved a hand to stop her, as he was uninterested in her voice. Julious stared at her with contempt.

"It doesn't matter. Your summoner ability needs to be

enhanced. I have the tutor, and he will start in two days. Now leave us. I have to have a private discussion with Julious."

"Sire, will you let me see the city?" She asked, a tear running down the length of her face, already knowing the answer.

"No!"

She almost ran, upset and hurt by him, cut deeply by his lack of love. She walked quickly away, the tears running.

After she left, the Emperor smiled to Julious. "A toast!" Julious stood with his glass. "To the death of the republic." The two clinked glasses and gulped the juice down, allowing it to run down their chins.

"Remember, Julious, do not lead the siege from the front. You have officers for that." He told him, and Julious nodded in agreement. "Damn the gods! I can't wait for the destruction of the Imperium." He grinned and Julious echoed it.

"Father, should I heed the advice of Samiaraita or Petrovic.?"

"Don't be foolish. Anyway, I have Samiaraita on a mission dealing with something important... And Petrovic. You have enough colonels. And with only a few regiments in Eastania, this is the perfect opportunity to strike. I can't see you losing. It will be a triumphant victory."

Σ

Isis sat motionless by the side of the pond at its edge upon the grass, her knees wrapped in her arms. Feeling lost, she didn't even notice Leena and Leeron come to her side. She started as Leena's hand rested upon her shoulder.

"I'm sorry, Leena, Leeron. Surely the army will win, even with Julious at the helm."

"We can't be so sure," Leena sighed. "He has moved the forces under us. The Emperor's Guards have already left for Caracoa."

"What do you think will happen?" Isis asked.

37

"Without the support of the Adinan Empire, who will not support this invasion... We will be overwhelmed."

Isis sank deeper into her own sorrow.

"We can only pray to Odin and Castelli, that they will once again come and rescue us."

Isis looked at Leeron. "I cannot help you. But I wish for you to help me. Please, will you help?"

"Anything, ma'am."

The princess smiled at them.

5

ADVENTURE ON THE RAIDEN

"Hey! Wake up." Zidaini shook Calum awake, forcing him to open his eyes. Which he did ever so briefly, and closed them straight away. "I'm having a wash."

Calum heard him walk to the front door, and its bang as Zidaini deliberately shut it firmly. The noise brought his eyes open and closed again.

Zidaini came back with a newly sewed black t-shirt and the accompanying black boots, and threw them at Calum with a smile.

"Hey!" Calum groaned, pulling the shirt from his face. He sat up to the pouring of water, his muscles straining. He could not believe that his friend could possibly be up and wide awake like he was. He threw back the covers and hopped out, and stepped over to the window. He opened it and went out onto the balcony, staring out to a street that was barely alive. A couple of old Adinans walking slowly along chatting, and a few young Adinans, looking barely awake, walked out of an alley and crossed to another.

He turned from the sunrise glow, and stood at the end of the bed. He begun to stretch, smoothly transferring his weight and stance, like a slow dance, stretching out a foot to his head height, and holding his foot in the air before switching sides, bringing his left foot up and out.

"You've got agility," Zidaini said, quite impressed.

Calum brought his leg down. "Take it you're finished."

Zidaini stepped aside and waved out an arm. "All yours, senor," he said, with a cheeky smile.

Calum walked past and pushed Zidaini, who quickly returned a kick at Calum's butt as he tried to dodge laughing into the bathroom.

"Don't take forever." Zidaini threw himself on to the bed, gazing at the ceiling. He had already considered there was more to Calum than he had at first noticed. His future missions might not be as daunting as he had previously felt. He was sure there was trust between them, certainly on his part.

Σ

The two ate greedily at the bar of the Night Owl before stepping out on to the street. A couple grey-haired men played chess outside one of the old men's house. A pair of boys younger than the old men was playing with hand-sewed pictured cards.

"What are they playing?" Calum asked, as he watched them scan through their cards, searching for the highest stats.

"That's called Seraphim. At home it's Cheriphan, and Zorastron in Lulsani. Extremely popular across the eastern continent," Zidaini told him. They continued walking along the cobbled road and headed towards the harbour. Its water was visible at the road's end, and the amount of people increasing as they went closer.

"There's a shop just across the road. Wanna take a look?" Zidaini asked, already going towards it.

"Sure!" Calum smiled at Zidaini's obvious eagerness.

The two wandered over and through the entrance as a few young Adinans played cards outside.

Calum wandered slowly through the shelves of the shop, gazing at the illustrious games that filled the shelves. "There's quite a lot of rubbish in here," he whispered. The store manager looked up and across at them, from behind her desk, and Calum made himself busy as he blushed, certain the manager had magical hearing.

Zidaini dragged him over to a selection of cards and they looked through them next to one another. Zidaini spoke in a whisper, "The better the card, the more you pay," he said taking up a card and showing it to Calum, "this is Quetzalcoatl. Very, very rare," he said, wondering on Calum's expression. "What?"

"Quetzalcoatl, the god of white lightning."

Zidaini gave a raised brow in wonder. "You remember a god, but not yourself?" Calum shrugged with a smile, and kept the temple to himself.

"Guess so."

Zidaini took a more careful look at the front and back. "I'm buying it." He looked Calum up and down. "How's the shirt and boots?"

"Did you just realize I was wearing them?"

Zidaini turned grinning and strolled to the counter. "Yeh! They're fine," he called out.

The pre-age girl took Zidaini's money with a smile towards them. "You're lucky. There's only one of those."

"That's a good omen for the day," Zidaini said and walked out with his tail gently swaying, dulled in its blond colour by the light.

Σ

Reaching the riverside, the area was full of cafes that lined the harbour-side, with the smell of coffee mixed in with the dozens of fresh market goods on offer. There were chickens clucking frantically in their cages. The Adinan specialty, the Amimnas, a creature that looked like steak upon the coals of a barbecue, eaten with the pink still showing, was cooking. A famous delicacy that is usually eaten only at the weekends was now leaving its smell drifting through the air to mingle with the coffee.

At anchor beside the pier were three ships; the Liberian frigate, the Restitution, being fitted with the latest weaponry.

"Cannon will change everything," Zidaini said quietly, watching a culverin being drawn by a horse to the frigate.

"Better hope swords stay the weapon of choice, or we'll

be obsolete." They continued on, silently walking past the large blocks of stacked cargo, supplies and wares.

"That's the Ciarli; it has a bad reputation," he said, referring to the humans' three-mast caravel.

"Why?" Calum stepped aside to let others pass.

"Humans are always trouble. Guaranteed a few brawls per trip. Which is why they always take the extra crew, and they still need to try and recruit new crew members, after suffering several deaths by blade. And you can't leave anything out of your sight, for if a human sees it, they think they can take it. Thankfully not too many come up this far," he said with a note of disgust.

"What about her?" Calum asked staring up at the large carrack. It was the final ship in port, and was bustling upon deck.

"The Raiden," Zidaini answered. "Come on!" He walked up to a booth, a one-person shed with a bored woman inside, and her face in her palm. The sun picked up a little, with a sign that it was only to get hotter as it glared down on them.

"Yes. Can I help you?" She questioned, gazing at Calum's emerald sword.

"We need a ride."

She failed to answer. Zidaini tried again.

"Excuse me!"

"Now, where did you get such a lovely sword?" She asked, admiring his sword with a dazed look.

Calum stuttered in thought. "Lon-Londinium."

Zidaini sighed beside him.

"Londinium makes swords like that?" She looked bemused.

"Gaian seller, charged a lot," Zidaini said. "Tickets?" He added trying to revert to what they came to her for.

"Oh, yes. Only one left, the Raiden." They both groaned with disappointment.

"What do we do?"

"You get this. I'll head off later," Zidaini said, pushing money into Calum's hands.

"What! No way!"

Zidaini pulled him to one side. "Trust me. I'll see you later."

Zidaini shot off, disappearing further along the pier behind the cargo the Raiden had left for the town. Calum suddenly felt lost as he left alone to pay for his ticket, and the world of Gaia became somewhat daunting. Calum looked back at the woman, and passed over the money to pay for the ticket.

"Here ar!" She swapped the money for one and continued to look just as bored. "Up the plank there. Have a safe trip," she said.

"Thanks!" He replied, stepping around the booth and staring up the side of the carrack, and looking along the wood deck, and the three masts across its deck with sails hoisted, and flags of the Raiden flapping above the crosstrees. Both its fore and aft castles were bustling with personnel, and the single crow's nest lay empty. A giant four-armed man covered in hair guarded the end of the gangway. As Calum reached the guard at the top, he could see rich people dotted about, mingled in with the likes of those that carried less obvious wealth.

The ship's wheel was at the rear where the captain stood giving orders. The four-armed guard looked him up and down, taking in his weapon. "Ticket please, sir." The politeness startled Calum momentarily, it didn't suit the giant man.

"Here!" He passed over the ticket.

"Thank you, Sir. Passenger's quarters in the aft. Remain off the bridge sir, unless invited, Sir."

"Ok!" He walked past while the Elseni continued his watch. Calum eyed the axe on the man's back, a double-headed battleaxe, and decorated in red and burgundy patterns, then went walking down starboard side to aft. He looked back and caught sight of Zidaini, who was upside down, shuffling up the ropes that kept the ship steady at the jetty. Calum quickly removed his eyes from the sight, trying not to reveal his friend.

The stairs downwards into the passengers' quarters were in the centre of the ship's aft. The mizzen mast was level with the door. Stretching upwards, it was overlooking the doorway.

The captain watched Calum go down. He called over his first-mate, the four-armed beast of a man.

$$\Sigma$$

Calum walked slowly through the creaking corridor. The rocking made him wonder on what it would be like once they were out at sea, being sent to and fro in the swaying ocean. At the end of the poorly lighted corridor lay his allotted quarters. He pushed open the unlocked door to a simple desk with feather quill and its corked vial of ink, a single bed and a small open window with a worn fabric tied to the side of it, giving cover from the light of day.

Calum stepped up to the window that looked out from the rear of the ship, and could only hear the slapping of water against the hull and the seagulls squawk as they flew over looking for food.. A hand slapped on to the seal of the window and Calum jumped in fright.

"Hey, Calum!" Zidaini popped his head up, and Calum helped him over, once the fright wore off.

"You scared the crap out of me."

"Scared? You?" He looked in a mocked incredulously. "I thought you couldn't be scared."

"First for everything," he replied, letting Zidaini go once his feet found the floor. The ship lifted in commotion as the anchor was winced up, and the sails came tumbling down and extended by the light wind. The vessel bobbed about as it moved out to sea.

Zidaini laid on the bed in satisfaction. "See if you can find me some meat. There's usually a cook who has fresh food available, and I would think dinner will be a while and I ain't gonna be waiting that long."

Calum sighed. "This ship goes all the way to Libera?" Calum asked, listening to the noises.

"Brief stop in Los Santos, a rich person's paradise." Calum sat on the corner of the bed, and looked at Zidaini clearly waiting for something, and even palmed his hand out.

"Money!" he said, realizing that Zidaini wasn't getting it. His friend just laughed at him.

"Ok, ok. Take this, it should be enough. Something with meat, yeh!" The ship shifted, forcing them to hold their balance. "It's gonna get interesting. Once we get to Libera, you're gonna learn lugarta, then-"

"Who's a what?"

Zidaini smiled. "I'll tell you after you get some meat." Zidaini sat up and patted him on the back, with his usual smile.

"Yeh, yeah!" Calum got up, and went to the door to leave, opening it to the six-feet five Elseni first-mate who towered above him, staring down at him with a grin upon his face.

"The captain wishes to speak with the two of you." The first-mate turned to leave from the shocked boys but stopped in his tracks. "Don't try to escape from the window. It's covered." He left them, his feet thudding on the floor.

Calum looked out of the window to see a grinning man who was hovering on a rope, dangling upside down. Calum mumbled under his breath while Zidaini stared out in fury at the hanging man.

"Great! I thought you were good at stealth." He was angry at being caught, rather than at Zidaini, who had to sneak on for them to travel together. He still had no memory, and the thought of travelling alone wasn't that appealing.

"Sorry! Guess we'll have to talk to the captain. We should force him to take us," Zidaini said, pondering the possible judgement from the captain.

Calum held the hilt of his sword. "Let's show some strength. If a lesser option appears, we'll take it. Aye?"

"Aye!" The two walked along the corridor. "Why does this passage rock so much more than our room?"

"Huh?" Calum wondered for a moment on how Zidaini

couldn't care about their situation.

They stepped up the stairs to the deck slowly. Drops of perspiration ran down their foreheads. They remained poised, ready to strike, as they took each step cautiously. The top of the stairs they found to be surrounded by crewmen armed to the teeth. Dinero was fading towards the horizon. And neither let the contemplation of swimming to the ever-distancing town remain in their thoughts for too long.

The opposing sailors gripped their swords expecting a fight from the two, and Calum took in those they would have to go through, if they took up the sword and dagger.

The captain smiled down at them, hiding a feeling that this could go horribly wrong.

Calum pondered on what the captain has running in his mind, having no memory he had no clue as to what punishment a ship would dish out. The scene had attracted everyone on board, and audience of Gaians, Adinans, and the odd human passenger. Calum could tell from the eyes of the Gaians that they were tempted to take out their swords and side with them, their natural allies. One even hung on the shroud leading up to the crow's nest. His tail was wrapped around the netting and his hand loosened the katana in its sheath.

The captain had noticed the problems arising and knew he would have to be careful and delicate on how he would proceed. "One of you hasn't paid. I suggest you both accept the punishment given, and the consequences of your actions."

"Or what?" Zidaini laughed at them. "You wouldn't last five minutes against us. We'll kill half of you before you've swung a sword in return."

The captain walked from the aft castle, down the steps to them. "You're certainly confident. I'll tell you what. I won't get you banned from every single ship and airship on Gaia."

'Airship?' Calum thought bemused.

"If you work a little for the trip, both of you." The captain finished talking as he came to stand in front of his sailors.

"Give us a minute."

The captain moved away, hoping he had defused the situation to his advantage.

Zidaini stepped into Calum, and whispered. "We'll have some serious travelling problems if they do what he says. I take it he's a member of the East Alliance Trading Association."

"So what are our options?" Calum asked. "Work would be safe."

"Are you boys finished yet? We're waiting," the captain sarcastically commented.

"Why should he be punished, he didn't stow aboard."

"But he did see you climb up the rope, and thus, let you aboard."

Zidaini moaned in frustration. "So what needs doing? I don't feel like a blood bath."

The captain raised a smile. His crew still clung to their weapons.

"Dismissed!" He shouted to his crew, alleviating their tension to concentrate on the ship itself, or the typical games of dice. "Follow," He told the boys.

The boys followed at a distance as they were led up to the ship's wheel, their eyes watching those around them. The first-mate was at the helm, his four hands taking the wheel in a gentle grip. He barely gave them a glance. His eyes keeping a keen look at the Raiden's path, following the deep sea along the distant coastline.

"Now, young'uns. Choose your job: cooking, cleaning the deck, or you can walk the plank."

Their heads dropped in a moan.

"Should have fought," Calum remarked. The captain grinned.

"Cooking? What if we can't cook?" Zidaini questioned.

"Ha! Don't you worry. You just need a knife."

They looked at each other. Cleaning was an appalling thought, and they weren't going to jump overboard.

"Cooking." Zidaini murmured.

The captain grinned widely. "Good choice. Now report to Tifa in the kitchen. He'll need a thousand carrots and potatoes to dice, and our favourite, Gooladi."

"Crapt Frelling Gooladi!" Zidaini looked horrified. The captain and first-mate were grinning away.

Calum tried to hide his lack of knowledge, turning his face away from their eyes.

"Ramuel, take them to the kitchen."

The first-mate swapped positions with another sailor, while the captain went off to his personal quarters, stopping half-way down the stairs.

"I'll tell you what. Give me that there emerald sword, and I'll forget the whole thing." He said, still smiling broadly.

Calum looked at him and lifted the hilt out of the sheath. The captain smiled at the boy and continued downwards as Calum's face said it all.

"Cheeky bugger," Zidaini said for him.

The first-mate, Ramuel, took them across the carrack, and then down the stairs before the bow's castle. The sunken stair case led straight into the kitchen. Above it was the captain's quarters.

The kitchen's door had *Tifa* scratched with a blade. Ramuel opened the wood door, and immediately Tifa greeted the first-mate, quickly moving around his bench for food preparation and to face the mate.

"Ah! Ramuel. Well now, look at this, helpers, and Gaian. Or, are they new crew?" He asked his face worrying, his four arms pressed into his thighs, his voice old and crabby.

"Your favourite; a stowaway and his friend, the accomplice."

"Ha, Ha! Wonderful. Well now, Gaians. You love Gooladi now, then?" He asked, smiling broadly.

"No!" Zidaini moaned, his face unable to hide his displeasure.

Calum still looked confused, but his friend's sulking was concerning him.

"Well, now. You're not the first, but no stowaway has

ever survived the trip without getting a waft of fresh gooladi. Ha, ha, ha." His laughter seemed unnecessary. "Can't wait. Can't wait. Very tasty though."

Ramuel left them to it. Tifa reached into a cupboard and removed two very low and small stools from the cupboard that was across the room of bubbling broths that lined the coal stoves along two sides. And placed them by sacks of potatoes that stood in the corner, He even leaned one sack between the stools and let the few potatoes tumble out on to the floor.

"Names?" he asked, with four hands gripping around his hips.

"Calum," he said, sniffing the smell of rice and meat.

"Zidaini."

"Hmm! Unusual name from someone of the Liberian Empire." He looked over them. "Now, then. Tails out of the way when you're peeling, no one likes hairs in their food, not a nice surprise. And remember, we Idonians like our food, so don't spoil any. Now sit."

The two boys sat on their given stools in a slump. Tifa went to another cupboard above a steaming broth, taking out two large jugs already resting upon a tray with clay goblets. "Drink up. Fresh juice, and the finest rum. You kids like juice over there, don't ya?"

"We're not kids," Zidaini said.

"Really? How many years are you then?" The smiling Tifa asked.

"Eighteen," Zidaini answered, unsure whether he should be stroppy with rum being offered.

"Eighteen? Ha, ha, children! Even by Gaian standards." He laughed boisterously, and plonked the tray down between them. Within moments he returned with a bucket, filled halfway with water.

"Now, then. Put the peeled potatoes in here. They need to be softened." He also gave them simple three-inch knives. "Well, now. Cut them in half before putting them in the bucket. He went off to prepare some large lumps of meat for more dinners, and checked one last time to see

49

whether they had started. Both were staring at the knives.

"Well now, get peeling," he ordered.

Calum and Zidaini stared at him. Tifa laughed and started slamming a meat cleaver through a lump of meat.

"What the hell is he trying to pull on us?" Calum asked.

"Who cares? Rum!" He said grabbing the jug and pouring a goblet full, and gulping several mouthfuls. "Maybe the Elseni's grateful for help. Cheers."

Calum grabbed the other goblet and clinked Zidaini's "How long till we reach Los Santos?"

"A few hours. It won't be a long wait while they pick up passengers. It mostly depends on their cargo."

"Hey! What about this lugarta?" Calum asked while he peeled.

"Ahh! Awesome game, two teams, six aside, and you basically have to get the ball into the try zone. You can only tackle the player with the ball. It would be a dumb sport otherwise. You can only throw the ball backwards, but you can kick forward."

"Can I run backwards?" Calum suggested, with a cheeky grin.

"No, you doughnut, it still counts as forward," he replied.

"So you've been asked that question before." He watched Zidaini smile.

Tifa looked over at them, he frowned as he noticed the drinking was lacking. He walked over with a mug, eager to increase their intake. "Now, then! How about giving me some?"

Zidaini picked up the jug and poured him a mug full of rum.

"Perfect! A salut, to the trip."

"What? Boring!" Calum said.

"Well, now-"

"Hey! Got it. Here's to '*well now*'." The two laughed and clinked goblets, adding rum to the floor, and ignoring that, gulped down a few mouthfuls of biting brown rum. Both boys quickly swallowed and took some juice along with it, to fade away the taste.

Tifa wandered away to leave them peeling.

"Hey! How about, *'now then'*?" The two gulped more rum down, following with juice to take the taste of rum away.

Tifa watched them a moment longer. "Won't be long now," he said quietly. *'Although you are being cheeky. Maybe I should give you the special cocktail,'* he thought on it for a while, *'shouldn't need it for young'uns like you.'* He decided on not giving them the special, certain the two Gaians couldn't last long on alcohol.

The boys were drinking quickly, not even noticing the Raiden docking at Los Santos. The number of drinks they had seem to outnumber the amount of potatoes that they had peeled, and Tifa made regular trips to them for a heavy shot, encouraging them further, to their demise.

"Bloody potatoes," Zidaini said, his voice beginning to slur.

"They don't have blood on them. Where's the blood?"

"Ohh! They healed." Zidaini giggled.

"I think we should make faces on em," Calum suggested.

"I think we should throw them at Tifa," Zidaini said.

Calum laughed. "Do you think he'll notice if we hit him? He's rather big isn't he? Easy target."

"Hang on. I throw on-"

"Stop it! Have another drink," Tifa interrupted, before any throwing took over.

"Oooh! You made him angry." Zidaini blamed Calum.

"As if! He must be chopping onions."

"Ah yeah! That could be it." Zidaini's and Calum's eyes were beginning to glaze. Grabbing the goblet, Calum aimed it high. "To Foresta Nero." Calum clunked the goblet back down, empty.

Tifa watched them as they drunk more. The forest was an interesting statement. The thought of the two having a tough history was attractive for conversation, but he had other things to think about. "It looks like you two will enjoy the gooladi," he whispered.

Σ

The ship lurched away, to continue its journey, both boys falling back off their stools, with their cries sounding and groaning at the connection with the planks of the floor.

'If you don't knock yourself out,' Tifa remarked in his thoughts while the boys struggled in lifting themselves up.

Time had passed and the boys had forsaken the juice, sticking unwisely to the rum.

"Err! I. We er. Going to seeee," Zidaini slurred.

"Wh'ers a what?" Calum gave a prolonged burp.

"A potatwo!" Zidaini shouted.

"A tatoo!"

"A what?" Zidaini struggled to remain on his seat.

"Potate!" Calum barely said.

"And a nuther."

"Amn a nothing," Calum said, picking up another potato. His knife missed the brown dirty skin.

The cook whistled away, looking forward to his favourite part of the stowaways' trip. The two boys were calling for more drink, just managing to remember it was a drink they wanted.

Tifa grabbed two gooladi, the thin appendage creature's had a flat belly, with bony fingers. Its head was rounded, and its closed eyes were otherwise large upon its face. He chucked them at the boys.

"Urgh! Whhat's thiss?" Calum stared at it with a confused look.

"Goolish."

"Gost!"

"Goolioos."

"Gooladi! You two are past drunk. Right! Chop their heads off, then arms and legs. Remove the neck bone and.. Well, go on."

"Ah, a, a, a dagga... Calum?" Zidaini held out a dagger in Calum's general direction. Calum swung out a hand and missed. After another attempt he grabbed hold of it.

"Tanks!" He said looking down at the grey meagre form.

A delicacy of bones.

The two lifted their daggers over the gooladi, aiming ever so carefully.

"Yahh!" They swiped down. Tifa's excited face dashed as they both missed. "Oih! It. Burp! Moved," Zidaini explained.

"How the hell did you two miss?" Tifa's eyes were wide open in shock.

Calum attempted again. "Na! Na! Na! Na! Er! Na!" He said at each missed strike.

"Calum?" Tifa questioned.

"It moved. Yo'er given ba'ad apples," he blurted the words.

"What? Oh my gods! How are you even awake?" Tifa asked himself as Zidaini's blade still hovered above the gooladi, having forgotten how to chop down.

"Hey! Goolish fight," Calum suggested. Zidaini eagerly taking to the suggestion.

"No! No!" Tifa said quickly, taking the gooladi's from them. "Gather round."

They etched in, intrigued at the moving apples.

"Zidaini. Aapples, move lot." Zidaini hummed in agreement.

"There not apples. How can you being seeing apples?" He questioned. "Right enough." Tifa slammed a carving knife through the necks of both creatures. The stench ripped out at them, penetrating their noses, and seeping down their throats. Instantly they both heaved, puking over the floor

Tifa watched in laughter, proud of his achievement, while Calum and Zidaini stumbled up across the kitchen and up the stairs outside, desperate to get away from the vile gooladi. Reaching the deck, and completely unaware of anyone around them, they rushed, swaying, to the side and began vomiting into the water, which slapped the sides of the carrack. The crew watched in amusement, having waited for most of the day for this particular moment.

Calum watched the churning ocean below his spinning head. His body felt like it had wandered off to another plain.

He had no idea that Zidaini was beside him in the same condition. He heard a voice somewhere near him. Then the sea spiralled until he was being carried on someone's shoulder. And the crow's nest shouted muddled words. And his stomach churned again.

Already Calum regretted drinking. Even before the morning hangover would begin. His eyes kept closing to the still shining sun. But he wanted to see where he was going. Someone was carrying him to his room. He was sure it was the first-mate, Elseni. Maybe even Tifa. He was slowly placed down on his bed. Zidaini was let down beside him, already passed out.

Calum, feeling safe upon the bed, drifted off to his dreams.

6

NORTEDES PONDERS

His path back to Eastania had been blocked off by Imperium fleet ships. He knew it had been done deliberately, and he was certain they would fire at his flagship, so he had ordered the Viracocha south to the town of Regan. Londinium was inland, and had no port, and he would disembark there at Regan, rather than the treacherous rocks of the nearest coast to the city.

Nortedes watched the waves rock the carrack, thinking back to the days when the senate favoured him. A time when the eastern continent, and the Imperium were still fighting against the Asucion factions, although not as allies. He had helped to end a war between his people and the Gaians and Adinans, for the Imperium to concentrate solely on the Asucions. He was even a hero to the Idonians, when, without other humans, he helped Idona survive against Asucion invasion.

Now he seemed a distant memory to the senate who had once idolized him. In their lust to become a super power, they had loved, and gave him the means to fulfil their desires, of world domination. Convincing themselves to concentrate on one enemy at a time.

Yet in all he had achieved, that love for the fight had faded over time as he realized the desires and actions of his leaders were incompetent and inappropriate. Now with Bushia's need to start another war, it was wrecking his passion, his own heart, making him feel depressed. His love was long gone for both his people and its cities. Centrali, once his home, now meant barely anything to him, as his people embrace hysteria, thus being easily controlled by the senate. His fellow people were tearing themselves up, from the inside out, and he wanted to fight it, but people do not listen to something unless it reflects what they want.

As the rain begun to come down from the dark grey clouds turned a dreary blue from the night sky, he remained, with no wish to leave the deck. He had thought about his path, and nothing seemed certain. For the first time in his life, he felt lost in the world.

His mission to kill a Liberian colonel would lead to all-out war. He did not wish war upon his people, although in defeat, it would probably help to clean up the mess that had infected the people's minds. But he could not fathom why this particular colonel should have to die.

His major's lieutenant came to his side while the ship creaked with the rolling sea, and the wind pushed the sails. "Perhaps you should sleep, sir."

Nortedes stared out from the ship at the cliffs and beach-laden haven of the Idonian shore, shinning with flames within their sconces from the locals huts, away from the beaches.

"I cannot sleep, Veneris. I fear my command is to be taken from me."

Veneris would usually crack a joke, but he could see now was not the time. "Your Specialli would not desert you, sir."

"They won't have a choice."

The lieutenant said nothing. He left to resume his post at the aft castle.

Nortedes would be on the Viracocha for quite a few days, according to his major, Graneria Nivedes. He thought about his future victim.

"You had better be worth ending my career."

7

CITY PORT OF LIBERA.

With head pounding, Calum awoke with a groan, his stomach churning, and face feeling like it was covered in dirt, the alcohol-driven perspiration leaving him uncomfortable and irritated. Zidaini lay sleeping beside him; his and Calum's weapons leaned against the wall. And the ship kept the sickly stomach from feeling even remotely better. He tried raising his head and it throbbed severely in answer, and he laid his head straight back down. Instead, he turned it sideways to face Zidaini.

"Hey! Wake up." He nudged him, receiving not a stir. "I think I'm gonna puke."

The Raiden rocked about, and with it Zidaini stirred in some lost dream.

Calum rolled over and stumbled off the bed. "Oh! Think I'll just sit a while," he sat in a slouch. Uninterested in moving any further, he simply was not able to get up.

Zidaini rolled over and fell off the bed over the other side. "How did the floor get in bed?" He asked anyone, confused at the possibility.

A large gush of water was thrown over Calum. "Ahh! What the....?" he cried out, as Ramuel, with his two right hands, poured a second freezing bucket of water over Zidaini, who was shocked to his feet, sparking into life. Both Calum and Zidaini were dazzled and screaming for air with water dribbling off them.

"Get up and about. You need to eat." The first-mate smiled at them, grinning at their soaked bodies. "You young'uns were some sight last night. Drunk more than the guests. Now Tifa's got food for you in the kitchen, so go eat." He left them to their hangover.

Calum's eyes reverted back to their waking moments, where with eyes difficult to open he took several attempts to take hold of his emerald sword. Once he held the belt of his sheath, he gave up, and leaned into the wall still standing.

Zidaini took up his and leaned into Calum for support.

"I ain't ever drinking again," he murmured. "I don't think I want to be seen, either," he said thinking of the remarks and jokes at their expense.

Calum had finally got his belt wrapped around him, and pushed Zidaini upright, and they stumbled slowly out of the room, heads heavy and eyes disliking the light. Walking through the hallways, they dragged their feet, while to their eyes and senses, nothing but the desperate bodies of rejection followed their slow lumbering movements.

Calum stepped out on to the deck first. His eyes, blinded closed by the sun, shocked into closing, he struggled to re-open them against the light, as he stood motionless at the bottom of the stairs.

Zidaini, fairing no better, the sun paining his eyes and staining to remain open, with weak groans following.

"This is gonna be a slow, despairing day," Calum said still with his eyes closed.

"Aye!" Came Zidaini's short reply.

Calum attempted to keep his eyes open, looking through a small slit of open eye, trying not to squint while he took in his surroundings. Climbing the stairs to stares of amusement and laughter from other passengers, his eyes were unable to tell if it was directed towards him.

The captain watched them come on to the deck, the sight of the pair bringing joy to his heart, he had always enjoyed the stowaways, the event always cheered the crew and passengers, and not once had any stowaway survived the gooladi. "Well, if I have ever seen such a sorry pair of young'uns. You look abysmal." He grinned. "But I had great entertainment when you two charged from the kitchen." The captain teased as he walked down from the bridge. The boys had already given up on standing, and had sat on the deck floor. The captain stood over them. "I apologize for not introducing myself. I am Captain Naruda Vilo Sienta. It was very nice to have the pleasure of introducing you to the great cooking of Tifa, and his specialty, the gooladi." The captain was quite pleased with himself. "We should arrive in Libera in a few hours. You slept for most of journey, and the Raiden has made good time." He couldn't help but grin while they sat on the floor. He went back to the bridge and paused on the stairs. "I'm sure you two could've taken on my crew. Why didn't you?"

Calum looked up at him. "Never sailed before," he said.

Naruda raised a brow.

Zidaini grinned, completely understanding; neither could he sail.

"There's food awaiting you," he said and left them.

The two boys helped each other up and made their way to the kitchen. Calum gripping Zidaini's shoulder.

"Don't ever jump ship again."

"You didn't like getting drunk then?" Zidaini said smiling.

"I didn't like golad, goolad, whatever." Zidaini laughed. And they walked into Tifa's kitchen.

"Ah! Young'uns. Have a drink of the finest water." He poured a jug out into mugs, and passed them over. "Thanks for the fun. Now, then. You two spewed your guts all over the place. Was worth the cleaning though," he said and took another mug for himself, as he pondered the pair who ate slowly the food in front of them.

Ripe and fairly fresh fruit.

They ate what they could and went back up on deck, standing at the larboard side on the fore castle, looking off at the approaching city. The Raiden was venturing into the massive dock of the biggest port in the Liberian Empire that was jammed with merchant vessels, frigate warships and schooners, fishing boats and rich people's yachts. Large piers covered the front view. Behind were the tall buildings, with blue and white flags on almost every one, and cobbled roads that linked the city together.

Cathedrals to Odin, Shiva and Castelli reached out into the skies. Statues of gods and heroes, and famous mythical creatures lined the city's edge. Inns, bars and hundreds of shops, that had every item from every city across the north, east and south continents. Even rare items from the western empires, could be found here.

One of the two buildings that stuck out most was the city's oval stadium, for the Gaians' favourite sports. Looking overshadowed by the great new skyport, it was draped by a huge blue and white flag that, ruffling in the light breeze, went from its top and fell halfway down. The skyport, to Calum, seemed odd for Gaia and its technology.

As did the sight of a flying ship moving across the city towards the tower, its propellers protruding from a hull like frigate, carrying above the city. Everything was even stranger, but at least now he knew what an airship was.

The city of Libera had a railroad that linked it to the three empires, and the biggest cities on the continent.

Sea birds and all types of gulls swept from the sky in hope of another fishing vessel, as the Raiden etched into port, moving slowly through the many docked ships, and their allotted piers.

Calum stood in awe of the big city. He could tell Zidaini was excited to be back, as he took a sideways glance at him. The passengers were even getting excited at the coming alighting of the Raiden.

"Zidaini! How the hell do you have airships?"

Zidaini grinned at him. "The Adinans found a great ancient library of a lost people at a ruins near San Adina. They've found quite a lot. Trains, flying ships. Even muskets. They shared it all with us." He stared out at the city and his face became a touch disheartened. "Unfortunately, the Imperium spies were able to get their hands on airship and cannon designs. That could haunt us."

When the gangway was lowered, the crew stood to wish good journey for the passengers and thanking them for their patronage. The captain and first-mate were the last in line.

Calum and Zidaini cautiously, and trying to hide, walked through behind the passengers.

Captain Naruda was desperate for one last comment. "Aye, we're gonna miss ya," he said, trying to keep a straight face. "You're welcome back anytime, you hear."

The two nodded ever so slightly, keeping to themselves they had no plans to ever take the Raiden again, and walked off the ship onto concrete. The feeling of no longer swaying brought back their normal senses.

Σ

"So now where?" Calum asked, looking up at the weather. The sky had begun to turn a hazy twilight, with the darkness of night soon to stretch a hand and engulf the city.

"The train station. They completed the track a month ago... What? You look concerned."

Calum frowned at him.

"Don't worry. I'll pay this time," Zidaini said.

"So where exactly are we heading?" Calum asked, wanting more information.

"We're going to get the train to stop at about thirty kilometres outside of Libera."

"You can get the train to stop?" He asked as they moved through the crowd.

"Yep! We are going to see Hecate," Zidaini said. "He's a mage, and the best there is."

"A mage?" The two took a road leading away from the bustling port.

Zidaini gave him a look of amusement. "Yeah! Someone who can make fire and other elements appear," he said, weaving pass Gaians.

The train station lay ahead at the end of yet another cobbled street. A few shops lined its entranceway and the leading road on either side, each with a dozen or so people looking through the wares. Gaians were outnumbered in their own city, living for two hundred years. They never grew old

61

or frail, their hearts usually stopped and took them away. The Liberian Empire only ever had old people if they were foreigners.

Calum enjoyed the friendly buzz the people gave off. Splendid and vibrant colours were everywhere. Flowers never copied the neighbours, and an array of colours followed from house to house, each person to their own, and the same variety matched the hair styles, vivid and crazy, like Zidaini's spikes.

"See that?" Calum looked over to where Zidaini pointed. "That's the card tournament building. If you get the chance, you should play there." They walked on past. "Don't worry about missing anything, we're coming back for the lugarta tournament that's held here, so we will be back, and if you're in need of new clothes, head to Luminousa; more variety and cheaper."

"This is a big city," Calum murmured.

Zidaini smiled. "Every city in the Empire has something unique about it. Libera has the lugarta championship and the largest port in the Liberian Empire.. " he stopped talking as they walked up the few steps, and through the open iron gates. "And this is where my friends' headquarters are." Calum glanced at him

"A base?"

"We'll go there after I see Hecate," he answered.

They went up to the ticket booth where Zidaini organized the drop-off point with the Gaian at the check-in.

"Come on. Platform two. One goes to Libernian then Luminousa. And three goes south, straight to San Adina. By the way, so your amnesia brain knows, there are no trains to Caracoa, Redroa or Lusa, Dinero and Los Santos, hence taking a ship."

Calum looked over the black beams that held the roof in place. A walking bridge, painted dark green and made of iron, went over two tracks and the flying Scotia's red carriages. Two small stalls were on platform one where Zidaini grabbed some sandwiches, and together they crossed the bridge, taking a long look at the view of the station as they crossed.

"What's the emblem for?" Calum questioned, looking at two flags with the hilts of swords joining them together.

"The flag of the Liberian Empire. Which you must know without me telling you, as you've seen it flying above the city, and the flag of the Adinan Empire. A sign of union between us, combined with the fact that we worked on it together."

A Gaian shouted the next train was departing, and they quickly got aboard to find their cabin as the Empress Express to the Lulsan Empire pulled in. Their train departed almost before they found their paid-for seats within a compartment.

8

PALACE TRANQUILITY

Isis sat alone by the palace pond, high white walls hidding it from the rest of the world. The pond was rippled by ducks and their bobbing heads. Fuchsia's and roses of magnolia, amaranth and terra cotta dazzled her view. A setting that would please most, yet her heart just didn't respond, not even to the dozens of tweeting tits and chaffinches with beating blue yellows, black and whites.

No guards guarded by her. They patrolled the inside, and the entrances, deliberately trying to make themselves less of a nuisance to Isis.

She sat drinking from fine china and then was alerted by the break in the surreal atmosphere as the gates were being opened. General Leeron had entered the pond's setting and strode to her and the small table. She lit up as he came to her and stood awaiting him as he walked up the garden path toward her

"Ma'am!" The blond general called as he approached.

"Leeron, good to see you. Would you care for some tea?" She asked, wanting friendship to give her release from the dullness of the palace.

"No, thank you, Isis. I've come to tell you that our plans are in motion. My friend will be your guide, and your bodyguard. He is very loyal, and would never even dream of betraying you, not even to your father. Trust him with your life, for he will give his," the general said. He looked over her and smiled slightly at her shyness.

"How can I ever repay you and Leena?"

Leeron shook his head. "There is nothing you can give.

You will never be indebted to me. We do this because we want to."

Isis smiled shyly at him, her eyes borderline tears. "Thank you. I'll be ready."

"Goodbye and good luck. I won't be here when you leave," he said. Isis reached out and hugged him.

He was shocked for a moment but then caved in, and returned the gesture. He marched quickly away at her release, leaving her feeling excited at the future prospect of leaving the palace and the city. She longed to explore the world of Gaia, and its people.

She sat back down and leaned back in the chair feeling somewhat happier, and looking on the garden pool, she felt the beauty in it once more while she dreamed of what her adventures would give to her. What sights and sounds she will see and hear. She was to have her desired wish released for her to feel and touch, and it made her loll into the chair, feeling nothing else could be bad for her.

9

REALIZING. UNDERSTANDING.

Aboard the Viracocha's creaking quarterdeck and tight shrouds and square sails, Nortedes frowned; irritated by the length of time he had to wait onboard the carrack as it traversed the ocean. He was still dwelling on the reasoning for killing the colonel. Outside of war, it was a wasted endeavour. He, of course, being a general, knew of the build-up of Imperium forces at the Great city of Centrali.

'What are you scheming, Bushia?' He asked amongst his thoughts. *'Are you moving for war? Are you the aggressor?'* He asked himself.

The sky was patchy with plump white clouds. The odd ship appeared on the horizon. And the lands had long disappeared.

'You must be trying to rid your armies of me.' The thought sent an avalanche of understanding. *'Relocation of forces to Centrali and the moving of both Arosian and Hastati Specialli means a likely invasion of either La Agarve or Bamtam. I, being the only general who would oppose an invasion against an ally of the Liberian or Adinan Empire, must go.'* He was being kept away. But that still didn't explain the colonel.

'An invasion of Niguaraga is almost acceptable, as they used to raid our small villages near the border, there for a viable target,' he pondered. *But the officers had all been in Centrali.* The majority of the Arosian Specialli were still near Perpious, the capital.

'The senate wouldn't attack, surely?' He stood, angered,

still trying to piece together the situation. Wondering whether he should turn back, and meet Bushia's assassins.

'But if the Liberians really were to invade, he would need my Specialli to defend Eastania, as they're already there.' "What is going on?" He asked out loud.

The crew briefly looked at him before returning to their own business, scared by his stern face turning to glare at them.

'Hastatia wouldn't care about war either way, he'll jump on in if there is war. General Aros Narsisis would do any murderous bidding if it increases his reputation as a power-ful general. Grand general Bortedes would love to kill the little Gaians, and the fame and glory for himself. And the desire for the position of tyrant would gratify all of them.

"Why me?" *'I would defend from any species invasion. So he must be attacking. But why strike first, and risk a war against four species?'*

He walked away from starboard side towards the ma-jor's private dining room. His stomach calling to be filled, and he accepted the desire for food.

'I understand, Bushia, you want me gone because in an unjust invasion, the people will rally to me. I realize now… No general will resist war, but me. But why send me on an errand. Why not just kill me now. And just how have you secured the senate on your view?'

The questions he was sure would one day be answered. He stepped through the door and into his major's dining room and adjoining quarters. The major looked from his open door, from behind his desk.

"Nortedes, sir. Please make yourself comfortable, and take my servant, he will serve your food, and requests." The major gave a cheerful smile. He was a long time friend of Nortedes and the two had always maintained the friendship.

Nortedes gave a nod and sat down as a young man came from the office of the captain and into the dining room. The servant stood at attention beside the general. "Get some food from the chef boy, and make sure there's meat in it." Nortedes told him, leaning on the table to ponder more.

The major came out as the servant left through the door from which Nortedes had come. "Are you still thinking about your objectives?" The major asked.

"Yeh. Perhaps I should just forget about it. How's your life as a major for you, Nivedes?"

The major gave a smile and sat down. He poured a jug of wine from the large dining table and filled two goblets. "It is interesting. But so far, just like being a captain, except I'm not. Although the title has certain appeal, and I have more sway with the inner circles now," he told him.

Nortedes stared ahead.

"Come now. Stop this thinking, as it will not do you good. Think about the finer things in life." Nivedes told him.

"That is difficult. Bushia plans to wreck my reputation."

"Then fight him," the major said. Nortedes shook his head.

10

THE CAVE OF GOD.

Calum and Zidaini had their heads hanging out of the carriage windows, the wind brushing their hair while they took in the landscape of scattered pines and rocky terrain. The sea appeared within the intervals of broken walls of mountainous cliffs and hills. The pines were climbing up, and taking their places on the peaks of the hills.

"It's like this all the way up to Angus Dei." Zidaini shouted above the puffing and rush of wind, as they watched the pine trees drift pass.

The train whistled loudly in a long siren, signalling its intended stop for the two boys. The train was to stop precisely at the thirty kilometres asked for, and the engine slowed and the carriages nudged each other in its deceleration. The Gaian conductor reached them, looking out at the side of the track. "Funny place to stop."

"Aye, it is. But I've got family out here."

"Really?" The conductor reached for a handrail and leaned out of the threshold of the doorway, to peer down the track.

The train had almost reached a halt, and was in its last motions of the stop when Zidaini spotted the tell-tell signs of a track leading to Hecate's cabin. Two pine trees cut at the base, either side of the trail, helped to reveal its hidden route.

"There it is!" He called to Calum, who took a quick look out, wondering how many people live out in this wilderness. The train pulled to a stop, and they jumped down on to the sloping track, on to the gravel. While the conductor waved his green flag to get moving again. Calum and Zidaini waved the train away, and walked to the cut pines.

"By the way, it might be pretty, but keep an eye out for dangerous animals, they do get troublesome," Zidaini said.

"We'll be alright. I'm sure."

The track they walked on was badly kept and grass sprung up, sensing their passing. New shoots were trod underfoot as their feet found the ground, trampling them before reaching the height of the Gaians, like the grasses along the side of the trail that kept trying to brush them, curious as to what walks their path.

The boys spent a lot of time with their hands at their heads to fend off the too-friendly grass while mammals climbed the pines that provided shade from the sun and protection from the predators, and smothered in the vines, that carried red berries.

Eventually they came to a cliff face, with an entrance to a cavern at its base. Zidaini gave just a brief glance at it and continued past away along with the cliff, crossing wet stony ground that had been soaked by water that had run off both cliff and out from the cave.

Smoke rose from a cabin's chimney, its porch decking greeting guests. Sitting on a cushioned chair within the front porch was an old man, with deep sangria eyes and dark brown hair, watching them as they neared. On a small table in front of him were three green glasses and an accompanying jug, as if expecting somebody.

He didn't bother to shout a greeting, nor to stand up. He watched them scanning around, and brushed off a crumb from a long-gone sandwich that had fallen on to his sangria long coat.

Zidaini was smiling broadly. "Hey, old man! You still got that magical touch?" He shouted out. And Hecate quickly stood from his chair and hurled a rock of ice that formed in the air before him. Zidaini bolted from one side to the other, as he ran dodging several more balls of ice, until he reached the steps to Hecate's hut. The Adinan pushed a wave of wind into Zidaini, lifting him from his feet, and back on to the wet stony mud.

"Ah, unfair!" Zidaini said, not amused at the mud that caked his clothes and hands.

"Nothing's unfair in battle, I taught you that once. At least your speed's better." The mage sat back down in his chair. Calum walked over and sat down in the seat beside. Hecate watched him sit.

"Another without manners," Hecate said.

Calum noticed a look of remembrance. "Do you know me?"

Zidaini took a glass, and waited for an answer for Calum, thinking Hecate might actually pierce the bit of amnesia.

Hecate stared at the emerald sword a touch longer.

"No!" He answered, dashing both boys hope. "Here! Have some lemon. I was expecting you monkey-tailed brats."

"Really?" Calum asked, surprised.

Hecate didn't answer; he just took a sip of lemon.

"So what's up, Grandpa?"

Calum shot a look at Zidaini.

"Just the usual training that I expect you to keep at," Hecate said and lean slightly in Calum's direction. "Do you like the glasses? I made them myself."

"This one is alright," he replied, taking a gulp.

"They do the job," Zidaini added.

Hecate frowned. "You two brats want my help, don't you?"

"Maybe. We thought you would like the company." Hecate huffed at Zidaini, who grinned back while Calum sat wondering why they would want a grumpy strop of a man.

Hecate lolled into his chair. "I have a condition. You must head into the cave and retrieve a treasure chest, or at least what's inside."

The two boys became attentive. "So how do you know this treasure is even there?" Calum asked, cupping the glass with both hands as he leaned forward, with his elbows upon his knees.

"Because I've seen it."

"So why didn't you take it?" Zidaini questioned.

Hecate became reluctant to answer.

They stared at him, waiting.

"Well, I couldn't climb the cliff face down to the beach, and the nearest way down the sea's edge, has jagged rocks in the water... And the cave was to.. Resistant," he said irritated by his failure.

"And he wants us to go through the cave," Calum remarked.

"Some of the creatures inside the cave are resistant to magic. Ok?" Hecate argued.

"So, use a sword," Calum said.

Zidaini laughed.

"Be quiet, Zidaini. I don't have a sword."

Calum was amused. A great mage that wasn't able to achieve a task because magic was useless and he didn't have a sword. "Why don't you have a weapon, just in case?" Calum asked.

"He won't go and buy one. Thinks the Emperor himself will come after him. And I won't buy one for him." Zidaini mocked and received a stern expression from Hecate.

"And we want him why?"

"Listen, you little monkeys, as I've already said. If you do the task I've set for you, I'll come. I haven't any doubt that I will have any problems once back into one of the cities. I will though act with a touch of caution."

"Ok, me and Zidaini will be back in a minute."

"Zidaini and I," Hecate corrected. "Don't be long," he said while they walked confidently to the cave.

Zidaini was eager to enter. And Calum clapped a hand on his shoulder.

Zidaini stopped, wondering about his friend. "What's up?" Crimson red flowers fluttered at their feet.

"Considering your great mage grandpa couldn't get the chest doesn't mean we'll be able to walk in and out with ease," Calum said, bringing out his emerald sword.

Zidaini understood and brought out his daggers. "You

should really get a short sword at least," Calum stated.

Zidaini smiled as usual, and the two walked through the threshold.

Only to be greeted by a snarl from a sharp-toothed beast that was welcoming them into the cave, its head long at the end of a lengthy neck, with body that was plated all over. Short spikes pointed up along its tail, covering every inch of the top side. The twelve-feet long creature was angry at its shelter being trespassed.

"Pretty thing, isn't it," Calum said; he was getting excited at the prospect of a battle. The beast roared with defiance, a putrid smell forced from its breath towards them.

"Oh, by Baal! That's disgusting." The two choked on the stench. The beast was taking the time to move at them.

"I've had enough of this thing. Let's kick butt," Zidaini called, and attacked to the right. The beast's head ducked the silver-hilted dagger, then tried to swing its head to snap its jaws into the furry blond tail of Zidaini. With the beast at Zidaini, Calum lashed down upon its neck. Sapphire blood splattered out over the wet ground, the emerald sword passing through the thick scales.

The beast staggered as it tried to swing a tail out and scrape the spikes across one of them. Zidaini nipped in and stabbed his two daggers through its side. Responding in pain, the creature tried another attempt to sink its teeth into Calum, who slipped around the neck and hacked clean through the exposed neck. The body collapsed to the ground and its head dropped to a splatter into the wet surface.

"Easy!" Zidaini said.

"Would've have been easier if you had a sword."

"Yeah, yeah!"

The two went into the darkness, assured that the rest would be easy. The tunnel became too dark to see, and they only knew they were together by the sound of each other's footsteps bouncing off the walls, and the breathing from each other. Their hands felt along the soggy walls, and Calum was sure they weren't alone, by the scraping and scratching noises they could hear.

"Calum?"

"Yeah?"

"Can you use some of that magic of yours?"

Calum halted in shock.

"Heh!" Zidaini called as he walked into Calum.

"You see that?" He was sure Zidaini hadn't seen anything.

"How could I not see a flash of bright white light in a dark forest. So give us some light, please. Por favor."

Both of them could hear and sense the creatures coming nearer. Gurgles of sound drifted to them.

Calum brought his left hand to bear, holding it ahead of him, palm upwards. Amongst the sounds was that of water being splashed from a distance echoing in the cave. Flames licked around his hand, illuminating the surroundings, revealing the wriggling insects, and centipedes and other critters that crawled on the rock.

"Urgh! What is that?" Zidaini cringed, realizing it was what he had been putting his hand on. Furry flax-coloured moss gripped to the rock, ground and walls. Zidaini regained his composure. "Well, your flame's not white. What else have you got under your sleeve."

Calum shrugged in response.

"You can lead," Zidaini added.

"I was, anyway," Calum said.

They ventured deeper towards the gurgling noises, rounding a slight bend and into a large cavern where stalactites were hanging down from the ceiling over a clear pool surrounded in stalagmites and eight-legged reptiles.

"We have company," Zidaini said into the flickering cavern of glowing orange.

Their side of the pool seemed free of the beasts, and the creatures were reacting to the flame of Calum's hand and were stirring.

"I'm ready. Bring it on," Zidaini said not realizing the fact they were actually completely outnumbered, and the creatures were entering the water to get to them, sliding off the rock and into the water.

Calum took in his surroundings, the body of water that took up most of the cavern and even wondering if they could use the stalactites. "Get the ones I miss. I'll deal with these. His sword remained sheathed, and he walked to the pool.

Zidaini looked worried as he moved forward.

"Don't get in the water," Calum told him. The flame extinguished and they were plunged into darkness.

There was just the sound of the reptiles coming through the pool, leaving the edges and sliding down the sunken rock.

Zidaini was amazed by bright sparks that flickered and zapped around Calum's hands, brightening his body. He used the light to stab a creature several times in a fright, as it had crept up on them.

Calum forced the lightning to streak across the pool, ripping through the conducting waters. The reptiles writhed in pain, the lightning surrounding them and searing the skin. Their strange, gurgled screams echoed throughout the cave, a thousand sounds at once that combined with the electricity that scorched across the pool, killing the creatures. Water bubbled and turned to steam from the immense heat. The vapour rose and made the boys perspire fluidly.

Calum stopped.

The light died.

Blackness blinded them.

Zidaini was in awe, and could hear Calum breathing heavily. He went to him, crouching beside where he was sure he was.

"That was frelling awesome!" He heard Calum laughing. "Lightning, as well. You might give Hecate a good fight."

$$\Sigma$$

Hecate stood at the edge of the cave, worry on his face. "Where are they?" He questioned the air. He had expected them to return, and not fight in the dark. "Surely they wouldn't fight blind," he said, staring into the cave. "That

Zidaini, always trying to win, needs to learn how to lose."
He took a deep breath in, releasing it, he walked in. "Troublesome rascals, probably playing a prank on me," he groaned at the lifeless and headless body, of a reptilian. "Well they've started well."

He went in with fire on his hand, to light the way, furthering the distance of the darkness.

$$\Sigma$$

Calum stood up and gave off a small light to guide them. "That water looks cold"

The two hesitated at the edge.

"Perhaps you could warm up the water," Zidaini suggested. They were too warm and comfortable to go into the pool. They both continued to stare. "You first."

"Why me?"

"Because!"

Calum shook his head and smiled, and with a thought of encouragement to himself, he dropped down into the cold water that froze his skin at its contact. He held his breath to the cold so as not to reveal the true freeze to Zidaini, who dropped in after him.

"Hahh!" He breathed deeply, his chest feeling the icy water, and becoming tight. They were shivering as they climbed up the rocks on the other side and soaking wet, they went through another passage.

They came around yet another corner where the cave became more closed, due to fallen rock. Calum let his light die as it was replaced by a glow from outside, coming from the tunnel's end.

"See, easy. We're outside already," Zidaini boasted.

"You think Hecate will be jealous?" Calum grinned.

Zidaini smiled happily behind.

"Whoa!" They both exclaimed, walking from the cave to bright yellow sand.

"Do you think it'll attack us, if we go near it?" Zidaini asked, staring at a giant eagle cooped up beside a treasure chest.

"You should know these things," Calum stated. While Zidaini shrugged. "It doesn't look bothered by us at the moment," Calum answered. "Why though have we the giant bird? Hecate said nothing about it."

Zidaini mulled over it and shrugged again. "We could wait till it leaves."

"I'm not staying here forever. I need to eat one day."

Zidaini sat down on the sand, which clung readily to his wet clothes.

Calum leaned against a rock, where water and sand grinding had left indentations at its base. He rested a hand on the hilt of his sword. The sun's rays dispersed from sight, just a slight haze of light, to remind them the sun was behind the horizon.

The eagle shuffled in the sand, making itself more comfortable.

"It doesn't look hostile, looks friendly," Zidaini said, examining the creature from afar. "We'll go see in a minute," he said quietly.

Σ

"How on Gaia's wor..." Hecate became overcome with awe, as if the heavens had granted his every wish. "Well, I'll be, if it isn't an Azael eagle." Calum and Zidaini looked at each other, as Hecate walked towards the eagle.

"I guess it's friendly," Zidaini said standing up. The two jogged to Hecate, reaching his side; they came up in height to his chest.

Hecate was dwarfed immensely by the Azael, its head as big as Hecate's whole body. He stopped short of the eagle, admiring its form.

"This, boys, is the very first Azael eagle I've ever seen," he told them, a broad smile alighting his face.

The eagle fluttered the feathers of its head.

"It's sitting on our treasure," Zidaini mentioned, desperate to grasp the contents inside. Hecate frowned at him.

"Shall we scare it off?" Calum looked at Zidaini, amused at the suggestion.

"If you hurt it, I'll punish the both of you. It's a harmless bird, unless it meets its nemesis, the Baalier eagle, then it is very ferocious," he said quoting the history books.

The eagle rose on to its talons, bothered by their intrusion, lifting itself from the ground with a beat of its wings. A gush of wind was thrown out, and the boys dove for cover as a feathered wing rushed out at them. Hecate dropped to a knee. The eagle soared into the air, a haze of sand left in the air from its departure.

Hecate was mouthing something inaudible, in wonderment of the Azael eagle. His words were abruptly stopped by the sight of Calum and Zidaini eagerly at the side of the treasure chest, their eyes on the prize inside.

Hecate was enraged, not understanding how they were more interested in the treasure than the beauty around them. "You little brats, can't you appreciate what's around you?"

"Hey! We are. This is beauty," Zidaini said. He picked the lock, with a lock-pick he had hidden in his trousers. The two lifted open the chest, and beamed with delight.

"Whoa! How much do you reckon that'll fetch us?" Zidaini asked.

Calum realized what it was, and knew they wouldn't be selling it.

Hecate looked at Calum "You know what that is?" he asked. "That, boys, is the diamond of the white bird of lightning, the god, Quetzalcoatl," he said proudly.

Zidaini was delighted. "Cool! That's number two."

Hecate tried to keep his uncertainty from his voice. "What are you two up to?"

"I acquired the Sunstone of Shiva from San Adina, under the Emperor's orders," Zidaini explained, looking at the stone now in his hands.

Hecate knelt on a knee looking at the sand at his feet. "If you let these gems fall into the wrong hands, thousands will die. I am aware of your path, and I sense a perilous one."

Zidaini sat on the sand, listening to the words. Calum sat

down beside him, waiting for something further.

"I had a dream, maybe a vision. Told me that you two should get as much help as possible."

"In other words, you were going to come anyway." Calum realized.

"Cheeky Grandpa." They were smiling at him.

"I don't know what'll happen. But the gods have clearly desired it," Hecate said.

"Hey, we are gonna be the greatest team on Gaia," Zidaini informed them.

Calum grinned back. "Are you talking about kicking butt, or playing lugarta?"

Hecate peered into the chest to see if anything had been left behind. A piece of papyrus paper sat at the bottom. "You should really check everything," he told them. They shrugged. "The dark god is a stone's throw away."

"See, useless," Zidaini exclaimed.

"Zidaini! This is not useless, and you know what part of Gaia is called the stepping stones… As a god lies there, you might want to remember." Zidaini raised his lip. Not angrily, but knowing he had been caught out. "Now I don't want to see either of you two abusing your strengths along the way. Understand?"

"I wish I had some magic powers," Zidaini said, looking down and playing with the sand.

"You don't need powers, your speed is unmatched in all of Gaia, and your strength is pretty high, as well."

Zidaini beamed with delight.

"Hecate. How did you not get soaking wet?" Calum asked, still being tugged by the soggy clothes he wore.

"I turned the water into ice and walked across," he said, without thought of how amazing that was.

Zidaini smiled at Calum.

"Now, what about the resistance to magic creatures, because we didn't meet one?" Calum asked.

Zidaini folded his arms and waited for an answer.

"You killed it."

Σ

When they returned to the cabin, Hecate had organized beds and fed them, sending them under their protests to bed. He sat in front of the fire, with cauldron raised above it, wondering on their future. He would have to get back into practice. He had just been made to look quite inadequate, his magic skills needed to be restored to his usual status.

He woke them up in the morning as the sun climbed the first break of the horizon. "Breakfast!" He said, shaking Zidaini awake.

"Wh-What?" He sleepily called.

"Eat. Then we will get going," Hecate replied, walking back out of the room.

Leaving their weapons by their rumpled beds, the two boys joined the old mage at the table. They ate the meal silently, and Hecate took it as a sign they enjoyed the food, preferring the silence. He looked over their sleepy eyes, and was reminded of past memories, as the two swallowed the bacon down.

Zidaini's tail came round and slivered to the mug wrapping round the handle, his eyes looking in concentration. Calum was smiling, wondering whether he should try that himself.

"Zidaini! Do you mind not playing at the table?" Hecate ordered. Zidaini smiled, and his tail—which would've no doubt dropped the mug—safely swayed behind him.

Calum looked over Hecate's clothes. "I still think you need a sword," he stated, wondering if there was even a quill-sized knife hidden away inside the sangria and cardinal coloured long coat, that Hecate wore.

"I have my dagger," he muttered.

"What's with the daggers?" He asked as Hecate took their plates and dropped them into a bucket of water.

Σ

After the plates had been cleaned, Zidaini had leapt from

the porch playfully. They trekked through the worn track, Hecate moaning at the boys' comments about the trail.

"Clearly looked after by misfits, who never bother to keep it tidy," so they reckoned, teasing him.

"I hope you learn to understand the limit of your powers as we travel along," the mage said. "You'll learn. I'm sure. I will train you if you desire it," he added.

"Na! Zidaini says he's gonna train me," Calum joked.

Hecate looked shocked until he heard them giggling.

"I do hope you two will not be a hindrance for the entire journey," he said, while they continued to smile.

"Do you think we could have missed it?" Calum asked when they came to the stumps of the two pines.

"It'll be here. I didn't hear it going past," Hecate said, sitting at the side of the train tracks, and began meditating, crossed-legged on the gravel.

"What he doing?" Calum asked Zidaini.

"His asking the gods to turn us into quiet and good little boys, that we'll never ever bother him."

Hecate ignored their laughing, and tried to clear his mind of everything around him.

11

A PRINCESS SEARCHES

Isis ate at her personal dining table, hidden away from her father's attachment of advisors and spies. She was perky this morning, as this was the day that she was to leave; to finally see what she had always wanted to see. Her father had kept her away from society; a society that joked on her existence.

Now, though she had another something important to achieve as part of her objectives. She had been after a key to the hidden archives: archives where past discrepancies of secret vices, and clandestine operations against other kingdoms, of important events and even the birth list of every Gaian born. Most importantly to her were the archives of the gods. Past and present. Every known detail, and some stolen articles. A room that was hidden beneath the main structure. A place where Emperor Lousous had spent much time searching through the papers for any clue to the whereabouts of the gods.

General Leena had managed to have a key replicated, and passed it over to the princess. Now the emperor had gone to Libera for the lugarta, to make an obligatory trip for the opening ceremony. Isis held the small chain of the key as her maid walked in, and to her table, placing a letter addressed to Isis before her. "Ma'am. I've given you some food and medical supplies and tucked them into your bag, with a few potions, should you need them. It's already with your guide." The maid became teary-eyed, and Isis stood to greet her.

"Don't worry about me. I'll be fine," Isis said.

"I'm sure you will," the maid wiped away a tear, "I'll miss you, ma'am. Make sure you come back."

"I will. Thank you, Sierra."

"Don't you get into any trouble now. I'm sure your guide will be able to care of everything. I was told he is an El-seni," she said, almost in a whisper. "He's supposed to be well travelled and has a vast knowledge."

"It may be a long time until I return," Isis said, looking around the small dining room.

"I know. Now I have some work to take care off, so I'll get busy," Sierra said, leaving.

Isis picked up the letter, and unfolded its content.

'You must search for understanding of who you really are. Learn to be everything you can, but most of all, never judge others, and never anger with ease. Most situations can be solved without violence. Which is only for use against those that refuse to accept truth and justice, that are unable to open their mind.

'Embrace your skills as a summoner. I have left you with a gift that remains in Leena's hands for when you leave.

'Don't rush, take your time. Most of all, enjoy yourself.

General Leeron.'*

Isis finished reading the letter, and wiped away a tear. She had bonded with only a few, and Leeron and Leena were two of them. The two generals had always taken the time to tell her about the life of the world around her, they were her closest friends.

She placed the letter inside her pocket, and she headed for the library that concealed the hidden archives. The library was her favourite place in the palace—a world of knowledge that she thirsted for. As she walked past the one of the few lounges, she thought back to when she had summoned an aeon, which had then trashed the room, tearing apart the chairs and the couches to shreds. Her father hadn't become angry. Instead, his face had glowed at her ability, and seemed so pleased that he immediately went and got her a teacher, and a empty room to practice in. Of course, the teacher didn't last long. Lousous got rid of the Gaian for teaching her subversive thoughts.

Σ

The path to the library went through a corridor, too small for any past-age Adinan, or any human. The passage led down into the one of the many cellars. Encased in stone, this was where the supports for the main palace went deep beneath the surface. Staircases ran off at the sides to secret rooms. Some were used as dungeons for those the Emperor never wanted to see returned. But most of the rooms hid treasures: forgotten relics and artefacts, gold bullion and jewels from across the world, riches kept safe inside the walls.

She walked into the poorly-lit library, void of anyone. She went straight to the location of the secret room, past the stacks of books. A long gothic table took up the center. On the table were candles unlit across its length, for the few that used it infrequently. At the end of the concrete floor was a section of manifests and documents of laws, and deaths. Records of the people. Simple facts, nothing that takes away the freedom or privacy of the Gaian people, just their recorded existence.

One book was perched upon the shelf, the 'forever after'.

Isis could see it was out of place. It even looked fake. She had never bothered to look through the papers within their folders. Births and deaths were something she wanted to see, not read. These weren't stories, but figures, dull meaningless figures. Of people she would never meet.

"No wonder I never found this room, previous emperors put the boring stuff here." She pulled out the fake book, and a clonk sounded as a lever unlocked something behind the shelves, the book stuck at an angle. Nothing else had moved.

"Now what?" She looked over the books and papers, and could see nothing obvious. Nor anything else useful. Instead she looked down the side of the bookcase. 'Hinges!' She pulled on the end, and the bookcase creaked open. "Anything else?" She asked as she opened the bookcase further.

A cast iron door lay locked in her path. She pulled out the key, and slipped it in, and turned. A vault lay inside. A single desk strewed with papers. Around it, were eroded statues of ancient gods long replaced, no longer worshipped upon the planet, they had found a new home, to be forgotten. These deities were replaced by the likes of Odin and Bahamant. The ancient gods were in existence long before the first recorded Gaian history.

Stacks of papers had been searched through and Emperor Lousous had been clearly busy in his obsession.

She sat down and looked at the papers of his search. "The gods? Why are you so obsessed with them?"

12

NEARING LUGARTA

The train let off a cloud of steam, as it finished its journey into Libera. Calum and Zidaini leapt off the train, and like kids, rushed off to the nearest food stand. Hecate alighted the train slowly, then walked in their direction while they scrambled for some scones. By the time Hecate had caught up with them, they had already eaten a scone each and were in the throes of another.

"Got ya one," Zidaini said, handing one over, then with Calum went off, still eating and leaving Hecate wondering what they had in mind. He really felt like leashing them, and was sure they were up to no good.

Calum walked the streets with Zidaini while Hecate followed behind, keeping himself at a distance. Calum's eyes rolled over the sights of the city, taking in its architect. Zidaini was taking them through the back streets of Libera, the quickest route to his target of the Luverii stadium.

The city's kids watched Hecate walk by, curious about the Adinan. He wondered if any of their parents would recognize who he was, or perhaps to them he was another strange foreigner, lost in the empire's second city. Being lost in their young searching eyes under the shadow of the multi story buildings was for him, preferable.

They went along shrub-lined streets. Drapes of vines, smothered in flowers, fell down from the banisters of balconies with their windows open to the air. The narrow streets gave a scene of a vigorous and vivid life. Zidaini was taking them down streets that tourists seldom travelled; away from the sellers and their wares, just the home life of the Gaians.

It was a shock to Calum when they came to a sports field beside a park. Filled with families and friends, they were using the posts for friendly games of lugarta and park games. The park itself was covered in chestnut trees, standing high and wide, with small gardens dotted around, and Zidaini took them through.

"Seems a little out of place," Calum said.

"Got to have somewhere for space and play."

"True. It's nice. Mixes well."

"Sure does. I would stay here a while but I want to get to the stadium."

"You're not getting tickets to that ridiculous sport, are you?" Hecate questioned from behind.

"Not exactly. Tickets to watch, no; tickets to play, yes." Zidaini smiled at Calum, he knew what was coming next.

"Don't expect me to watch," Hecate said with a grumble.

"Yeh, yeh. I'll give you a supplementary ticket. If you want to use the bar while you wait for us, you can."

Zidaini walked them down the last street that wound to the stadium grounds; a bustle of teeming motion, as crowds gathered for tomorrow's tickets, stretching from the stadium grounds, to the outlying streets, all excited and eager for those priceless tickets, and chatting away to pass the time, the talk of the tournament was on every tongue.

"We aren't gonna queue here, are we? It's huge!" Calum's eyes were wide with shock at the possible long wait.

"Nah! Team admittance is separate. Come on, it's over there." He walked them over to the team entrance booth where a dozen foreigners were also signing up. Daggered eyes pierced the air at them.

"What's this? Easy meat, for the taking."

"I don't have time for nobs, Vaaska. Your pathetic Head Crushers won't stand a chance against us," Zidaini said. He walked on past, uninterested in the human.

"You got the guts, but have you got the skill?" The Regonian grunted. His other human friends gathered around him.

"They're kinda sad, huh?" Calum said, walking past Vaaska's friends. Their eyes shot towards him. Hecate looked amused trying to hide his smile at the contesting group.

"You better watch your mouth, boy," one of the followers said. Vaaska had taken notice of Hecate's big frame, knowing the Adinan was powerful. He even recognized the face, but couldn't place the mage.

"This is a waste of my time. See you on the field, boys!" Vaaska said. He walked off with his colleagues in tow and their attempted strut.

"The uneducated persons need to attack others. Simple minds," Hecate said, referring to Vaaska's crew, "are a waste of people's time. It should only matter what happens on the field, not off it."

"Yeah! But I'm still gonna kick their butts." Zidaini wrote down some team members, even though he didn't know whether they were still alive, and gave it to the Gaian girl, behind the counter.

"Make sure you're here early. As you're not a seeded team, you'll have to play the opening qualifiers," she politely said.

Zidaini nodded, and then went back to the others. "Right. Let's go."

"And where are you planning on staying?" Hecate asked.

"You'll see," Zidaini's answer was vague. And immediately Hecate knew he was hiding something.

After a short trek across the city, Zidaini took them down a street of pattern corbels and neatly decorated frames and houses with pillars supporting roofs at the front of the building, each even had its sides and backs done with beauty. The Gaians prided themselves on making the place beautiful. Not just the fronts, like the humans did, to make themselves look richer, or important, but every section, to make themselves feel better and prouder about what they have.

"A hotel here would be very expensive," Hecate remarked, looking at the houses of the city's suburbs.

"We're not staying in a hotel," Zidaini smiled as Hecate frowned.

"So where?" Calum asked.

"There!" They had reached the shabby-looking Mary Rose Association.

"Criminals!" Hecate fumed. "I thought you weren't doing those offensive acts anymore."

"I'm not," Zidaini replied angrily, "I was on a mission for the Emperor."

"What does the Emperor want with thieves?" Hecate queried.

"I'll clue you in after I've spoken with the first Royal. We have to see him to deliver the package."

Hecate said nothing as Zidaini knocked on the door, just in case someone was actually in. "There shouldn't be anyone here except the housekeeper."

The door creaked open, and a hairy bare chest leered at them. Calum and Zidaini looked set to vomit. Their hands were covering their mouths. Then Zidaini realized who it was, holding back the sickly feeling that the grotesque stomach of the Adinan was giving him, and the shock of who it was.

He tried to speak. "B-boss! How the hell did you get back here?" He found himself able to speak as long as he remained focused on the Boss's face.

"I suppose I should tell you.. Come on in." He rubbed his hairy flabby chest, even making Hecate feel a touch revolted.

They followed him through a corridor that was open to the sky hall. Clearly the Boss once had plans for the place. Mattresses ran along the walls on one side. A few were slept in by bandits. Some grimaced and murmured in pain. The smell of blood drifted across from them. Then the Boss took them outside to the patio steps where a neighbour's barbecue sent over the scents of cooked meats.

The Boss sat on one of the three steps that joined the patio to the garden's poorly kept lawn. Zidaini sat next to him, while Calum sat leaning against the wall. Hecate stood over them, patiently waiting for the boss's explanation. The smell of food, he noticed, was being sniffed at by the boys as they fidgeted.

"After we sent you on ahead, just in case we were followed, we entered Foresta Nero. Only to be attacked by vicious goblins," he said clearly thinking back. His eyes looking upwards to the clouds. "They killed several of my crew, before we forced them to withdraw. We decided to get out of the forest to the west."

"What about Jazz and Osera, Vasca an-"

"You're thinking about your lugarta team! You cheeky little brat," Hecate moaned.

The Boss looked on angrily at Zidaini, who shrugged with bemusement.

"Keep going," Calum told the Boss.

"Well at least someone is listening. Well, they survived, by the way. Anyway, it turned out they hadn't retreated, but had just regrouped. Little bastards charged us. We fought like gods. It was clear we were surrounded. Sure it was to be our end, would've been. But then big balls of trailing white fire from this great dragon came down upon the goblins. Kinda like rain."

Zidaini shook his head looking at Calum, who smiled back.

"It was beautiful..." His eyes left them, deep in remembrance, of a past moment, that only a few will remember.

"Hello!" Calum called.

"Sorry! Sorry. This beast was being ridden by a dark being, like no species I've ever seen, called himself Hades. I knew there was something about him not to be trusted, something not right. This Hades told us to climb on the strong dragon. Once in the air, he headed towards Libera. Kept asking about the Sunstone to Shiva.-"

"You stole from the Adinan royals. You-" Hecate slapped Zidaini across the head.

"Hey!" He rubbed his spiky hair and his face pouted sulking.

"They are a noble pair, the Queen and King Alvares, and you are risking the alliance between our two nations. You must return the Sunstone," Hecate fumed.

"We should worry about this later," Calum said, "I want to know more about this Hades."

The Boss continued under Hecate's scornful gaze. "This Hades got real angry because we wouldn't tell him where the Sunstone was. He shook the dragon violently. Lost Learkra, fell to his death... Then he questioned again. I told him it had been sent to Lusa, with a girl. Simply described you with brown hair instead. Stupid dope!" He laughed thinking back on it. "He dumped us to our bruises, tipping the dragon upside down. We fell off, obviously. Hurt like hell. Right near Libera, though."

Zidaini was looking at the floor. "Er? Oh! Is that it, finished?"

"You bloody nuisance." The Boss stormed off, and headed for the small second floor corner office.

"Looks like this is getting bigger. What have you two got yourselves into?"

"Three!" Calum corrected.

"Did you find all that really boring?" Zidaini asked looking at Calum.

"Yeah! Couldn't even handle a few goblins. But I do believe we need to think about this Hades, or at least be wary of him."

"We can worry about him later. I've got to teach you some lugarta."

Σ

"Well, what have we here?" Zidaini's eyes lit up as three friends walked in. "Got ourselves to the lugarta sign-up. And low and behold, someone had already put us down."

"Jazziera! Vasca and Osera. How are ya?" He said giving Jazz a hug. She responded with a peck on the cheek.

"I see you survived," She said releasing him.

"Of course. Goblins stood no chance against Calum and

me."

"Yeh! Unfortunately we lost a few of our crew," Vasca said.

"But the Odinian Demons are alright?" Zidaini asked.

"We managed to all get out of there, even Bawn and Jalerik." Jazz said.

"I like your purple hair, it suits you." Zidaini complemented Jazziera.

The Gaians looked at Calum. "We take it you're Calum?" Osera asked.

"Aye!"

"That's a cute sword," Jazz said, admiring the emeralds. "Cost you much?"

"Yeah, it did. So, shall we get some practice in?" Calum questioned looking at Zidaini.

"Of course," came a cheery reply from Zidaini.

Hecate watched them all go outside, chatting away. He sat himself down on the patio and watched.

13

STADIUM LUVERII, CITY OF LIBERA

Bands played in the corner of the stadium, their songs sounding up into the oval Luverii. The crowd was dancing and enjoying the entertainment provided. The beer flowed to many of the visitors of Gaian, Adinan and Lulsani populace. Thousands of souls had come for the opening games, with an arrange of attire that was both colourful and bizarre. Faces were alight with glee at the prospect of drinking to the lugarta's first tournament of the year, and calling out in support for their love of skills and plays from each of the teams.

Teams of sellers carried trays of fluids and freshly-made pasties filled with meat on their rounds throughout the stadium.

In all of the crowd there was just one who sat without laughter, and without any love for the tournaments proceedings. Hecate sat still, waiting and watching for the boys. Nothing else was on his mind to do with lugarta, not the banging and singing of the bands or the dancing people within the crowd.

Beneath the mass of cheers were the Odinian Demons, kitted up in their yellow and black. Zidaini came through the dressing room door, a smile lit upon his face.

"What is it?" Calum asked, unable to stop himself from smiling with Zidaini.

"Who are we facing?" Jalerik added.

Zidaini's grin continued as he spoke, "Our stupid rivals, we play the Head Crushers."

They sat now looking forward to their encounter, ready to take on the humans they hated so much.

Σ

At either end of the stadium Luverii were two Gaians acting as announcers, with their cone shaped speakers at the ends of their mouths, calling out the games events. A belief that the crowd would get into the game more led to the calls from these announcers. And as the food and drinks flowed, they shouted:

"LADIES AND GENTLEMEN, WE'RE HERE FOR ANOTHER ACTION PACKED SEASON OF LUGARTA. THE FIRST TOURNAMENT OF THE YEAR. TWENTY-TWO TEAMS HAVE SIGNED ON, ALL HAVE NEW PLAYERS FOR THEIR TEAMS THIS YEAR."

"Right, we're second on, after the Libera Angels versus the Redroa Rocks." Zidaini said.

Calum looked around at the nerves itching the group. Tapping of feet and fidgeting fingers were telltale signs of nervous players.

"You remember what I taught you?" Zidaini said looking to Calum.

"Yeah, sure. One thing though, I've never played before." Zidaini smile broadly.

"Don't worry, you're starting as sub." Calum's heart sank. His friend could see his desire to be a part of the team, and a part of the atmosphere that was affecting the crowd of watchers above, but he had to be sure he was ready.

The calls for the beginning of the first match came through the tunnel, with the Libera angels and the Redroa rocks racing out behind them.

Calum and Zidaini walked out towards the touchline to watch the game, and were hit by a roaring crowd, excited and enthusiastic supporters, their outrageous costumes, a colourful array of dress, combined with a euphoria that lifted up both the boys. Their eyes glowing with excitement, as they rolled them over the crowd.

Calum looked to say something, but words never exited his mouth. Zidaini was not much better, lost in his infused state.

The game was quick to burst into play. The Libera Angels steamed into the Rocks, showing their previous year's power.

Calum was quick to admire the Angels who worked the oval ball far too quickly for the Rocks to keep up with the fast pace. A breakthrough came straight away, the try line coming up with a few steps. The Rocks left behind.

"TRRRYY!! ONE TO NONE. FIVE POINTS TO THE LIBERA ANGELS. THEY LOOK ON FIRE."

Music blared out around the crowd. They leapt with joy and continued to dance to the band that played with every stoppage. Hecate was still in his gloom, high up in the stand, he felt the enormous desire to leave the stadium, instead of watching the cheering crowd.

"OOH! LIBERA ARE ON FIRE. ANOTHER TRY!"

$$\Sigma$$

"Sir?" A crewmen called to Nortedes, regarding the general with a passive face. Nortedes had begun to have a few drinks, and was thinking less of his future. "We should be in Regan in a few days." The crewmen quickly faded away from Nortedes, who was clearly not interested in talking to anyone while he hung over the side of his usual spot.

'It would be quicker if I got some sleep,' he thought to himself. He had decided to venture on the mission. He would do what he had been ordered to do, what the senate had asked of him. It was not the time to go against the senate.

He strolled, less than steady, to his lavish quarters, with

a wide king-size bed. Traditional colours of black and grey covered the room. Large cushions and a duvet were draped over the edge of the bed. A huge bird of prey emblem hung above the bed, on the back wall; yhe national symbol of the Imperium, which adorn the royals.

He took up a jug and filled it with rum. He saluted the eagle, holding the salute with sarcastic attention. "To the fall of the Imperium, my beautiful home. See you at my fall," he said bitterly. His actions would ultimately start a war between the empires. In his eyes, the Imperium couldn't stop the combined forces of the eastern continent. He downed the mug and sunk into his bed. He lay staring up at the ceiling. The hours wouldn't be passing quickly. Thoughts of his past and future, would keep him awake. Dreams of the bad events in his life would echo viciously through the period he will try to sleep. Good times are always forgotten in times of stress, and the low feeling that was eating him was forcing his mind to run cold parts of his past through his head; every last detail, easily remembered, to never forget.

He closed his eyes anyway, trying to close his mind off, to simply see blackness within his eye lids. But the dreams of his future and the memories of his past continued to strike him. Even the rocking and swaying carrack, which usually wouldn't bother him, was clearly heard, and felt.

He rubbed his face and stared upwards. Another drink entered his mind, he would fight the temptation though, a clear head for the day was always his preference.

$$\Sigma$$

The first half was over and the teams begun to walk from the field. Both Calum and Zidaini were still at the tunnels entrance while the beleaguered Rocks went past to the dressing rooms, with heads down, revealing the story of the half upon their faces.

"These Angels will go far," Zidaini said, watching the Gaians go past, confidence across their faces.

"Four tries to none. They're looking tough," Calum added.

"They always get far in this tournament. Think you're up to it?"

Calum smiled at him. "We're gonna kick their butt..." He was alive in the stadium, a familiarity. "You know what. I feel like I've played this game before, just feels like I know what to do and expect." The feelings he were having in the stadium was close to his heart, something in his past echoing within him.

"Maybe you do. You'll know for sure when you're out there." There was a certainty in his voice, a belief in Calum's past.

"HERE WE GO. THE SECOND HALF TO BE-GIN. FOUR TRIES TO NONE, THE ANGELS OVER THE ROCKS. CAN REDROA COME BACK FROM SUCH A DEVASTATING START""

Calum hoped for a stronger half from the Rocks, a comeback for the troubled side. Their faces had showed an eagerness to play, as they return to the field. They delivered.

Their tackles were more ferocious, attacking with more desire, a need to prove themselves. The Angels were being kept back from their half. The tackles were timed and painful.

Calum watched the oval ball kicked up and over, the Rock's chasers racing for the ball's target. Underneath the ball was an Angel, wary of the incoming chasers. The ball entered the usual safety of his hands, and he was smashed by a chaser. The ball fell from his loosened grip. And another Rock came pouncing upon the ball.

"TURN OVER! TURN OVER! THE ROCKS HAVE POSSESSION AT THE ANGELS TRY LINE."

The Rocks were on the offensive, cheered on by the crowd. The ball was being passed across the line, with the intention of finding a way through the opposition.

Calum and Zidaini shouted out support to the Rocks as they assaulted the Angels. A player broke through, and charged towards the try line. Caught up and tackled, the Rock player laid off the ball to a team-mate, who dived for the line, slamming the ball down behind the try line.

The crowd roared. Calum and Zidaini leapt with joy.

"THE ROCKS HAVE PULLED ONE BACK,
AND ARE LOOKING THE BETTER TEAM."

Stadium Luverii was in the party state. The people clapping their appreciation for the revival, and a huge cheer was sounded as the kick off was launched by the Angels, who were unfazed by the points against them. The Rocks were met by the Libera Angels line, trying to regain their previous superiority. Only to have one of their players misread a feint. The Rocks poured through the gap.

"NUMBER TWO, NUMBER TWO!"

The Angels were stunned, their eyes looking in disbelief, with hands on hips. They were a strong team that was looking vulnerable.

$$\Sigma$$

Hecate had found the bar as the game went on. The bartender was stunned by someone using the seated bar area, instead of buying a dozen from one of the kiosk which dotted the underpass around the stadium. He was grateful for the attention, as only a few came into the bar area away from the lugarta fans. He was just as bored as Hecate, and grateful for the attention.

"Take it your here with your kids?" The stubble face Adinan asked.

Hecate saw the irony, and a small smile creased his face. "You can certainly say that." He took a sip, and listened to another eruption from the crowd. Another try from the Rocks. "When does it end?"

The bartender barked a laugh. "At least six hours"

"What?" Hecate's face dropped. "By Horus, no!"

Σ

"IT'S OVER! FOUR TRIES TO THREE TO THE ANGELS. THE ROCKS GAVE IT THEIR ALL, AND TOOK ON THE GREAT ANGELS. BUT THE ANGELS ADVANCE. NEXT UP, THE ODINIAN DEMONS VERSUS THE HEAD CRUSHERS."

Minutes later Zidaini was leading the team on to the field, leaving Calum to head for the dugout. The two sides took position on the field. The dugout of the opposition with manager, trainer and sub sat ready while Calum wondered about the Demons' lack of off-field leadership.

Vaaska held the oval ball, and in a parabola, swung his boot through the ball, his weight pushed forward, his studs ripping the ground in a scar, while his boot launched the ball high in the air. The Crushers moved quickly forward, chasing down the receiver of the ball.

Zidaini, beneath it, moved forward, passing the oval ball off to Bawn, who was instantly crunched in a tackle. The ball fumbled from his hands.

"OOH! THAT MUST OF HURT."

Hecate had returned to his seat, beer in hand; he had decided it would be dutiful to watch the boys, and he looked out over the crowd at the attacking Demons. A prang of emotion touched his heart, softening him to that of a pillow, rather than the rock he usually was, as he caught sight of Zidaini carrying the ball forward.

He came up from his seat, uncontrollably rising as the Demons picked and drove for the line, his voice shouting out. The Crushers stopping them just before the try line, meeting each drive inches short of the line.

"WHAT DEFENCE! THE DEMONS AREN'T BREAKING THROUGH."

Calum couldn't contain himself, he was screaming out encouragement towards the team, and finding himself irritated by Bawn's lack of ability. Hecate was now shouting his old head off. His cool had faded. An uncontrollable allegiance to Zidaini and the Demons had taken over; his passion had risen with roars of support. While on the field, Zidaini had recovered from a Bawn mistake, and tackled Vaaska who had broken through, and Zidaini had chased for half the field before taking the player down. But it wasn't enough, Vaaska was able to pass the ball off for another Crusher to race through and score. The Demon's defence had failed.

"TRRRY!! TO THE CRUSHERS."

Hecate threw his beer in angered frustration. It flew to the steps lower down, covering a rather overweight, beer-bellied human fellow, right on the head. Quickly, he ducked down to hide behind the seat in front, embarrassed by his outburst. Calum's heart had sunk; he felt with Bawn on the field, that the Demons were with a huge weakness. He was desperate to get on to the field, and was pacing in frustration.

Vaaska pushed Zidaini in the head as he walked snobbishly pass. "No chance!" He sneered, and walked back to the Crushers half. Zidaini stayed sitting on the ground. He looked at Calum pacing in front of the dugout, he was seriously contemplating bringing his untried friend on to replace the incapable Bawn, who was making even Jazz angered.

14

AROSIAN SPECIALLI

Columns of black-armoured foot soldiers and lightly-armoured archers from the Arosian Specialli trudged through the brown-stained snow, which squelched beneath thousands of feet. The wind carried a blizzard of snow across the landscape of perfect white that covered every bump, hill, tree and any plant life that existed upon the land. It blew, swirling through the air and into their eyes, and chilling them further in the gruelling march, and adding a blanket of snow over them.

Watching them head past, while he sat saddled on his mare, and wearing no extra blankets or clothing around his body of armour, sitting warm against the cold, was General Aros Narsisis, a vicious human who considered Nortedes not just his rival, but an enemy. His hate for Nortedes was surpassed only by his disdain for the Niguargan people, the intended target of his very own Specialli. He was ignoring the many white flakes of snow hitting his face and drifting into his eyes. He surveyed the long stretch of his army with an aloof pride. His colonels, Rika Liarta and Relarus, both of which despised each other openly, like a Nortedes and Narsisis to each other, were beside him.

"It's about time we received these orders. Those scum have been a thorn shoved deep in the side of the Imperium and twisted in her very heart," Aros said. Sitting tall on a still and well-trained horse, his face was bitter at the thoughts of his enemy.

Rika turned his face in response. Hearing Relarus agreeing irritated him. The colonel was covered neatly in a thick fur blanket, and Rika didn't try to hide his hate for Relarus; the general knew of it anyway. Relarus's opinion was irrelevant for Aros.

To Rika, the Niguargan people were no longer a nuisance. Neither side had come to any kind of hostile engagement for the past thirty years; both sides had come to a mutual non-aggression pact, without any calls for one. The results, now, were simple trading between the nearest village of the Imperium and the city of Niguarga. A harmony, as Rika saw it.

Aros adjusted his breastplate with a hand; he took pride in his black armour, and loved the feeling of power that came with the patterned uniform of armour. Wearing the dark cloak gave him a sense of class and added transcendence. He would have preferred if only the generals could wear the black cloak, but that was not the case. His face was far from beautiful, coming off as a tough but scary feature, with scar across his face. Women would not fall for him; if it wasn't for his position he would never have one, and he knew it.

Rika on the other hand, was a beauty, his good looks and his almost white hair upon a young healthy face, made Aros despise him. The general was always to feel outdone by the colonel.

His eyes went to the far end of their columns of soldiers. To the new stolen technology, the Iberian artillery, cannons. The stallions were easily pulling the heavy weapons behind their well-groomed hides.

"Walking death," Liarta said, audible enough for Aros.

"Yes! Yes, they are. Niguarga and Cravi should suffer quite nicely."

'Under the white of Gaia's beauty comes a plague to swallow everything.' Rika kept his thoughts to himself, then guided his shining white horse away, leaving the two behind.

Colonel Relarus stared at the leaving colonel, and spoke to Aros when Rika was out of earshot. "Sir. Why did you keep him? He is like Nortedes," he groaned.

"Exactly. Left to rise to general, he would become a threat to me. Under my control, he will not be able to challenge me; he is beneath my feet to be trampled on." Aros laughed above the noise of the marching men and women of the Specialli.

Relarus smiled and watched the soldiers marching on, not even noticing that what Aros Narsisis said could also apply to him.

15

LUVERII WATCHES.
ANTICIPATION AND EXPECTATION

Hecate sank into the crowd heading for the nearest toilets and kiosks, his chest sore from shouting and throat feeling tight and dry, he was angry with himself for cheering and shouting when no one on the field could hear him. The thought of them finding out was far worse. He was, though, in dismay at the one try to nothing score line, and shocked by the way it was eating him, as he walked through the happy and bustling crowd.

He noticed the amount of Gaians draped in the colours of the Liberian Empire; the blue and white cross, with a second angled behind the first. He loved their sense of pride, and wished he could join in with this happiness that surrounded him, abound in all those here. Yet something was beginning to plague him, a scratch inside his mind, something was to end that laughter and joy until tears doused that happiness away. A darkness was coming, and he felt it, was sure of it, knew that it was going to cover the empires. The pain and sadness would replace this, that he could see. It all made it so much harder to embrace a happy state. He had even begun to pray to the gods, even the human ones. The bar he was heading for brought him back to a clear frame of mind, and he was quick to order.

Once again he was rushing back through the throng, to get back to his place in the blue seats of the stadium. On his return, he sat impatiently waiting, trying to see down into the tunnel, an impossible feat as the tunnel went beneath him.

He stood up in a shot as Vaaska led his team on to the field, the mostly Liberian crowd booing the Crushers. Vaaska didn't take it to heart.

Σ

Zidaini and the Demons followed straight after, to applause from the fans. Hecate immediately entranced by Calum's entrance to the field of play, to a confirmation from the announcers.

Calum, excited and eager to play, took up position on the field.

Zidaini shouted out to him, "Remember! Charge the player who catches the ball. And no magic." Calum grinned back as the magic comment was made note of by the opposition.

Zidaini signalled he was to kick by raising the ball up above his head and down to his feet. His boot swung through and launched the oval ball high up into the air. Vaaska came beneath it, and the ball was caught in enfolding arms. Calum, at full speed, dropped his shoulder and launched into Vaaska's gut. The crowd gasped in awe, while Vaaska's face turned to anguish. The execution of the tackle was so perfect that the ball was lost by Vaaska and he was left writhing on the grass, curled up in agony.

The ball was seized upon by Jazz, who was quick to lay off the ball to Osera, who pounced through.

"TRRRY! THE DEMONS SCORE. LEAVING
VAASKA IN BREATHLESS PAIN"

Zidaini leaned over Vaaska, looking into watery eyes. "Perhaps you should sit this half out. Eh?" he suggested.

Vaaska groaned in response, and a Crusher teammate in Larka picked the man up from his grave.

Zidaini threw an arm around Calum. "Wow! You kick

105

butt" Calum was grinning. His entrance to the team had left a huge statement to the crowd, and he felt proud by it.

$$\Sigma$$

Hecate was deep into the game, forgetting the world around him, and roaring on the Demons, and their crunching tackles. The score remained the same for a long time. Yet the crowd thoroughly enjoyed the spectacle, they lifted once again as they see Jalerik pass the ball out to the left. Osera sucked in two players before just getting the ball out to Calum, who raced through the gap created by Osera, straight through the centre. The Crushers chased the speedster, but to no avail. Calum drove the ball down and roared to the crowd in celebration.

The elated team cheered the try as if it had assured victory, embracing each other as they crowded the try scorer.

A worn-out Vaaska felt like it was. His colleagues had their heads down, and arms drooping down, eyes revealing a picture of despair and loss. It wasn't the end just yet, but for them it was.

The Demons celebrated all the way back to the half-way line. The Crushers slowly took their time going back, gutted to be viewing the faces of their opponents.

The referee, waited for the kick to go up. And once again Calum crushed Vaaska to the ground, leaving him bruised and battered. The full-time whistle blew a second after and the Demons went wild.

Hecate jumped into the air, screaming out.

"VICTORY TO THE DEMONS! AWESOME PERFORMANCE. BUT DO THEY HAVE THE ABILITY TO GO ALL THE WAY?"

$$\Sigma$$

The announcer's voice was faded out as Calum and the team went down through the tunnel, faces filled with cheer.

They were past their first opponent, a second would follow. For now they would talk and boast with each other within the dressing room.

On arrival, Zidaini grabbed Calum from behind, clasping his arms around the top of his shoulders. "You're a star."

"Yeah, I am," he said, cheekily. "But it ain't over yet."

"Nah, not yet. Cracking tackle on Vaaska, by the way. The idiot didn't get up for ages." Zidaini let go and sat on the bench, leaning into the wall, and resting his head against the solid concrete wall.

Calum sat down next to him. "That was fun. He won't be giving any big talk next time."

The others sat along the bench opposite.

"Oh, so you'll be continuing the lugarta for the future," Zidaini smiled.

"Yeah, yeah." Calum leaned into the wall.

"So who's next?" Jazziera asked.

"The Regan Racers will be next, and they'll be fresh," Zidaini answered.

"Yay! So, who won last year?" Calum asked. He see Zidaini smile. "What? You're joking right?" Calum shook him playfully, while grinning.

"We're playing them next."

"No, really?" Calum double checked. "The Regan Racers, where are they from?" He whispered. Zidaini laughed. "What? Don't tell me. Regan."

"First time humans have ever won. Very disappointing." Zidaini raised a lip, slightly disgusted by a human team from the dirty continent winning. "So do you think Hecate managed to watch us play? Zidaini questioned, changing the subject with an instant return to a smile.

$$\Sigma$$

Hecate took a large mouthful of chicken off the bone, delighting in the tender taste. He stood to the side of the field, his eating stopped as he heard from the wall's edge the announcer called the Regan Racers versus the Odinian

Demons. The match was about to start. He looked back up the rows of seats to his own, and sighed. He began the walk back up. Accompanied by cheers from the crowd, the Demons were coming back on to the field, and the crowd were right behind them, wanting the former and shock champions to lose and be out of the tournament, and bring back the normality of the competition.

Hecate was unable to walk without taking constant looks toward the boys coming back on to the field, not realizing how desperate he looked to those who were around him.

16

THE SAPPHIRE OF CASTELLI

After several hours reading and absorbing information on the gods, Isis had found a text that had caught her attention. Among seemingly random writings and the obvious selection of information about the gods was the mention of a name, Colonel Samiaraita. He had been sent on a mission to Londinium to collect the gems of gods, and the name, Mary Rose, a group that was to meet him there.

It was clear her father was searching for the stones; perhaps he was looking to strengthen the military with the power of the gods. She was scared he had other thoughts in mind. The power he could yield would be immense. War would be easy with gods that could wipe through regiments with ease. She pondered their strength, their awesome power and magic that they have. In history they have helped armies massacre other armies, hundreds of people in single hits, then to disappear into the history books, as heroes or if the enemy survived somehow, feared as great villains.

Princess Isis nervously walked through the corridors, and expansive halls, taking wary looks at the guards lining the halls, staring endlessly ahead, silent amongst the statues of past heroes and gods. She knew the guards had seen many things, and had kept those secrets hidden from the world outside. Voices that had stayed in the dark, never revealing the gossip of the palace.

She had made notes of what she felt she needed to keep; the mission of Samiaraita was first to her mind.

She reached the servants' quarters which were empty of the lines of guards. She sighted Siera walking along the dark corridor with a basket of laundry.

"Siera!" She called, stunning briefly the maid, as she walked quickly towards her.

"Ma'am. What are you doing here?"

"Please find a pouch to put these in and leave them in my carriage," Isis said, and placed them on the laundry, then rushed away, without a further word. Siera went to speak, but stopped short, leaving the princess to disappear around the corner.

"What is she up to?"

Σ

Princess Isis walked into the centre chamber, a room never guarded within. A single statue of the god Castelli, the god of fire, was roaring at unseen soldiers, its two legs and arms ready to pounce upon its enemy. In its chest, an empty hole that once held the sapphire of Castelli. Now the glazed green and white gem had been removed and hidden from the view of the guards, and anyone else who could find themselves gazing at the stone.

She recalled the conversation between her father and a mysterious stranger; a being that had somehow gained the trust of the Emperor, a solid black creature that had the deepest eyes, that to her were like a bottomless abyss, the depth never to be established.

Σ

"Emperor Lousous," Hades said, as he reached the Emperor's side. "This sapphire, it holds great power, yes?" The demon asked.

The boy Emperor's eyes crept over Castelli, admiring the god's historic power; the lessons of his childhood, running through how powerful the god was, travelling on in his head.

"It is like a god, only it is called by a summoner; a good summoner, not just some mage of magic and aeons. Those abilities of calling fire and beasts are not enough, you must be gifted be able to hear their voice, to speak to them. Very few have the gift, very few. The stupid humans have even slaughtered their summoners, through fear of them. Not us, we protect ours," he paused, and looked at Hades, "unfortunately, we have not had someone with the ability since the Asucion war. They just seem to be a lessoning breed." Hades did not add anything for a while, just stared at the statue with the Emperor.

"What about this Shiva in Adina? Is that just like Castelli? I was told it resides with a person of power."

"Power, power! With Queen and King Alvares. You imbecile!"

"You need these stones. Perhaps I can find a summoner," Hades said, ignoring the outburst. "Perhaps you will not require their help anyway. Although I suggest retrieving these gods; they will be a great use. Especially as the Imperium looks for war, would they not?"

The Emperor turned away from the statue. Hades moved from his way with bowed obedience. "Hades, your knowledge of the gods is poor, so keep from trying, as it is clear I surpass your level. As for Shiva, I'm already trying to find the appropriate people for the job, and they will be collecting the Sunstone of Shiva. Thankfully, Hades, you do have some use, your reports on the Imperium are being put to immediate use. Now I suggest finding yourself a further use."

The Emperor marched away. And Hades was escorted out by the Libernian Royals.

$$\Sigma$$

Isis had seen the sneer upon the demon's face, although she felt it could've been a strange way of showing happiness. She wondered on his intentions, and was scared of her father's.

Now with the Emperor in Libera, for his usual obligatory showing for the lugarta tournament, she stood looking over

Castelli, which was encircled by six great pillars; each having the same code engraved into a scroll like bronze plate. Above the statue, the ceiling was a stained glass that resembled Castelli and Odin, standing strong together.

IUYXFC VON FXMN ZUM VON WXGNH XA
APHN GPVO VON UZSN XA VOPD WXM

She knew it was a code and it was one of those things she enjoyed doing. This code, her father had created. A loyal mage though, had sealed the sapphire beneath the statue in an iron box. The renovations had taken a month. The Emperor had closed the chamber on its completion and had the workers imprisoned. The sapphire had been put in the secret compartment once the site had been cleared and anyone with knowledge of the renovations secrets were out of the Emperor's way.

Isis moved quickly through the code, even as she took her time knowing no one would be disturbing her. It was forbidden to venture into the chamber unless with the Emperor himself. For Isis the code was simple, having had plenty of time to learn such puzzles and even past civilizations languages. She was quite adverse in ancient Amarian and all of the languages of modern times.

She voiced the code which echoed off the acoustic walls. The magic seal was broken with the call. The statue of Castelli shook and moved. The ground shook and the pillars signs glowed briefly, as Castelli's movement allowed her to see the small hole with a simple iron box resting inside. No key hole had been placed on to the box, the Emperor clearly not thinking it a necessity.

She opened it with a glint in her eye. Seeing the smothering rag that hid the sapphire, she grabbed it, grinning. She was going against her father, and as she moved the rags and revealed the glazed green gem, she knew she was hurting him and his plans. Her fingers wrapped around the small sapphire, she placed it into a small purse hidden away in her pocket. She was going to find Colonel Samiaraita, and get him to help her; she was sure he would.

She glanced around at the two entrances. No one had entered. Perhaps they heard and knew it was Isis. Someone would find out about the missing sapphire. That was obvious, as the Emperor was a regular visitor to Castelli, always checking on his prized possession.

17

AND LUVERII SEE

"WHOA!! AGAIN THE DEMONS TACKLE A
RACER AT THEIR OWN TRY LINE.
THEY'RE UNDER PRESSURE FROM THE
HUMANS."

The Demons had spent most of their time defending
their own try line. The Regan Racers once again had the
ball, and a player tried to get through the centre, running
straight forward. Zidaini drove a shoulder into the stomach
of the racer, forcing the player to the ground. His teammates
pushed off Vasca, who went down to make a grab for the
ball. The ball was thrown out wide and Osera and Calum
were covering. The Racer on the ball reversed direction and
launched a hospital pass over the head of his nearest colleague. The ball came down into another pair of hands, and
Zidaini charged into the receiver, shoulder into the ribcage
of the human, putting the guy to the grass. Jazziera picked
up the ball from the clinging hands of the Racer, and with
support alongside her, she went forward. She was tackled
by a chaser, Vasca launched in over her, and protected the
ball as Zidaini laid it off to Osera. Taking on an opponent
he laid off the oval ball to Calum, who charged into his
tackler. The human bounced off, dropping to the ground.
Calum stepped over and raced through their lines. The try

line seemed to be in distant lands to him as he raced for it.

He could hear Zidaini shouting him on. The ground echoed of thumping feet chasing him from behind. He did not look back, and just took in the rising hum of support from the crowd.

Hecate roared out, as Calum reached the try line. The chase had been in vain, The Demons led, in a game they had been out-played in, all throughout the match.

The Racers though, did not give up, and heads did not drop. They continued as if their lives consisted of nothing but the title. They went on the offensive just as they had through the game. It was like an endless tirade of tackles. The Racers would not lose hope, and could see the Demons were tiring.

The clock was counting down, the crowd was cheering for an upset.

Calum brought down another player. The Racers secured the ball within their ruck. He laid underneath two players wondering if it was going to end yet.

The crowd called the countdown, roaring on the seconds. Zidaini made another tackle, himself thinking the last ten seconds were taking forever. The siren sounded, the ball needed to be sent out of play. Osera took out another Racer, and Jazziera followed suit near the touchline. Calum moved behind the ruck and lined up the next opponent who took up the ball, and went straight for the man who pushed Jazziera off. Calum wrapped up the legs and lifted them off the ground in a spear tackle, the human's head smacking on to the floor. The ball fell free, and Osera booted it off the field.

The Demons erupted in celebration, jumping into the air, and crowding each other in their rejoicing.

Hecate melted into his seat, glad and proud of the victory. Across the other side he noticed someone, in all his surrendering to his feelings, he hadn't noticed until now. He could see Emperor Lousous, surrounded by guards. From the distance he couldn't see whether the Emperor was happy or not. His past echoed within his mind. Contempt passed through him, and he pushed it away, wondering if he would ever see the boy face to face again. Hecate stood up and made his way out of the stadium.

$$\Sigma$$

The changing rooms were alive with the noise of joy. Wine was being thrown upon each other, of which Calum found the taste too bitter for him, and tried to get away from Zidaini and Jazziera, who were covering him in the wine from their large bottles that took both hands to hold.

"Get away, will ya," he shouted out. The rest of the team was laughing and continuing to pour over each other. He left the room to rid the taste of the white sparkling wine, changing into his clothes as he went. He was hot and tired, and felt the need to escape the celebrations.

He walked through the hall and out to the fountain that was gushing water out from the mouths of four little'uns and into its fairly deep pool. He stood resting his hands on the sides, staring into the water. He was a part of a winning lugarta team. He had been thrust into a world that he couldn't remember. It all seemed so bizarre. He wondered if he would ever know his past, and if it was as interesting as it was now, and whether he had ever been doused in wine before, something which now lingered on his clothes.

He sat on the edge and let himself fall backwards into the water, which engulfed his body. As he went in and dropped to the bottom, coolness smothered him, and he relaxed. His eyes closed, the water rippling in dazzling light that flickered and flashed in his eyes.

While the water caressed Calum's skin, Hecate had walked to the fountain and stood looking at him. Calum opened his eyes and was shocked to see Hecate's big frame, and sat up quickly, embarrassed by being caught lying in a fountain.

"Hi!" Calum rubbed his forehead, sitting with the water at his chest.

"You know, some people would think it strange to find someone alone in a fountain," he smiled as he said it.

"Yeh, yeh," Calum replied and crashed back into the water.

"Very strange," Hecate added.

Calum came back up and sat there with a confused expression upon his face. "I haven't breathed since I ran for that try." Hecate looked up at the sky in thought, as he sat at the edge. "And yet I know I'll need to breathe in a few hours."

"Sometimes there are no answers. Maybe as time passes you'll get what you seek," the mage replied, and Calum looked at him thoughtfully. A silence came over them until Calum broke it with a splash, as he climbed out and sat on the edge. The water running off him, and soaking the wall that he sat upon.

"Did you watch us play?" Calum curiously asked.

Hecate was quiet for a moment. "I managed to sit through your two games."

"Games, huh!' Calum said, grinning at Hecate's hidden reply.

"Hey!" Zidaini called, sitting beside Calum. "We have the Habana Bulls next, and we don't play for a while. So we're gonna deal with some business in Libernian," he said, still excited from the game and not taking in Calum's soaked body.

Hecate rose from his seat. "I'll pick up your weapons," he said and wandered off around the stadium, and leaving them alone.

"You ok?" Zidaini asked his friend.

"You know, I can hold my breath for ages."

Zidaini just laughed at him. "Wow! You can beat me at something."

"Oh you!" Calum bowled him over into the water. Splashes were thrown over the edge and on to the floor outside of the fountain pool. Zidaini came up from the water grinning at the laughing Calum, and he leapt out after him. Calum raced off. Zidaini in hot pursuit. Zidaini caught him quickly, and took him to the ground at the corner.

"Ah! You bastar-" Zidaini tried to pin Calum, who

struggled to block Zidaini, and get him off.

Hecate was walking back looking at the bundle of weapons he carried. The crowd was drinking at the gates of the Luverii behind him.

The hilt of Zidaini's silver daggers and Calum's emerald sword glinted in the light. There was something powerful about the sword of Calum's, something worldly.

Calum and Zidaini came to a crushing halt before Hecate, as he stared down at the weapons

"Some would think it strange to stare at swords," Calum echoed Hecate's original words. They seem to be just as excited at having their weapons back as winning lugarta, making Hecate wonder whether they should be allowed such sharp objects, as they swung them and admired their blades.

"Right, let's get going. Shall we?" Hecate asked, watching them finally put their swords away.

The two boys followed Hecate through the thin crowd heading for the station of Libera.

Calum leaned close to Zidaini. "He watched us play lugarta."

"Did he?" Zidaini beamed. "He's a cheeky old man, isn't he? Bet he cheered his heart out, never admit it though."

"Did he ever have any sons or daughters?" Calum questioned.

"He's never told me."

Calum wondered on the statement, while they walked past dozens of closed shops and cafes, only a few remain open. The usually busy streets had just a few walking through the bars. Until the end of the day's events, the streets would remain this way, then the throng of supporters would congest the bars that would open with the end of the day of lugarta, filling them full and drinking the rest of the day away.

The station lay ahead. And very few were there awaiting their train home. "Come on, you two," Hecate moaned at them lagging behind. He was walking up to the ticket office, as a train hooted from inside the great station. The boys went racing off for the train.

Hecate shook his head and watched them enter. "Not even our train yet." He could see them slow down across the station as he walked in with tickets in hand. Both slumped onto one of the black benches. He noted their tired postures, pleased they were. He might get some peace on the ride. He laughed at them, while he went over the station toward them.

18

REGAN'S HAZE IN SIGHT

Nortedes was at the bow of the Viracocha. The distant cliffs of Regan's shore were coming into view, and were covered in a haze of fog, with clouds of still grey drifting overhead. He was here to kill a Gaian, and this was the first port of call. And awaiting was a lengthy ride, even assuming he could find a horse, for the long ride to Londinium. Yet, it wasn't on his mind; his uncertain future now plagued his thoughts.

'If I go back. He'll finish me I'm sure of it.'

The clouds dropped down in drizzle. Another hit of depression to his face, as it blew over him, adding to his sadness.

All his life, he had fought for the Imperium, stood side by side with the black army, fought and served with honour and fortitude. Now the senate was to oust him. He had known his powerful position had installed fear within the senate. An army had signed allegiance to him, thousands of soldiers that were his alone. They would follow him to his death, even if it sent them to their destruction, they would sacrifice themselves. He knew this had distanced the senate from him. But why not General Aros Narsisis, or Hastatia? Both equally powerful, and he knew Aros had no love for the senate. Were they to suffer the same fate? Or was all this paranoia? Is he believing in what Bushia wanted him to believe? Make him turn against the senate, was that it? To make him make the mistake of turning against the senate, and give fuel to his own burial pyre.

He would find out from this colonel, force the Gaian to

reveal why he was there. Perhaps the senate really believed there was something for them to fear from this one Gaian, but that just didn't seem right.

Although the senate could oust him if he killed the boy, yet even with the distance that was creeping in the shadows, he was sure the senate still loved him. Perhaps Bushia, in all the man's stupidity, had somehow convinced the senate to fear its generals.

What he did know while he looked out to the hazy Regan was that the end of his career was stirring, and it would be painful to lose everything he loved.

19

FOUR ARMED MONSTER?

Princess Isis rushed through the halls of the palace. She was awash in happiness; the constant dreams of seeing the city were to be realized; a reality. Even now as she ran past the tall windows of the palace side, she lived the ideas of what the city would look and feel like from the stories told to her. Joined with what she could see of the city, she had pieced together Libernian. The biggest of the Gaian cities, the capital was far wider than Libera, and had buildings away from the palace as tall.

General Leena watched the princess enter the kitchen, lacking the decor of a princess, and wearing the clothes of her servant. It made the general a little less sad, and made a small smile rise across her face, helping her to hide the truth from it. She wasn't getting the princess out to experience the world; she was protecting her from the Emperor, whose plans were less than kind for Isis.

"What do you think?" Isis asked, with a twirl.

"I think you make a servant dress elegant," she said, and received a blush from Isis. "Come on, it's time to leave."

Isis felt her heart tighten and beat faster, while she followed Leena out of the palace kitchens. The rooms were empty on Leena's orders. There was no one within the palace walls that didn't know of Isis desire to leave the hold of her father. They had done the bidding of the generals without remark. Leena took her out from the backdoor of the servants' section to where a carriage lay waiting, simple in design, no emblems or patterns, a poor man's travelling compartment.

Isis couldn't help but stare at the Elseni sitting at the reins. The chosen guide had two of his four arms taking hold of the reins, while his other two rested in his lap. The man from Bamtam carried two decrepit axes, old and rusted, and at his side, so as not to get caught on the carriage when they were at the normal place upon his back. Two swords hung loosely at his sides. His revealing clothing allowed for the sighting of hair across his chest.

He looked over at her while she stared at him, and she could see he recognized her. Those dark Prussian blue eyes, had taken her in, remembered her from somewhere. But she didn't recognize him. He seemed to shake his head, as if to rid his thoughts.

"That is Valkesies, he will guide you, and protect you. Listen to his words," Leena told her, breaking her stare. She placed a chunk of pyrite into Isis's hand. "Horus is strength," she added.

"Thank you!" She said, under a swell of tears.

Her maid came to her side. "I noticed you staring at him," Siera said. "He's a giant."

"And he has lots of hair. I wonder how he brushes it," Isis grinned.

"I don't think he does." They giggled together.

"I guess I should get in." Isis climbed the steps of the carriage. She turned back. "I'll be back."

"One day. Just remember not to stare too much, for humans will think they can cheat you so hide your money, especially in human territories," Leena told her, knowing Isis was still safer leaving.

Isis waved them goodbye as Valkesies was nodded away by Leena. The gates were opened for them. Leena and Siera watched them leave. Siera wiped away a tear. Leena walked back into the palace, leaving Siera wondering why Leena wasn't more upset. The generals loved her just as much.

Σ

The rickety carriage's iron-strutted wheels clattered across cobbled paths and roads, the trip a constant smooth-less ride.

She took in a deep breath as the palace grounds disappeared around the corner of a junction. She would have felt small in the carriage built for an Elseni frame if it wasn't for the fact that this was the first time she had seen the houses and people of the city, and she tried to take in every detail of the surroundings. These were her lands; her people. The Gaians' home and she was mesmerized by it. A new experience and it was dazzling to her. Each person that walked the darkening street; she could see the closeness between the Gaians, the way they embraced each other like a close family. It was what she was desperate to see.

With each street that Valkesies took she saw something that made her want to take a look. A theatre, quaint shops that were small and homely. Even a Gaian sitting on a bench just watching the people go pass, was a welcoming feature. Each street was filled with Gaians relaxing or playing the evening away. Each of them she wanted to meet. But she found herself too shy and without the confidence to ask Valkesies to stop. He seemed to be taking her somewhere, and he hadn't spoken yet, not even a simple call back to check on her. She hoped that on her journey she would gain that courage.

Valkesies had taken her through the back streets of Libernian, away from the main road. He had no desire to cross paths with the Emperor on his return. The Emperor would be back from lugarta on the next train in.

The carriage pulled to a halt. Isis looked out from the window, trying to see where they were, and why they were stopping. Valkesies jumped out onto a narrow road outside.

Isis waited inside for Valkesies to open the door of the carriage, like she had been taught by her tutors. Royalty, after all, did not let themselves out.

"Are you coming?" Valkesies called out. Isis abruptly stopped in thought, and became embarrassed by her situation. She forced herself out of her embarrassed state, and opened the door herself, and stepped out into the new world. She stood on a pathless road, just the narrow street. She watched the few Gaians that chatted in the street. She felt nervous and a little uncertain. She walked hesitatingly to where Valkesies stood, before an open door to a flat-faced wall of a three window house.

"Will you invite her in?" A friendly voice called from inside the house. Isis tried to look through the doorway. Valkesies stepped, in taking a last look down the road. Isis followed him inside.

"Hello! My dear, please come in and make yourself at home now, young'un." Valkesies' wife took her over to her couch and sat her down. Isis looked around at the towering ceiling. The woman was excited, clearly happy at the opportunity for conversation with a princess. "Valkesies! Go get the tea and biscuits." He sighed and left them alone to get the prepared tray. The smell of brewed tea came through the kitchen to the room, a delightful scent that lingered throughout the lounge.

"Now, my husband said, no calling you princess." She was nervous speaking to Isis, and it showed clearly in the way she stuttered, clearly unsure how she should approach speaking with a princess. She sat on the edge of her chair, two of her four hands fidgeting. The others holding on to the seats, tapping away. "He did say that calling you Isis should be fairly safe, as there's a few of those named Isis, unless you think changing your name would be better."

Isis was distracted by Valkesies returning to the room, with a tray in hand. He walked across the blue and white furred carpet, past shelves with ornaments of Liberian and Elseni designs.

"We believe that no matter what, you should embrace the culture of the country you're living in," Valkesies said, noticing her looking around their room. "You haven't answered Deerdra."

"Oh, I'm sorry. I will keep my name," she answered, taking a cup from its place upon the tray.

"Now, Isis. You have to wait here a while to avoid the

Emperor. Then you'll be free to explore the distant lands first."

Isis face dropped.

"I'm sorry, dear, it's for your own protection. The Emperor will send people to search for you. Both you and my husband will be safer in faraway lands."

"But I so wish to see Libernian, and the Liberian Empire," she said, feeling hurt.

"We will need to keep on the move, spending more than a day in one place is too much. We'll make our way south," Valkesies said.

"Oh don't you make her miss the lugarta," Deerdra told him. Isis smiled briefly. "After all, it is a showcase of Gaian celebrations, and it is pure madness," she said smiling.

"That will be dangerous," he huffed.

"Don't be silly. You just protect her." She turned back to Isis, taking up a biscuit. "Now make sure he makes it exciting for you. He is under my orders to give you an account of each town and city's history. Plus I want him to make sure you get to do something that you want to do in each place you head for." Valkesies shook his head as Deerdra spoke.

"I will," Isis said.

"Remember, I have experience, and seen things you will never see. Done the things you'll never want to do. I've killed to survive, and killed because I was ordered to. I travelled to distant lands. Been in wars. Shared conversation with pauper and rich alike. I've experienced every type of person imaginable-."

"Oh, I doubt that" Deerdra interrupted. "My husband may be experienced, but he has a lot to learn about dealing nicely with people. Just make sure he's nice to others."

Valkesies decided to leave them to it. Deerdra smiled as he left. Isis grinned at her.

Once he had left and she had swallowed a bite of biscuit, she leaned towards Isis. "Listen, he does have a lot of experience, and endured a lot in life. Just don't let him get a big head."

"Has he actually worked with royalty before?"

"Of course, dear. But please don't remind him of it. Something happened a long time ago. He and his friend lost someone they loved and protected. Well, they're not so much friends anymore, drifted apart you see."

"Oh, how sad," Isis said.

"It was... Oh, that's his name, Hecate! Almost forgot the grand mage of the Liberian Royal Bodyguards."

20

THE GODS WATCH WITH
POTENT ANXIETY

The train dropped its speed, and came to a stand-still, leaving Hecate angrily looking down the track from the carriage window. The distance held the capital city of Libernian that sat across the large lake of Farii, which the train rounded on its way into the capital.

Hecate fumed loudly out from the window. "What have we stopped for?" He shouted. The sound of heads thumping on ceiling and bunk came from behind him.

Calum turned onto his stomach, rubbing his head with his hands.

"What are you shouting at? You moron."

Hecate pretended to ignore his low outburst.

Zidaini stumbled from his bed, his tail just as limp as he was, to stare blankly out of the window. The lake was the only glittering movement under the white moon.

Calum laid on his back, and stared out at the stars through the small window; one of four that dotted the ceiling. The sparkling specks of light seem closer to him, like he could be amongst them. Beautiful to his eyes, he lost himself in dreams of them, not even listening to Zidaini and Hecate talking, while he searched the stars. Shouts and sounds that weren't there flowed in and out of his mind, not there long enough to grasp what the noises were.

"Hey!.. Hello!"

Calum snapped back from his trance, reality returning.

"Huh?" Calum found himself being stared at by Hecate, whose face was a sign of disbelief, while Zidaini was giggling with laughter.

"Where were ya, K? Stuck in the stars?" Zidaini mocked.

"You weren't listening to a word I said, were you?" Hecate questioned.

Calum momentarily hesitated. "Not really," he answered, lying his head back down.

Hecate frowned at the boy's response. "When we get to the palace, and see the Emperor, you must show absolute respect and dignity at all times, regardless of how he acts." Hecate was interrupted by a train going past, only two carriages; it was gone just as quick. "That was the Emperor's train..." He said, staring out after it. "As I was going to say, the Emperor has become more irrational over the years. I don't want to find myself trying to rescue you from the palace dungeons. Understand?.. Calum?"

"Wh-hat!?"

The train had begun to move again. Zidaini jumped back into bed, sinking his head into the pillow.

Hecate sat on the bench. *'What am I doing? Going near the palace.'* He was becoming more worried, nervous of the possible encounter with the Emperor.

Σ

The train pulled into the cathedral designed station. Along both sides of the track, pillars crafted with intricate patterns of climbing ivy, towered high for support of the awesome depicted ancient battle between the Liberian Empire and Asucion Empire, painted over the ceiling of the Libernian station. A marbled floor, adorn with granite statues of gods was presented to passengers alighting the trains.

Hecate was first to step off, attracted immediately by the white pillars and green painted ivy. The huge scene above him stopped him in his tracks. He had been a part of the campaign in the war against the Asucion Empire. The sight of its depiction was truly impressive.

Calum stepped off behind him, in awe of the station, and still heavy from need of sleep.

Zidaini was worse and had glazed eyes.

Hecate looked at them and knew the perfect remedy, his very own energy drink. It will wake them up with a single sip.

They walked along the almost empty station, a few passengers followed behind, giving the station a sense of life. Passing the station cafe on the way out into the plaza, Hecate refused their stated need for coffee.

The plaza had horse-drawn carriages waiting to pick up travellers, to take them further, at a small cost. The drivers were waiting patiently, an unwritten rule never to approach and irritate people. They wait for a signal from someone, who wants them.

Hecate ignored them, and went across to a stable owned by the coaching house next door.

"Wait here," he said. They stood, glumly waiting, while Hecate went into the coaching house, as no one was within the stable walls.

"What's he doing?" Calum asked, without thinking.

"Oh, I don't care," Zidaini replied quietly.

The gates to the stable were slung open by a Gaian, who said nothing to them while a carriage was pulled out by a trotting mare, Hecate sat holding the reins.

Calum and Zidaini stood staring.

"Well, get up here." Red eyes looked down at them in bemusement. They climbed the steps slowly up to Hecate, who pulled out the smallest of vials. "Drink just a sip, no more, clear?" He received just a vague murmur.

The two swallowed a touch each.

A feeling of euphoria gripped the two of them instantly, before fading to just the feeling of being awake.

"Whoa, awesome! Can I have more?" Calum beamed. The tiredness was gone, and he sat on the seat at the reins.

"He said a sip. Do you really think he'll give you anymore?" Zidaini said.

"Well, he might be nice..... one day."

Hecate sighed at Calum's comment.

"Yeah right. He would never give us anymore. Think

about it, he even carried it in the smallest of vials, because he was too stingy to give anyone more than that."

"Yeah! But surely he would give us some to keep our reaction speeds at the highest."

"Yeah! But-"

"Boys!" They both looked at him, as he guided the carriage down the streets towards the palace, the couch bobbling along the traditional cobbles.

"Did you enjoy lugarta?"

Hecate sighed, realizing he should have given them the vial later.

Calum interrupted Hecate's answer. "Did you see that tackle I did; floored that guy."

"Hey! I was trying to get Hecate to admit to watching lugarta."

"He already has," Calum replied, looking bemused.

"Ohm right. Awesome tackle, I loved it when Vaaska was stuck on the ground, unable to rise. Sucker! Did he say whether he enjoyed it?" Zidaini asked Calum.

Hecate's head dropped.

"He lied. He said-"

"Calum! Be quiet. Both of you..." He could feel them staring at him. *'Maybe the potion was too strong,'* he thought to himself.

"How many years are you?" Calum asked.

Hecate closed his eyes, reminding himself never to give them the drink again.

On the main street, the 'Castela', shop signs leaned out from above the shops, signalling their location, to lure new and old customers to their wares. 'The sunny café,' 'the Great Ritz night club,' 'Jackion bar,' and even 'Thee Old Potion shop,' all along a line of other shops.

"He isn't answering," Zidaini said, giving up with waiting. "Shall we guess?"

Lanterns followed along the paths, patches lighting the night for the late-nighters. Many Gaians were still out on Castela, traversing the bars and streets, the night clearly not over for some.

"How come you don't know? What about, we make him tell us," Calum said.

"Yeah! Good idea.-" Zidaini looked seriously at Hecate, who was laughing at the thought of them trying to make him tell them anything.

"Yeh, punk!"

"Don't think we can, eh?" Calum asked.

"Will you two be quiet? For that matter... I do not think it wise to hand over the Sunstone of Shiva," he said changing subject. He was worried about handing such power to any nation's leader.

The two boys remained quiet as Hecate took the carriage from the pavilion and on to the palace road. A change of scenery was made from bars and shops to trees and shrubs with centre statues leading up the middle of the road to the palace that sat at the road's end upon a Gaian-made hill.

"Will you make a reply," Hecate told them.

"You told us to be quiet," Zidaini said, quizzingly.

"Yeah! I just thought you might give us some more of that drink."

"Ok, reply to my statement, please," Hecate said, now absolutely sure they weren't getting anymore.

"Hecate, Hecate, I want money, the Emperor has tons of it, and is going to pay us a lot," Zidaini replied, looking out over the skyport that sat over the city's skyline.

"Are you gonna give us some more?" Calum asked.

"No!"

"That's not very nice. We're hungry and thirsty," Zidaini said.

Calum nodded in agreement. "Yeh. I think you should buy us some drink."

Hecate looked briefly at Calum, whose eyes began to search the stars. "Later, I promise."

Two obelisks were in their view of the T-junction, either side of the palace, with Odin, the god of death, looming over the front gate. Hecate turned away to the right, looking for the side entrance. Small iron struts, over a wood door, were tucked into the side wall, guarded by two Libernian

Royals.

"Let's hope this goes as well, as the stars shine brightly," Zidaini said, leaning into Calum, who was staring up at the stars of the night sky.

"Yeah, they are," Calum said.

Zidaini raised a brow. The carriage came to a halt. The guards watched them curiously.

"Em! Calum, you can stop staring at the stars now."

Calum gave him a shoulder. "Funny!" he said.

"And you can get off the carriage now," Zidaini grinned.

"Aw, you!" Calum's words were muffled by Zidaini pushing off him, while coming down off the carriage, using Calum's shoulders as support.

The two Royals, in their bright blue uniforms, watched slightly amused as Calum and Zidaini were pushing each other while they crossed the gutter on to the path before them.

"Stop, stop, stop!" They regained composure, at Calum's call. They stood still, with their arms folded, eyes focused on the guards. Hecate watched confused.

"Mary Rose Association," Zidaini said. The guard on the left, moved back to the side door.

"Mary Rose!" He returned to his previous position.

Moments passed, and the door was pushed open. A corporal stood within the doorway and motioned them in. They followed at a short distance behind, walking beneath an ivy trellis; the climber plant ran along the lattice work, dropping down pink flowers, pruned to precision. The little pink flowers were closed for the night, but still added grace to the brick paving. They ducked and weaved their way through the hanging flowers, wondering where a human or pre-age Adinan would go to, for those clandestine meetings.

They entered a room only to be separated by an oak kitchen table from the First Royal, whose eyes didn't seem right as he regarded them. He looked away from them, behind the solid wood, before he forced himself to look back, brushing away a lock of green hair from his face. "You have the stone?"

Straight to the point. Calum found it quite rude.

"An assurance of our fee," Zidaini countered.

"Stone. Then you two riffraff's can have your money."

"He's quite frustrating, eh?" Zidaini said, keeping his eyes on the Royal.

Calum had kept the corporal within his sights.

"I'm waiting.. Quite patiently as well. Let's not make it go sour."

Zidaini began to take the gem out from his pocket. "So where next?" He asked. He held the stone in his hand.

"You will head to Londinium. Colonel Samiaraita will be there waiting for you, he'll be in uniform, not hard to miss. The stone, now," The voice of the First was calm, but had a hint of distaste within his enunciation.

"I don't know. I still haven't decided what to do. I still see no money," he smirked. He knew this wasn't going to end peacefully.

"You brat! Give me the stone," he ordered.

"Sunstone of Shiva. Don't think you need it, do you? No money, no Sunstone. Time is fading."

"Corporal. Take it from them."

"Sir!" He looked across the table at the First Royal who was seething with open anger. The corporal turned his eyes to his fellow Gaians, showing none of the same emotion, but an embarrassment.

Zidaini whispered into Calum's ear. "Run. And don't kill anyone."

"Lock them away and get the stone." The First ordered. The corporal pulled out his sword.

Calum was first to shoot out of the door, Zidaini close behind. The corporal was hot on their heels, barking out orders to soldiers that neither boy could see.

"Will you run faster?" Zidaini called under the long whining trellis.

"I am, you cheeky doughnut," Calum shouted. Two guards blocked their escape, ready to tackle them down.

They ran hard, keeping just ahead of the corporal. Pink flowers were hit off the dangling vines to scatter on to the

134

pathway. Calum lowered to tackle a guard, grabbing the sword arm of the guard and launching his shoulder into the gut of him, flooring him in writhing pain. Calum rolled over the downed guard, and, quick to his feet, he struck out with a kick to the corporal's face. He didn't stay down, but slowly tried to get back up. The two guards were also trying to get past the pain.

Zidaini grabbed Calum and they slammed through the side door, and raced past two unconscious bodies. Hecate sat ready, reins in hand. The carriage door wide open. They clambered in over each other.

"Yaah!" Hecate whipped the reins and the horse galloped into life and left the corporal and guards standing helplessly at the gate, clutching their bodies.

Zidaini and Calum grinned from ear to ear.

"That was fun, huh?" Zidaini said, smiling broadly.

"Why did that just happen?" Calum questioned.

"I decided that I would jump at the chance to keep the gemstones. Plus he wasn't gonna pay," Zidaini shrugged his shoulders, "so we keep the stone."

"I take it you don't kill your own, either?" Calum looked at Zidaini, waiting for an answer.

"Of course not. No Gaian kills a Gaian, ever." They sat in silence, watching the cobbled street drift pass to the clattering and clonking of hooves.

Σ

With bright blue drapes at the windows, and his desk sat centre with a Liberian flag in either corner, a chandelier of perfectly cut diamonds adorning the candles, hung from a chain attached to the ceiling, Emperor Lousous watched after the escaping carriage from his private office. "Thieves, damn thieves. And that man, that mage, Hecate, of all the scum on the planet, Hecate."

"Did you see?" A voice at the back called.

"Of course I see. Those thieves were with Hecate."

"No, not that. The sword with emeralds."

135

"What is your point, Hades?" Lousous fumed. His eyes still watching the streets. No longer was Hecate in view.

"It is said that the Sparda del Dios is an emerald sword," Hades said, creeping up beside the Emperor; a small candle revealing his black face, forever twisted, even in the darkness. "Absolute power, the power of gods."

"And a thief was carrying it? I do not think so," Lousous stretched his words. "Do you seriously believe that the weakest of all the gems would adorn the Sparda del Dios, the sword of god?"

"Perhaps, but I think it would be wise to take the sword anyway, just in case," Hades pleaded.

"Get me the sword, Hades. Leave none of them alive. And if the sword is the sword of god, I'll give you your every desire... I'll get you some help, you could probably use it."

"All help is appreciated," Hades said, bowing his false obedience.

21

REGAN TOWN

Nortedes at last disembarked to a heavy-set, lingering mist. Only the dim lanterns at the piers edge had guided the ship into port. The gangway lowered on to the wooden pier with a thud, and he stepped off alone. The creaking of the pier, from the moving water, was seemingly one of a few noises within the eerie fog. Only a few people came out of the mist as he walked, to match the sounds he could hear as he moved.

Water brushed against the hull of the ships at anchor, barely seen as he went past them. Trying to peer through the mist, he could see nothing beyond a few feet. The seagulls above him squawked in series, as if they were communicating. The townsmen would say that they were indeed.

Piles of cargo, passed as he walked the unseen length of pier, were waiting to be shifted on to the nearby vessel. Now and then a face would fit the voice as he walked, and they would look at him warily, before averting their eyes, once the threat had been assessed.

Regan town, and its sister, the village of Regonia, and the city of Londinium, were all human colonies. Left behind in the economics of the world, they were all poor, and would likely remain so.

This port was rarely visited from the other civilizations. Only a few traders would make the journey here.

Nortedes reached the end of the pier and found the concrete stairs to the main square. The mist was more broken here. He could see the housing of painted black oak beams that crossed the buildings fronts, with white masonry, brick-ing the housing together. Each house, shop and pub was covered in thatch roofing. Fish were being sold along the square's edge, with a dozen sellers along the wall. Visitors from across the continent came here for the bountiful Meni fish, abundant in the waters surrounding the town. The stench of the fish went drifting up his nose, and he hated it.

The odd beggar appeared out from the mist, to be waved away by Nortedes, with angry face to convince them to leave. There just wasn't any point being nice and handing out money to one, it would only attract the rest. He didn't want too much of his money being handed out only to in-crease peoples' reliance on foreigners for handouts.

He left the fish market to begin his search for a horse to rent. The 'Old Smelly Fish', the aptly named pub, would only cater for beer and bed. Certainly no horses within the tavern's walls, or at the inn at the other end, 'The Night Catch.'

He made his way across the square and down Gretia street. Which he had been told, while in Perpious, led the way to the town's gate. He walked the way for twenty min-utes, passing many an odd looking and poverty stricken populous, wandering the streets within the haze of mist, mostly through their boredom.

The damp and puddled road, amongst the foggy gothic buildings, finally provided a stable, into which Nortedes ventured straight in through a tall black gate. Eleven stalls, three of which lay empty. Eight had occupants, the horses poking their heads out from their tight abodes of confine-ment to take a look at the newcomer.

An overweight seller came wobbling over. Trotting with a sly face, wiping his sweat ridden forehead. At once, Nort-edes realized this obese slimy man would try to take every-thing he could from him, cheat him in anyway possible and still look cheerful about it. There was no other way he could have got so fat without the money from cheating people. His eyes were even that of a scamster.

"Three thousand roubles sire, the finest horses in all of

Gaia. A small price for a general, don't you think, sire?"

Nortedes assessed him as a man who, if he see you pull out ten peso, roubles, whatever, he would think he could get eleven from you.

The general had already chosen the horse he wanted. He stared at the seller, stared into the bulging eyes that gave off such sleaziness. "One thousand."

The fat man gave a horrified look of fright, a fake response on his squirmy face. "Sire, that would ruin me. Perhaps! Two thousand, and seven hundred, cheapest I can do.

Nortedes continued to look down angrily at the man. "One thousand, or I take the horse, with you dead in the dirt." He pulled out the prepared bundle of notes, so as not to reveal how much he had. Anymore would be seen as spendable in this opponent's eyes. "No more. Accept it."

"We-Well perhaps two thousand. That's good isn't it?" The seller was covered in perspiration, even his armpits were wet and smelling. Nortedes wondered how the sly creature could sell anything.

"Fine! One thousand two hundred." He pulled another two hundred from his pocket. After handing the money over to the despairing man, he went over to the horse. He saddled the mare with the stares of poorly-paid stable hands following him. The horse shook its head as he opened the stable door and then guided the horse out.

The fat man looked on shocked at such a foreigner. To make the matter worse for the seller, he was witness to Nortedes over-paying for an apple from a stall opposite the stable and handing over the fruit to a child.

Nortedes climbed on the horse. He had no care for the creature, and no desire to ride them for fun, but he needed the horse for the trek to Londinium. He smiled back at the seller, who was still in the middle of the stable staring back at him. He took the mare into a gallop, fading into the mist. The lack of sight did not bother him. People would hear him coming and get out of his way.

A few minutes passed and he reached the gate of the town, guarded both on the outside and on the inside. Two pikemen stood unceremoniously, gaping up at him.

With a slow uneducated voice, one of them spoke through a wavy unshaved beard. "Ang about, int ya a general." His voice rang of stupidity.

"Of course e is, ya doughnit." His colleague blurted.

"Who da ya call doughnut?"

"Are you going to let me pass?" Nortedes asked, getting impatient.

"Well, ya is need be carefil oat there."

"E know ow ta take care of a banits."

Nortedes sighed in frustration, looking away from them.

"I suppose!" The pikeman thought for a moment. Nortedes began to worry for the sap, having to think. "Ow com ar generals ain't big like im."

"ENOUGH!!" Nortedes yelled. "I'm a busy general, so open the bloody gates." The two guards were shocked still. "Fine I'll do it myself." He dropped off from his horse, and begun to walk to the gate.

"Nah, nah sir! We is do int." Both quickly got over to the gate, and pushed it open while Nortedes climbed back on. As soon as the gap was wide enough, he charged the horse forward, and left a trail of dust in his wake, covering the hapless pikemen.

Σ

Mist was replaced by constant drizzle. Animals grazed freely either side of the track, owned by no one. The bandits had demanded too much money, regardless of business. These animals had been left behind, to become wild and roam the grasslands, to fend for themselves.

It was the sight of five figures in the rain that made Nortedes slow to a stop. He leapt off the mare, keeping an eye on the five armed humans who, so used to being stronger than their victims, no longer laid any traps; they took their prey head-on.

Nortedes wanted them to come, to fight them on his terms. Their horses were to the side, grazing on the lush grass, under the dreary drizzle. Nortedes stood in the road, and made sure his longsword was loose in its sheath, a habit he would never bother to break. He moved aside his black coat from the hilt of his sword, and waited.

They walked slowly, not used to someone standing their ground. "Come on! What's taking so long?" He groaned. At the distance they were from Nortedes, their nervousness was unapparent. Even though there were five of them, the prepared Nortedes had left them worried. Three of his opponents carried jagged-edge blades, teethed sabres. Of the other two, one held a cheap arming sword, a single-handed weapon, with a double-edge blade. The other attacker, the leader, she held a mace of spikes over her shoulder, and was the least nervous. The bandits' clothes matched their criminal intent. Bandanas upon their heads, with symbols of their gang on the foreheads. Torn brown shirts, and put-together sandals, and even their gang's colours hanging from the hilts of their weapons. Red and black, the Morics choice of distinguishing themselves from others, and to show the enemy (unintentionally), their targets.

Nortedes consider these sorts of people weak. They needed a gang, a group, to feel stronger, and with that false strength, they preyed on the others with their gangs, and very rarely alone, too weak to fight by themselves. He hated them.

He stood with his side facing them, and gripped the hilt of his longsword. When they came near, he could see them trying to hide their fear with anger, bringing a sense of security to themselves. The leader took her mace in both hands, and roared out her charging order. The five bandits charged for him.

"Unprofessional," he muttered, as they ran toward him. He had already decided how to kill them.

All five went to swing their weapons at him. In one motion, he pulled out his large double-edged, cruciform longsword across his body. "Shock!" White flame seared out from the blade, ripping off from the blade in one wide arc of flame, shooting out into the band of bandits, and lifting each bandit off their feet, and sending them flying backwards. It was like being hit by twenty tons at once, struck across the chest. Their rib cages and arms were crushed. Blood came out from their mouths, and the searing heat melted their shirts to their skin.

Nortedes watched them for a moment, noticing the leader was still barely alive, he stood over her. "You really know nothing. The lot of you are just pathetic."

She uncontrollably spat up more crimson blood.

He looked over the hills. Some children had seen his efforts, and were re-enacting his quick moments. He wondered where they came from. He could see no horses around, but the bandits. The children would most likely take them.

'Good for them.' He couldn't even see a house or cottage across the grass fields. He took one last look at the caved-in ribs and left, not caring. He had always been unattached to such weak minded people.

22

THE PROTECTORS

Isis's tail hung out from her bed, as she slept soundly, with the train clattering on. Valkesies sat beneath her on the floor as the bed was too small for an Elseni, his body not able to fit in the confines of the beds. He huffed in his boredom, and went to leave. At the door, he stopped to check if she was still deeply sleeping. He turned back to the door. His eyes widened in fright, temporarily halting him in his tracks.

Hecate was peering in through the small window, recognition across his face.

Valkesies opened the door, knowing he could do so. Hecate stared in, unmoving.

"Is it her?" Hecate asked, looking in wonder at her.

"I'm going to get some food," Valkesies replied. He began to walk off toward the cafe, the motions of the train carriage not even slightly making him sway.

Hecate stood still, hearing familiar feet. "Get back to bed. You need it," he said turning his face back down the hall, to face the boys. Valkesies could see around Hecate at the curious Zidaini and Calum.

"What ya doing?" Calum asked. Like Zidaini, he leaned out of their room, bare chest, and bare feet. Valkesies muttered under his breath as he remembered Zidaini, who did remember the hairy man for all the times the Elseni had told him off; he said nothing, but looked on curiously.

"Do you mind?" Isis said, her eyes filled with sleepiness, coming awake at the disturbance.

"Hi!" The two boys called. She smiled at them, and gave

a short wave.

"Well, I'm sure you can speak to each other tomorrow," Valkesies said.

Hecate waved them back to bed.

"Fine," Zidaini said, pushing Calum back into their room.

"Sorry for waking you, Isis," Valkesies said.

She slowly returned to her bed, although curious now to speak to Calum and Zidaini. It was something to look forward to in the morning.

Σ

Hecate and Valkesies walked on to the cafe, after they were assured the three Gaians had all returned to their quarters. Once inside the cafe, they ordered at the bar, and sat themselves down and waited.

"It's been a long time, Valkesies..." Valkesies nodded. "Back on protection duty, are you? I thought she couldn't leave," Hecate said, thinking back to the Emperor's silent decree.

"She can't. The boys? Zidaini?" They paused to receive their teas which were placed down on their tables, the brews simmering with climbing steam.

"Yeh. He's decided to get involved into gods."

"Ha, ha! Has he really? Who's he worshipping?"

"None. Don't ask. Maybe Isis would like to meet the two of them."

"I don't think so," Valkesies blurted quickly. "Don't you go setting her up with that boy! I don't want those thieves near her."

"They're not thieves," he disagreed, taking a sip of his tea. "Something big is going to happen, these two will be a part of it. You should come with us."

"No!"

A silence came between them, as they drank. Moments were filled with the clacking of the wheels of the train running along the steel of the track.

"I should have been able to save her," Hecate said; the past having bothered him for so long, he brought it up again.

Valkesies looked into his eyes. "You still haven't accepted that there was nothing you could do. What could we have done? She was stabbed in the back. Your black magic was useless."

"I should have been there."

"We both should have. He was still around." The silence returned.

Hecate changed subject. "How's the wife?"

"She loved having Isis over... She asked about Zidaini the other day."

Hecate smiled. "She was always the opposite of you. She was always nice, and you were always mean to him."

Valkesies laughed. "You never gave him a kick up the backside. Someone had to."

"I was always kicking his butt."

"No, you always thought you were. He always knew how to get around you." Valkesies couldn't help but smile.

"Are you taking her to lugarta?"

Valkesies shook his head at Hecate's subtle change of tactic. "Don't tell me those two will be there."

"Yeh!"

"Definitely not. Not till you teach that boy some manners. I thought you hated lugarta." Valkesies queried.

"I do. They will meet, somehow they will."

When the train had finally got to Libera, Hecate had pretty much carried both Calum and Zidaini from the train. Their sleepy legs were unable to walk themselves, leaving the old mage to say goodbye with a nod of the head to Valkesies who went off in a different direction, with Isis, who looked just as fatigued as the boys.

Σ

Hecate wasn't too surprised to find Mary Rose had become a guesthouse. The bizarre development wasn't totally unexpected. The Boss hadn't been around, and included in the new guesthouse was a poor fake ruby and obsidian chandelier, which had been put above, to hang from the new section of ceiling.

Hecate stared up at the poor attempt, wondering if he ever wanted to come back. At least they were trying to make their criminal reputation vanish.

Σ

Valkesies sat opposite Isis, having an early morning breakfast at a restaurant within the city. The smell of bacon and eggs drifted throughout the teeming restaurant, packed with almost a hundred guests crammed into the dining room, the bustle of fans enjoying the morning delights. They sat in the corner, where the non-Gaian guests could actually sit at the table and eat. A square red cloth was placed over the white draping table cloth. Valkesies was impressed with the way Isis was handling the new conditions. She wasn't concerned with the luxuries that she no longer had, although she was staring out of the window at the moving ocean, watching the waves roll.

"You ok?" He asked, expecting something his wife could deal with.

"Let's go to lugarta," she said, clearly hiding something in her reason.

"Wh- We won't be able to get tickets," he quickly thought.

She pulled out a couple from her pocket. His face turned to shock. She smiled as she placed them back. "I spoke to them last night."

"You spoke to them? You spoke to those ruffians."

"They were cute and sweet," she said cupping her chin within her hands.

"You-You spoke to- Those boys. He hasn'-" He had made a mistake, and she had caught it straight away.

Her mouth was wide open. "You knew them?" She asked shocked. Her hands had come down on to the table.

He leaned back into the chair. "Well... Yes!"

"Both of them?" She crossed her arms, frowning at him. He was sure it was a put on.

"Zidaini and Hecate. I don't know the brown-tailed boy."

"Calum," she told him. "How long have you known them?"

"Oh, Zidaini since he was a little'un. Hecate for decades," he said feeling caught out, and took to looking out at the oceans waves. "I hope that was all that happened," he said, looking directly at her.

She giggled at his words.

"Just remember you have a lack of experience with people," he said, "and Zidaini has caused his fair share of problems. He's a pain in butt."

"Well you'll just have to teach me to understand them."

He shook his head. "Just try to listen to me now and again."

23

SUBLIMINAL CONVINCING.

Valkesies and Isis had found their way through the crowd to their place on the concrete steps. Isis had sat, perked up, watching the Libera Angels and the San Adinan Storm, enter the field of the Luverii stadium, the crowd cheering them on.

Valkesies was already thinking of reasons to leave the crowd and head for something other than lugarta. Not that there was anything he could do; only the bar was the possibility for lugarta avoidance. "I'll get some food in a while, when the crowd lessens," he told Isis. She just nodded back, now involved into the game. He scanned amongst the people, a red long coat was all he could focus on. The crowd erupted, covering the man he had just seen. He didn't see the try for the Angels, he was still trying to see who it was.

Hecate was walking up the steps toward them, a big brown bag of popcorn in his hands and a jug balanced within the bag of corn. His eyes had taken them in, his face aglow while he moved between the people.

"Hey! It's Hecate," Isis said, smiling.

Valkesies was wondering where the boys were.

"Isn't that a rather large bag you have there, Hecate?" Isis asked, smiling at him.

"Well, I don't want to be going back and forth all the time, do I? Better to get something that will last," he answered, squeezing in beside her.

"So where are Calum and Zidaini?" she asked.

"You'll see them."

"The gods, this is-" Valkesies got up, and walked off to

get some snacks. He was craving some mussels. He knew she would be fine, and he was desperate to leave.

Hecate watched him go, then took the chance to talk with the princess, who he hadn't seen since she was ever so young. She no doubt didn't remember him. "Where's he taking you?" He asked, curious whether the Elseni had any clue to how he should deal with Isis.

"We're taking the train to Lusa, then we're crossing the channel to Regonia."

"Ah! Interesting. We'll see you there," he said. She looked at him surprised. "We're heading to Londinium for a meeting. You can travel with us if you like," He suggested, grateful for the opportunity.

"I'd love to." She smiled. Then she remembered the Mary Rose association and wondered whether he was one of them. Added to that was the mention of Valkesies' old friend, Hecate, the grand mage.

Valkesies returned after three more tries had been scored, carrying some chicken and a jug of juice. Isis and Hecate had finished his supply, and eagerly tucked into the chicken, turning their hands grubby with the very first touch.

"You haven't told me what you used to do," Isis said to Hecate, wondering what the red eyes held behind them.

"We were in many occupations, on the military side of things. Then, of course, protection; like now," Hecate answered.

She took glances at them both, and wondered what they were hiding. She was curious now to find out why Hecate would consider Calum and Zidaini would need protecting.

Σ

Calum kept pacing, adrenaline coursing through his veins, while Zidaini sat chewing his nails, and fidgeting his feet and toes. They weren't outside watching the Angels crushing the Storm, instead they were keeping to themselves in the changing rooms. They were ready for action, but wanted to remain focused on their game. The team flexed their arms and stretched their legs. This was the dream, to win the tournament. Each match now they had to remain focused on each opponent; to play every game with every ounce of blood. They would lose if any had the slightest of bad games.

The announcers called out the final score, attracting the teams' attention. The Angels had won. The Storm would leave the field knowing they would not return. The Angels would celebrate, for this was a competition they excelled in.

"You ready for this?" Zidaini asked as he got to his feet.

"Oh, yeah!" The team fired themselves up.

"Let our Demons loose, and make the opposition suffer. This is our tournament," Osera said. "Let's show the world, the Demons rule!" They all shouted together. Leaving the changing room with a vigour that everyone they passed noticed.

"THIS IS ONE THE ANGELS WILL WATCH. THEIR NEXT OPPONENTS, THE ODINIAN DEMONS, VERSUS THE HABANA BULLS."

Hecate rose in anticipation. Valkesies looked bemused with the mage's sudden release of life.

"Oh my. Look, Valkesies! There they are," Isis exclaimed, as she sighted the distinct brown and blond tails of Calum and Zidaini. Both she and Hecate had become clearly excited at the entrance of the teams. Valkesies stayed on his seat, irritated at their excitement, and took a bite from his chicken leg, the juice dribbling down his cheek. The shock of Hecate embracing a sport that they both used to disgust was sending him into a confused contemplation.

24

EMPEROR'S ORDERS

In the small dungeons of the Libernian palace, two be-musing creatures stood behind bars. Emperor Lousous stood on the other side, looking in at almost rat-like ears covered with course, unwashed furs that covered what the rags did not. The two looked scared, and cowered behind the bars within their cell, trapped here and forgotten, by anyone who would care.

The Emperor watched them silently as they showed their fear, drenched in perspiration. He took a single deep breath in and out, taking in the foul smell of their confinement. He had left them here for their betrayal, left them to suffer beneath the palace, in the blackened and solid floor of concrete where fungi was growing along its walls, fungi that would leave someone covered in a bleeding rash. Now he had come for them to redeem themselves.

"I have a job for you two, if you wish for your freedom to be obtained and kept." His voice was echoed by the close proximity of each of the walls, one of the many small sections of dungeons amongst the supports of the palace grounds. The two beings kept their heads down, lowering their eyes from him, their bodies shaking with loose nerves.

"Sir, yes sir. What is your wish, sire?" One of them asked, keeping the head bowed.

Emperor Lousous stepped close to the bars of the cell. "I require you to take an airship."

They looked at each other, the feeling of freedom coming to both of them, and they looked at Lousous with intrigue.

"A new airship, which you wouldn't have ever seen; fully laden with cannons, you will take it to Londinium, fly across the ocean to avoid being seen by your targets. I have written your orders clearly, and you will commit to only my orders. Clear?" They nodded in agreement. "This is essential, you must carry out my orders, exactly. Upon the targets' failure, terminate them."

They enthusiastically nodded in unison. "We obey. sire." "Obey we do. Yes!" The other said.

The Emperor brought keys to bear. Their eyes glowed at their imminent release. As he turned the key and unlocked the cell door, he spoke. "Gaia has changed a lot since you Traicans were free, it's more advanced. So listen to the advice of those I have assigned to your mission, when in relation to enemy weapons. Understand?"

They nodded at his unusual gentle voice. He spoke to them with kindness behind the words, to the two Traicans. He was hiding how important this mission was, or maybe he understood how difficult it is to come into a completely different world.

Their eyes searched the walls they hadn't seen for over a decade. The Emperor passed over his orders, and watched them walk away. Then the thoughts of ruling Gaia returned as he wandered up the stairs behind them.

25

SUBLIMINAL CONTINUES

"TRRY!! THE DEMONS HAVE SCORED AGAIN. AN ABSOLUTE CARNAGE. SIX TRIES TO ZERO. THE WHISTLE HAS GONE! THE DEMONS HAVE HUMILIATED THE HABANA BULLS."

Hecate and Isis were cheering, while Valkesies sat uninterested and bored.

"Who do they play next?" Isis asked excitedly, looking down on to the field of play. They watched the boys who searched the crowd for them while Valkesies noticed Hecate sitting down and trying to hide his own excitement.

"Wasn't it the Angels, Hecate?"

"Yes, the Angels." He could see Valkesies staring directly at him, in a stare of bemusement that was thrown at him.

"What?" Hecate questioned, still forgetting himself.

Valkesies had surreptitiously watched Hecate for the entire game, shocked by the Grand mage acting in such a lost control manner. Isis had clearly been an encouragement to the old Adinan.

"What has happen to you?" He asked shaking his head. "You don't like lugarta."

"Of course he does." Isis interrupted, taking one of Valkesies pastries from the paper bag.

Hecate stayed quiet, overcome by embarrassment, realizing he had been caught, his face red. Isis though, didn't notice.

26

NORTEDES TRAVELS

Golden reds and dull yellows stretched out from the setting sun, a strange comparison from the black storm clouds that chased the sun away. A breeze was whipping across with the pursuing clouds, into the side of Nortedes' face. He wanted shelter from the oncoming rains. Londinium was too far from him. The storm would catch him well before he could reach the dirty city.

Ahead were a few cottages, and were most appealing to him. The need for food was eating at his stomach. At one of the cottages across from two armed civilians watching him, he could see an old lady bringing in the washing off from her line, and into her weaved basket that a young boy dragged along for her. When they saw Nortedes coming along, a moment of hesitation came across them, before subsiding, and the boy rushed off from his gran, over the grass lawn, away from the cottage they lived in.

"Hey mister! Hello, mister!" He called enthusiastically. "Who are you?" He asked, smiling, and gaping at Nortedes. The old lady came over behind the boy. "I'm Verum. This is Gran."

Nortedes looked over them for a moment. "I am General Nortedes." The boy looked awe struck.

"You need somewhere to sleep tonight?" The gran asked.

"Yes ma'am. I don't wish to be caught in that," He said, looking across through the cottages at the dark clouds and the haze of grey rain beneath.

"Verum, show the general to the shed, so he can tether

his horse."

"Over here in the barn, sir." He ran over to the barn, pushing open the gate, the barn big enough for the horse to be left under a roof and some hay to be stored. Nortedes followed on his horse, watching the clouds light up with sheet lightning making its way throughout the clouds. He passed his horse to Verum, who put all his strength into pulling the horse into the barn.

"Hey, mister general. Have you killed anyone, have you, mister?" He questioned with a glow over his face.

"Huh?" The general was stunned a little. There were a large number of other questions the boy could have asked. "Well, of course. You don't make it that far in the Imperium if you don't."

"Whoa! Really? What was it like?" He asked, trying to help Nortedes with the saddle. The general knew not to let the boy take the weight, and kept it in his own grasp.

"Each situation was different." The boy looked on in awe, and kept up with Nortedes while they left the barn. On the way to the small cottage, Nortedes noticed the boy still staring up at him.

"Some were gratifying, like the bandits." The boy's face lit up. "Some, there was nothing. Sometimes it just doesn't feel right."

"Did you get some bandits here?" Verum asked, walking into the house.

"Yes!" Nortedes could see a sword that sat up against the wall by the doorway.

"That's awesome!" Verum cheered and told his gran straight away.

The cottage's main room, was lit up by a fire on the go; cooking above the flame, a stew the gran had begun cooking while they tethered up the horse. The gran sat in a comfortable couch, watching the flames lick up at the pot, "My son-in-law and daughter will be back later tonight," she said still staring into the fire. "Where are you from?" She asked.

"He's from the Imperium, Gran." The boy piped up, and she looked at him. He sat on the floor near Nortedes. The general sat on one of the couches.

"From Centrali."

"Tell me about your home. Is it a big city?" Looking up at him.

"Centrali has its beauty, and it's ugly. It could seem to be the greatest city in the world, with some of the greatest humans known to Gaia. Where my brother and I were born and grew up. But within the city, just like in all the Imperium, there are evil people, looking for power, and to control the people around them. With fear being cultivated amongst the people, instilled into their hearts, the mass hysteria has formed and is growing, the senate is creating it, to control the people who will do anything, even abandon their freedom for false security. Centrali is the least affected city, unlike Perpious. But if it continues to fester, the people will throw themselves into wars to do the senate's bidding. Wars that have no meaning, then these evil doers will have the ability to have absolute control. They will take over. If they win. I must make sure they lose."

"It sounds like your home land is suffering, and yet doesn't know it. You are clearly not happy there," the gran said.

"True, but I do have some good memories. Perhaps I should offer Verum some war stories."

"Yay!"

27

BUSHIA'S CRY FOR POWER

Hades, with his head hooded, entered into Bushia's private manor. The foyer was walled with white and light brown coloured, wavy and striped marble. The floor was a continuation of the traditional black granite. A staircase went up the centre. The first floor had the same sparse outlook as the ground floor.

"Hades, why do I have the pleasure of your visit?" Bushia called. He stood at the top of the stairs, looking down. Hades wondered if the senator had seen him coming, and placed himself upstairs to make a more deity look for Hades to see when the servant let him in. But all the appearance gave was a look at how much flab the senator had.

Bushia walked on the red carpet that paved the way down, stopping halfway and standing to one side.

"There is...a Gaian that travels with a sword, a sword that the Emperor has ordered to be captured. The sword is called the Sparda del Dios, the Sword of God."

"What are you talking about, Hades?"

"Sire," he frowned, "the sword is supposed to be able to gain the power of an army. For decades across the east continent, the stories have persisted, and continued to exist as fables and myths. But most of history shows, myth comes from truth. Could you imagine if it was true? The Emperor of the Liberian Empire seems to believe the history."

"A sword that controls armies would certainly be a battle winner." Bushia pondered the thought.

"It's two Gaians, one a petty thief, and an Adinan old mage travels with them. No one who will be a problem,"

Hades said, believing it himself.

"Fine, get me the sword. Kill all three, and any of the Emperor's own trackers," he said uninterested.

Hades cringed, disgusted with having to deal with such a moron. "Sire, perhaps you could lend me an airship or carrack for the task," he asked, wanting more than his own resources.

"Hades, you are not one of my officers. No soldiers will fight for you. I will have a message sent out to my generals though, perhaps they will help you. Although I'm sure you can get vast mercenaries of your own. I'll have some money for you in the morning." Bushia went back up his stairs, the idea of the emerald sword still a fable in his mind. Not like the gods; those were something he would sacrifice for.

Hades walked out from the manor with the servant closing the door behind him. He looked up at the sky and then at the expensive houses of the rich sector. At least the senator would be giving him some money towards his effort, it was a small token in his mind, and he thought about how he could use it effectively. Perhaps Londinium would bring him more favourable results. Drexaria, his white-skinned dragon, landed beside him; to the gawking of the manor hands. It shuffled its black and featherless wings, and lowered its body. Hades climbed on and Drexaria soared into the night.

28

ANGELS AND DEMONS

The ball came down from a high kick into Calum's hands. He held it into his chest, and wrapped around it with one arm, he went racing forward. An Angel coming in to tackle him. He fended his opponent off with a hand to the boy's face, but was taken down by another. Osera was in over him, protecting the ball, for Zidaini to take up and run across the field, laying off the ball for Vasca, who took it further on into Angels' territory where he was taken down. Jazziera, shouldering off an Angel player, who went for the ball.

The game was a constant back and forth game of tackling, and no breakthrough. Hecate was biting his fingers as Calum was once again taking up the ball and trying to find a gap through the Angels line. Again arms wrapped round him as he tried to keep on his feet to get a few more yards onwards. As he went down Zidaini came in, slamming off both Angels. Osera grabbed up the ball and torpedoed the ball into Jazziera's arms. The Angels picked up the move immediately, and plowed into her, the ball spilling out of her hands, and into the open.

Isis had her hands to her mouth, as Angels found an open space in front. "COME ON!" She called.

Calum and Zidaini led the chase, Zidaini leading the way, catching the Angel twenty yards from their own tryline, and bringing down the player who was secured in a ruck. Calum made it back around the defensive side of the

159

ruck as the ball was taken out. He went straight for the ball carrier, tackling for the legs. The Angel down, the Demons were able to get their defensive line reset.

Hecate blasted out encouragement.

Valkesies sighed at him. The old Adinan was standing up at each tackle. "Will you just stay standing, or remain seated," he moaned. He could see that Hecate ignored him, and couldn't help but smile. The old mage had found a love within their joint hate for the sport. Isis and Hecate jumped up as an Angel dropped the ball forward. The penalty awarded to the Demons; the defence successful.

Calum's heart was pumping. No matter what either team had done, neither could break through, and he was feeling the burn. The pace had been fast, and he had found himself running throughout the game. Now he held the ball, he was deliberately taking his time, he eyed up the Angels positions, took in those that were showing the most tiredness. He called over Zidaini. "Take it down the right." Zidaini raised his brow and gave a slight nod, putting his trust in Calum.

Calum tapped the ball from his foot, and sent it off to Zidaini, who raced zigg zagging forward. As an Angel came into him, he laid the ball off to Jazziera, who went off some more yards. Calum chased behind and looked on, pleased, as Jazziera broke through a tackle; the tired Angel unable to keep his arms around her, she ran on. The Demons on the offensive. She finally laid off the ball, to Calum as she lured another Angel away. He shot clean through, the Angels chasing. He ran straight for the try line, and drove the ball down for a try. The Demons celebrated in usual embracing fashion, leaping over each other.

Hecate and Isis went wild with delight, the crowd around them jumping with joy. Valkesies again felt nothing,

The Angels jogged back to the centre line, still wanting to get the try back, still with the determination to win. The Demons walked back, slowing things down. They scored, it would be their kick-off, and they were prepared to keep things at a nice pace, they wanted some of their energy back for the chase at the kick-off. Zidaini was going to kick short in the hope they could compete for the ball.

Isis was sitting upright in anticipation for the kick, she watched the Demons get back to the centre line, Zidaini looking out at the opposition's positions. She had enjoyed watching the tournament with Hecate there, and was wondering now whether they would be able to watch the final, especially if the Demons made it.

Zidaini put his boot through the ball, and launched it upwards, high into the air. Osera was first to the ball's landing location. An Angel waited beneath it. The ball took almost forever to come down, with Calum and Osera there to attempt a fight for the ball. An Angel went up for it, to get above them. Osera went up with him, reaching out a hand, not trying to take in the ball, but slap it back. The ball was almost in the hands of an Angel, when Osera stuck his hand in, and slapped back the ball. Calum dived on to it before it even touch the grass. The Angels on top of him. Vasca and Zidaini were straight in to thump off the two Angels.

Up in the crowd, the Demons biggest fans cheered loudly. The Demons' had regained the kick-off, and they slowed it down as soon as they reset the line. They kept the ball close, with a pick and drive after pick and drive. The Demons were securing the ruck ferociously, smacking and shouldering off their opponents.

The time was running out.

Valkesies looked upwards at the drifting white clouds, few and far between in the blue sky, far more interesting to him then what was happening on the field.

The announcers called the time down in the last ten seconds. The crowd echoed the call. The whistle went.

"IT'S OVER! PULSATING GAME FROM THE ANGELS AND DEMONS. ONE TO NOTHING."

The Demons cheered and celebrated on the field, embracing each other, under a haze of euphoria. Calum searched

the crowd for Hecate, an impossible task; he couldn't believe he was in a final of lugarta. He hadn't believed he was
in a tournament.

Zidaini grabbed him. "We did it. I tell you what, we're
gonna be champions," he said it with sparkling eyes, deep in
joy, and overwhelmed with euphoria, squeezing tight Calum
in his happiness. The two became surrounded as the rest of
team including the hopeless Bawn, came together shouting
over the noise of crowd.

Hecate had already left his seat, and had walked from the
tunnels, to wait for the boys by the fountain. He was trying
to keep his emotion in check, forcing himself to remain
straight-faced as he went along the hallway to the exits.

Σ

The changing rooms were just as loud as the field was.
Jazziera had found a bottle of rum to herself, not noticing
that neither Calum nor Zidaini were in the drinking mode,
avoiding the alcohol, while Osera gulped down mouthfuls
of another bottle of rum, running through the games plays,
especially his own tackling.

"Hey, Zidaini! We're supposed to be going," Calum
called.

"What? Well! That leaves plenty for us to drink,"
Jazziera yelled, finding Vasca tackling her for the bottle.
"Hey! I'm having it all, hah ha!"

"See you at the final," Zidaini called. Jazziera came
rushing over, and wrapped him up in her arms, and gave a
fake groan at his leaving, then took up another bottle, while
Vasca and Osera gave them a friendly goodbye. The two
boys left in a rush, racing down the passageways to get out
and meet Hecate.

"Do you think Isis came to the game?" Zidaini asked as
they jogged along, to bravo and claps from others wandering the hall, mostly stewards and soldiers at the odd inter-
val, watching the halls for those that shouldn't be there.

Calum laughed at the question. "Not if Valkesies could

keep her away. I'm sure Hecate forgot to say good things about us." They were both still in the excitement of winning, while they slowed with the exit in front of them.

"I remember that big lard being a nob. Probably still is." Deerdra popped into his mind, and her delicious cookies. "Saying that, his wife Deerdra was really nice. She used to tease him by giving plenty of reasons for me to stay; I always had to have some cookies, otherwise I couldn't leave."

Hecate, with sword and daggers in hand, watched them come up the stairs to him at the fountain. Their soberness was clear in the way they walked, and it made him wonder on their avoidance of drinking. He knew Zidaini was one to be cheeky, and get a few drinks where he couldn't be caught by him.

"We ready to go yet?" He asked handing over their blades.

"Ah hah! You enjoy the lugarta?"

Hecate looked at Calum sternly, trying to keep a smile from his face.

"Yeah! Did ya watch it all?" Zidaini added. Only to have Hecate breathe deeply and stand taller in defiance.

"I enjoyed the company of Isis," he said, quickly starting the walk for the train station. They followed straight behind, curious to know what had been said between the old Adinan and Isis.

"She did come, then. Where is she?" Calum questioned, the two boys trying to keep up with his quick walking pace.

"Hey! Hello!" Zidaini called. Hecate wasn't stopping.

"Will you two keep up? We have a train to catch." He didn't look back to see the raised brows of the boys who were right up with him. "Would you two like a beer?"

"Noo!"

A unison response stopped Hecate dead in his tracks.

"What's happen to you two? I am happy you two aren't stupid enough to be drinking yourself sick, and looking like idiots, but I'm certain you're hiding something." He waited for an answer.

"So are you," Calum said. The three were silent for a

moment.

"Let's get going." Hecate carried on.

"Weird!" Zidaini commented, looking at Calum. He shrugged and walked on.

Σ

The station was bustling with passengers. The train was already at the platform and travellers were boarding. Steam smothered the platform beside the engine, while people tried to keep away from the black plumes of smoke, instead of breathing in the black fog.

Calum and Zidaini had somehow gotten into a wrestling match while Hecate watched on, sitting comfortably on a bench. The two were blissfully unaware of those around them.

Calum was almost on top, and it was nearly enough to declare himself victorious, when two persons stood over them.

"Hi, Calum, Zidaini," Isis said. Valkesies was staring down with a scolding expression upon his hairy features.

"Hey, Isis," Calum said, still holding Zidaini down.

"We don't want to be around ruffians, Isis," Valkesies said, with his head held back, eyes leering down at them.

She grinned at their cheeky smile back.

"They are thieves, Isis, stay clear of them."

"No we're not, you overgrown tree trunk."

Valkesies turned furious.

"Is that all you can come up with?" Calum asked, sitting up.

Zidaini shrugged back at him.

"You two have the manners of a gooladi," Valkesies moaned.

"Do you think he needs to lie down?" Calum asked Zidaini.

"With all that weight, definitely. But I doubt he could get up again. His face is hairy, too."

"Why you li-"

164

"Valkesies be nice, please," Isis intercepted.

"Come on, K, let's go!" Zidaini said, taking Calum towards the train.

"Where am I going?" Calum asked.

"We're boarding."

"Well, why didn't you say so?"

Hecate rose from the bench and followed them. "You've done well. Valkesies."

The Elseni huffed, and walked towards the other steps up on to the carriage. Isis followed, smiling away.

"Later!" She said waving to Hecate, who politely waved back.

Hecate stepped into the compartment, only to find Zidaini moaning about Valkesies. He laughed at Zidaini's whining.

"Stop sulking, boy," he said to him. He sat opposite them. "He's an honourable person, who you very well know is. He just doesn't like playing around; most of his people don't."

"He's a nob. What's he doing with Isis anyway?" Zidaini was sulking as he questioned.

"It's weird. I just can't see her actually wanting to hang with him," Calum commented.

"Well, they are, so accept it. If you wish to be friends with Isis, you'll have to get by Valkesies," the grand mage added to the conversation.

Σ

"You don't have to be so mean to them," Isis said, sitting down in their compartment. She looked out at the station, watching the few Gaians going home early from the games, their faces painted in the colours of their home town. She could tell by the blue yellow and white, that they were from Los Santos.

"They're ruffians, Isis."

"They're Gaians, Valkesies. So I wish to know them," She said, "I'm thinking of going with them."

165

Valkesies face turned pale. "Please think about it."

"I have." Thoughts of meeting with Samiaraita had already crossed her mind, and it was clear she had more authority then she at first thought.

Σ

The sky had turned to night, with stars shining on to the departing train, reflecting in specks of sparkles, glinting from the carriage's roofs. But it wasn't just stars in the sky looking down; black snake eyes with dark brown iris's leered downwards, a naginata held in its free hand, the other clutching on to the reins of his flying beast, another naginata sheathed in the skin of the creature he rode upon. Blended into the sky, the demon creature with scrawny dried grape skin, commanded a creature of slick black, and with great wings that protruded from its body, its scaled tail swayed in the wake of its hind behind.

"Prey, do you feel safe? Do you think you should fear nothing? I am coming. Death is coming for you, stalking you in your movements, waiting for the right time to strike, and I will strike. I will gut you. Prey, I come for you."

The beast soared with a screech into the sky. A witch's echo squealed from its vile saliva ridden mouth, into the star covered night; the occupants of the train, completely oblivious to the stalking demon.

29

LONDINIUM

When the saddle was on the horse, he looked over the animal. He had always appreciated the look of strength it gave. He gave it a pat on its neck and walked it out of the barn, closing shut the door behind him. He put his foot in the stirrup and pulled himself up.

"Hey, mister Nortedes, sir." The boy came rushing out. "Don't go yet. Please stay and teach me to fight."

He felt a touch of sorrow for the boy. "I'm sorry, I don't have the time."

"Will you come back?" Verum asked hopefully.

"I'll be passing back through here," he said looking down at the boy. Verum became a little better, not so sad anymore.

Nortedes rode his horse across the lawn, the wet grass brushing the water across the mare's limbs. Taking the mare on to the track, he looked back at the cottage, then waved to the boy, who smiled and waved back. He called the horse to life, and it responded into a gallop, speeding off into the distance, seemingly racing the wind. The gust was following along, with the splashes of mud and water at each landing of a hoof on ground. Passing a horse and cart, the gust of wind from his travelling mare whipped up the hay, and sent it blowing over an old farmer, leaving him calling out insults after him.

After several hours of riding, Londinium was in his path. Its walls were only fourteen feet high, certainly not the highest city walls upon Gaia. Her city skyline was a haze of brown. The dirty city was well known throughout the world for its poverty and corruption; the least attractive of all Gaia's cities, unclean and unfinished. The city's roads were lined with sewage, due to a poorly kept and overrun sewer system. Alongside were the thousands of starving and homeless; desperate and destitute, they roam through the rubbish, hunting for the scraps of food to help them survive one more day.

This is a city where the people steal and cheat from you and smile while they do it.

Taverns and inns, coaching houses and dens dotted every street. The usual hustlers, beggars, real and fake waited beside the door of each. Even the city gate was rusted and only guarded at night.

The outside was smothered in shanties, stretching off into the distant hills. The south of the city was clear of the debris of the northern shanty town.

Those of the shanties that saw Nortedes come to the gate of the city feared him. Their eyes were gone, once he trotted pass through the worn gates. The streets leading to the center were filled with wandering souls, with nothing to do but hang in the streets of sewage, feet bare and clothes of rags upon their skin.

The center for Nortedes was by far worse. The affluent recognized him for what his uniform said. Here both his famous and infamous deeds were well know, his past victories and achievements the talk of many mouths across Gaia. The center held the most knowledge of his existence, the rich having the money to learn. The poor not having the time to listen; here his name had spread.

To many that saw him, he showed a figure, proud and strong. That strength put fear into those he walked past. This was a city where the weak were preyed upon. Nortedes hated the city, despised the coldness of the people who attacked the kindness of others. The dirty and stinking streets made him wish he was back home in Centrali, in his land far away from this poverty and sickness, and people who try to sell everything they can; the trash that they had picked through, useless items, and any wares they had, including themselves. Great for those who have no release, here they would find it.

He knew that spending even the slightest amount would leave him beset by everyone, harassed till he found a hotel or left the city. So he deliberately ignored them, and headed straight for hotel Rossiya, which was situated directly across from the central park. Leaving his horse to an attendant of the hotel, he didn't hang about outside. He went in, and immediately on his left was the restaurant, on a raised floor and open to the rest of the lobby. The reception was on his right, and he walked over to it, receiving the looks of those around him.

"How may I help you, sir?" asked a well-taught receptionist. This hotel was the gem in a disaster zone that was Londinium.

"Any room," he said.

"Ok, sir," she replied and looked through the folder. She reached behind her for a key.

"Has a Colonel Samiaraita checked in yet?"

"No, sir. Your room, sir. One hundred and three. Name, sir?" She looked at him, wondering why he of all people would want to see a Gaian. The colonel was also a famous figure across Gaia. His location would not be kept secret when the chance for money begs.

"General Nortedes." He took his key from her hand. He lacked any belongings, and went straight outside, walking across the road, shoving a beggar from his path. He went through the poorly kept park, and found a bench from where he could see a wide section of the center. People slept and begged along its paving, hoping for a dime or two. He grabbed the sleeping occupant of his chosen bench and threw him off and on to the path.

"Benches are for sitting, not for sleeping," he said. The bum spoke his insults and scurried away to another section of park. Nortedes sat and waited, watching the passing people who walked past the hotel, clutching tight to whatever they had bought, unable to afford a carriage to take them. Those that could, had bodyguards surrounding them who pushed and threatened any that came close to their employer.

The beggars were in large numbers, taking up the streets and benches. They veered clear of Nortedes, who kept them away by the caressing of the hilt of his sword.

30

TRAIN OF CARDS

The train that sat at the bottom of San Adina's stairway mountain, running along the centre of the steps was the newly developed Tram that took passengers that could afford it up the mountain while clonking up, or down, to the noise of its cogs at each end, that turned winching it along. The introduction of the tram took away the hundreds of steps leading up the mountain to the capital city.

Isis had her head out of the carriage window, keeping an eye on the doors of the train, in case Hecate and the boys were jumping off the train here.

"You're not looking out for them, are you?" Valkesies moaned, concerned she wanted them as friends. Although he could easily accept her new friendship with Hecate; but not ruffians and scoundrels.

"Of course I am," she fretted, wanting to go chatting with them; she had found an interest with the three of them, curious as to the way they acted.

"Are you going to wait there all day?" He said. "Now sit in here, instead of looking at the station."

"Nope! We're gonna spend all day in the dining cart until they turn up," she said pouting. She stormed out from the compartment. In almost a panic Valkesies leapt up, and quickly followed her, wondering if she was ever going to listen.

$$\Sigma$$

Calum and Zidaini were slouched over, sitting on their bench, boredom written over their faces; they were losing the battle against the long journey.

"Will you two play a game or something," Hecate said. "You're depressing me."

They shot a glance at Hecate. He laughed at them, and returned to his book.

"Do old farts always survive boredom on lloonnngg trips, or is he one of a kind?"

"Definitely one of a kind."

"Shall we go find Isis?" Calum questioned.

"We would annoy Valkesies." Zidaini's face lit up with glee, as he said it. "Perfect!"

"Fine, good, be off with you. Tell Isis I'll be in the dining cart in the morning," Hecate said. His eyes didn't leave the book he was involved in.

Calum got up first and left their compartment, his face grinning at what he saw down the hall.

"What?" Zidaini asked as he came to Calum's side. They stared at a passenger standing by the toilet, looking about to burst.

"Hurry up in there, will ya." he clutched himself, trying to hold it in. The toilet engaged.

Zidaini nudged Calum as he sighted something else to laugh at. A guy down the other end of the hall. The train jolted as it begun to make a move, and headed for the next stop.

They sniggered together at the bright pink hat worn by a human. His green trousers were luminous, his t-shirt was bright yellow.

The boys weren't hiding their giggling as they stared at the strangely dressed human, who glanced back, uncertain and perplexed.

Calum walked over, dragging Zidaini along with him; wanting to talk with the guy but didn't want to be seen alone with the weird person. "Who are you?" He asked quickly.

The man asserted himself, facing them with a tug on the

neck of his t-shirt. "I am Janus," he said proudly. The boys looked at him as if he had completely lost them. "I am the card master, fourth in line. Our leader is grand master Squall." They started sniggering again, at Janus speaking with a pompous manner.

"So you're good, then?" Zidaini inquisitively asked.

"The best!" he exclaimed.

"Fourth best!"

Janus didn't say anything to Calum's point.

"Give us a game then."

Janus laughed. The boys leered at him.

"Well?" Calum said.

"Let me see your cards then, and maybe I'll play you." He tried to give a sound of importance and failed.

They fell about laughing.

"Fine, I will win the money for the Eden card from somewhere else.

"Eden card," Calum said in remembrance. "Where is it?"

"Not in here, not onboard the train. In Libera." His lying was terrible, and convinced no one. The boys looked at each other.

"You go that way, I'll go this way," Zidaini told Calum.

"Come on! You don't need the card. You don't even play cards."

They stared at Janus.

He faced the window, trying to look out and away from them, realizing they would get the new card; all because the souvenir shop was stuck in his mind.

Zidaini went in the direction of the back end of the train. Coming into the dining cart, he raised a smile as he saw Isis. She waved him over and he walked past the tables to where they were sitting at a side table attached to the wall.

"Hey, Zidaini!" She said as he came over. Valkesies sat irritated.

"Hi, ya! How's it going, Valky? Looking too big for the chair, I see."

"Why, I will kic-"

"Valkesies, be nice. Will you join us, Zidaini?"

"Tell you what, we'll start the day off tomorrow, yeah? Breakfast, and you can hang out with us."

Isis gave a reply straight away. "Sure! After sunrise."

"Well I'm on a hunt at the moment. So I'll see you later," he said, and continued on to the next carriage.

Calum had found the small shop at the front end of the train. Like a cabin in its design, it had small snacks and treats along its few shelves. More importantly it had cards upon the counter to which he went straight away, looking through the cards at each of the choices.

An Adinan lady noticed his searching, and stepped over. "Can I help you young'un?"

"I'm looking for a card called Eden."

She thought for a moment, leaning her head round to the back of her counter.

"The Dark Witch." She took it off from its perch on the shelf.

Eden wasn't the typical looking human witch. She had a long black sleek dress, over a slim figure. She wore no hat, and had bats surrounding her, her lips were covered in a deep purple, and eyes were the black of midnight.

The card was high numbered, with no weaknesses. A special, with a special price.

"One thousand, dear."

"How much?" He cried. Not sure he should be contemplating such a price.

"A thousand." The second time made it no better. He reached into his pocket, and pulled out some cash. It was a price that stabbed his heart, and he grumbled under his breath.

"Here." She took it with a gracious smile. Calum hoped it was worth it.

$$\Sigma$$

Zidaini had reached the last carriage, the end of the train, and in it was a girl with long, cardinal red hair and dark burgundy eyes. An Adinan girl, she had yet to reach the age

174

of a hundred. She was still much like a Gaian, except without the tail. She was leaning against the wall. The black
stripes in her hair gave a match to the black and red clothes.
Her short skirt had a knife attached to its side.

Zidaini crossed his arms while he watched her. His
blond tail wagged slowly.

She saw him staring at her from the corner of her eye
and faced him. "What? You want a cracked head or something?" She stood and crossed her arms, unintentionally
mimicking Zidaini.

He was taken aback for a short moment, then he came to
a conclusion in his assessment of her. "Thief, huh?"

She tried to hide the fact he was right, but had no re-
course. Just the give-away in her shuffle.

Zidaini laughed and begun to move toward her.

"I suggest you don't come too close."

"You've not been a thief long, have you? Bet you could-
n't pick my pockets. I'd have you for breakfast."

He had clearly angered her, and she looked ready to
pounce on him; her eyes raging, ready to run her blade
through his soft skin. He smiled back and left the way he
had come.

Σ

Calum finished the quick drink of black currant, and
headed back down the passageway to Janus. As he went
through a carriage section, a foot came out from the inside
of the next carriage, straight in front of him, tripping him
up. He went straight to ground on his chest. As he looked
up from where he lay, he saw Hecate running off down the
hall. Two girls and their mother were giggling at him. Calum's head dropped down in embarrassment.

Σ

Zidaini reached Janus first; he began grinning at Janus's
choice of clothes. Calum walked through the intersection,

taking a brief wary look either side of the doorway. Then he couldn't help but grin at Janus. The two boys came together, their eyes on the human.

Janus looked at them, frustrated and nervous with their constant laughing. "You didn't get it, did you?" He asked, coming over nervous.

"Well, you can play us and find out," Calum said.

"Fine; kiddies' rules or proper rules?"

The two grabbed hold of their hilts.

"Proper rules!" He blurted. He pulled out a folded nine grid board.

"You always carry that?" Calum asked, amused.

"Well, he does wear stupid clothes. He can't get any sadder," Zidaini said.

"True," Calum said.

Janus sighed as he sat on the floor with his board. "You first?" he asked.

Calum nodded, and put an average card down. To a laugh from Janus, who placed a king card down, taking Calum's.

Zidaini let out a sigh.

Calum placed another down.

"So you do have it!" Janus cried as his king card was taken by the special Eden.

After a few minutes on the hard floor, with only one card to play and the center spot untaken, Janus was salivating, his score higher than Calum's after three more card placements.

"The Eden card is mine. You have no chance. It's all mine," Janus called, excitement riding him high.

"Eh, Nah! This one's a charm, meet Quetzalcoatl."

Janus's face dropped as the card turned over three of his.

Janus looked set to cry, his eyes brimmed with wetness.

"Don't forget to take his best card," Zidaini said, forsaking the mandatory money bet for the card instead.

"Please, no. Please." Janus was set to cry, he spoke tearfully. "Please don't."

"Thanks. Oh, how nice! The Vanelia, a ship?" Calum

was unsure whether this was a good thing, or worth it.

"That's one of Adina's finest battleships, a ship of line. One hundred culverins. Both our empires went crazy building the ships," Zidaini told him. The two stared at it. Janus put his head in his lap and cried.

Σ

The train had long passed Santiago Del Niro. In the far distance lay Habana town, the last stop before Lusa. The morning sunrise was shining through the red blinds of the compartment, illuminating the room a shade of red. Hecate slept opposite the boys on a bunk that he had folded down from the wall. He had wakened to the glowing red room. Stretching his arms out and looking across at Calum and Zidaini to see if they were still sound asleep, he arose, feeling refreshed and wide awake, and went to wash, closing the door behind him with a hefty slam.

Calum was jolted awake with a start, and fell from the top bunk, and landing on his side, a quick stab of pain coming over him. With the pain subsiding quickly, he sat up, the covers still around him.

Laughter came from Zidaini. "Nice fall, Calum," he said, having been awakened by Hecate. Calum grabbed him, and pulled him out of bed,and on to the floor.

Hecate walked in and looked once, shook his head, picked up his knife and left.

"Hey! Wait-" Zidaini called out as he was tackled back down.

Σ

Isis came to the window of their door. Valkesies also peered in to see the commotion. "What are they up to?" He shook his head at the two in just their pants. Isis couldn't help but laugh at them.

Valkesies called out. "Will you two get dressed, and hurry up," he groaned.

The boys had frozen.

"Did we get laughed at?" Zidaini asked, staring up at the window now empty of onlookers.

"Um. Yep!" Calum answered, not sure whether it was such a bad thing.

They quickly got their clothes on, putting their belts on, and weapons in their normal places, and went racing down the passageway.

They caught up to Valkesies and found it impossible to get pass his wide frame. His four arms were just able to squeeze through the intersections.

"Hey, tree trunk! Out of the way!" Zidaini shouted. As Valkesies slowly manoeuvred through the doorway to the dining carriage, he ignored their comment, continuing un-abated.

The dining room was being visited by a few passengers that were scattered throughout the carriage's tables. Hecate and Isis had left one side open for the others to sit. As soon as Zidaini see a chance to get around Valkesies, he led the way; climbing, then jumping from a table to get past Valke-sies. Calum came quickly after, landing right behind Zidaini, who sat himself opposite Hecate, and Calum sat next to him. The two glanced back with a grin at Valkesies. He was furious, and plonked himself down on a bar stool near them.

They didn't need to order breakfast. The food was a choice-less menu. It came via a waitress and they eagerly tucked into the dish.

Isis had been wondering about their purpose in Londin-ium for some time, guessing that they could be on the Em-peror's mission. Although the way they acted made her think the chance was slim. "So, why are you heading to Londinium?"

"We're on a mission," Zidaini said, taking a mouthful of food.

"Thievery, no doubt," Valkesies moaned, not consider-ing Hecate.

"We are searching for the stones of gods, my dear,"

Hecate said. He looked at Valkesies, who turned his head from him, a little sorry and embarrassed.

Isis kept herself from looking too much like she knew who they were now, as Zidaini and Calum looked stunned by Hecate revealing their intentions.

"What are you doing? You're not suppose to tell anyone." Zidaini complained.

"That kind of power should not be in anyone's hands," Isis said, looking for an understanding of their reasons for doing the mission.

"Emperor's orders," Zidaini said.

"I don't think it wise to give such power to the Emperor, or any other leader," Isis said.

"I completely agree, Isis. I know even Valkesies does also."

Calum and Zidaini were beginning to notice the way Hecate spoke to Isis, while Valkesies sat bemused, disbelieving they could be performing the Emperor's orders.

"We don't plan on giving the Emperor the gems, or to any of his lackeys," Zidaini said. A slice of bacon, which he had held in his fingers, went into his mouth.

"That is clearly a good reason not to go near these ruffians; they would chance the Emperor's wrath."

"You did once," Hecate clearly said. Everyone was looking at Valkesies, and he found himself looking away in embarrassment.

Isis again was left wondering on their past.

"Don't worry, we might sell them for lots of money," Zidaini said.

Calum seemed to not be too certain on the idea, and both Valkesies and Isis could see he wasn't backing Zidaini.

"You will not. We will store them safely from the reach of anyone." Hecate ordered.

Zidaini pulled a face in a sulk.

Isis looked at Hecate and smiled. "Would you mind if we join you?"

"Ma'am! Reconsider, please!" Valkesies became horrified.

Calum bit his bottom lip, hiding a smile from Valkesies.

Zidaini looked on in horror, desperate to intercept the answer, but knowing that whatever he said, Hecate was going to let them come along.

"Isis, it would be my honour if you were to accompany us," the old mage said.

Zidaini and Valkesies stared at each other.

Calum laughed and looked out at the passing scenery of tall deciduous trees; the leaves big and bold, the little white flowers being whipped in the wind.

Isis let Hecate out from the table. He left and took the four-armed Elseni to one side, sitting him down at a table, leaving the others to chat about the subject of lugarta that quickly came up.

Σ

The two had coffee placed in front of them, and they sip slowly. Hecate leaned close to his old friend. "Look, we could do with your help. The boys are good really. Just think, you'll be able to teach them some manners."

"If they annoy me, I'll kick their backsides."

"Sure," Hecate smiled at the idea. "Something big will happen, and I know it. It involves them. Let Isis be a part of it, it'll do her good."

Valkesies saw Hecate's face turn serious. In his eyes, he could see Hecate was concerned for the future.

"This world is heading for a disaster, something that will affect everyone alive on Gaia, even the gods."

Valkesies had long ago learned to trust his friend's instinct; even now he was beginning to accept his words.

"The other day, at the lugarta, I saw all those Gaians covered in their country's colours, and all I saw was pain riding the air surrounding them."

"An omen?"

"I think so. Please come with us. You know you can handle the boys," Hecate said.

Valkesies allowed the silence to come over them while

the carriage was becoming full with people wanting their breakfast. "I don't think I have to make the decision," Valkesies said, smiling, knowing that Isis had every intention of going with Hecate and the boys.

Σ

The cardinal-red-haired girl had seen her target. A bag that was sitting on the edge of the seat that Isis was on, and had been left beside her. The girl followed a woman heading for the toilet, and kept herself from Zidaini's sight, using the woman as a wall to hide behind. The bag got nearer, the table it sat upon got closer. No eyes from the table noticed her moving nearer to them; the woman a perfect shield. At the seat's edge, she reached out and grabbed the bag, stepping off into a run with the bag in her hand.

Startled into life, Zidaini leapt out from the seat over two customers, using their heads to keep his balance, and chased after the red hair.

"Calum, get her!" He shouted as the girl darted through the carriage, now with both Calum and Zidaini chasing.

Valkesies crashed through the tables, launching them and the passengers' breakfast into the air. Each person he touched was sent to the floor with the food and beverages over them. Calls of protest and shock, echoed out to him. The only thing reaching him was the need to catch the thief. A 'sorry' for each clumsy moment would have to wait.

The girl reached an intersection, and climbed rungs on the carriage wall to the roof.

Zidaini almost grasped her feet as he leapt at her, before climbing the rungs himself.

Calum ran straight through fast, getting beyond the girl, who had to traverse the moving train's roof and the smoke; a tougher task than just running along a safe carriage. On top they were more wary of falling off then the chase, balance a priority.

Calum got to the carriage ahead, cutting the girl off. Valkesies meanwhile struggled, having to crawl along the

181

roof. The thief laughed, and readied herself to jump of the train.

'What is she doing?' Zidaini thought to himself, the answer immediately apparent. The train was coming into Habana. Both boys raced to get her before she leapt off the train. Their hands outstretched, they jumped toward her, reaching out to grab her and the bag tucked within her short skirt. She leapt as they were upon her, and dove off the train, landing on the grass verge, into the short dry grass that cushioned her landing. The buildings shot by, hiding her from their eyes.

"Did you get it? Did you?" Valkesies called; he had been forced to stop, and was now looking on in horror.

Σ

"Aaahh, that hurt!" She writhed, as the pain of the landing wasn't the cushion she thought it might be. "Actually that really hurt." She lay still in the prickling grass, listening to the sound of a nearby trickle of water going along a stream within the trees.

"I shouldn't have dived off the train. Damn Gaians!" She forced herself up. Her black-striped red hair was now a scruffy mess from the fall, and her knife had pressed into her thigh, cutting through the leather and into her skin. A tear of blood fell down her leg.

"Where's my.....?" She said with a stern look, sitting up to look for the bag, as the pain gripped her. "DAMN IT- Ahhh!!"

31

NORTEDES AND SAMIARAITA

Nortedes placed himself by the windows of Hotel Rossiya's cafe. He drank slowly, taking his time, wasting away the hours, while staring out at the street that came from the northeast gate, and connected to the park's outer road that was being drenched by a slow drizzle. He watched the many humans, and the few travellers that weaved their way through the undesirables that took to the streets to intercept them, coming in droves for them. He even saw one killed, trying to steal from an old Adinan lady; her bodyguard gutting the thief of a man without the slightest of remorse. The blood spilled to the ground, and the poverty stricken stole what little they could find. The police didn't even bother to disperse the pilfering crowd, allowing the event to transpire before removing the body from the scene to burn to ash. The thief was quickly forgotten by everyone.

Shortly afterwards, a Gaian came from the path he had for so many hours watched. Wearing the bright blue and white of the Liberian Empire, he had his double-edged katana sword sheathed at his side. His hand rested upon the weapon's black-patterned hilt. He walked with a well-drilled military confidence, his chest up and proud, but not forced. He moved quickly through the throng of beggars that darted from his path. The soldier was a threat they would not attempt to engage. The colonel's green eyes scanned the crowd of people, and what lay around him. He seemed not bothered by the rain as he walked through it, and Nortedes could see a tail just poking out from beneath the black cloak that covered the Gaian's back, and which

183

made a good blanket in cold weather.

Nortedes stood up from his seat, and took just a few steps closer to the door of the Rossiya, and waited; waited for the moment he had pondered over for days.

Colonel Samiaraita pushed open the doors and went into the hotel; stopping at his step. His green eyes turned and sighted Nortedes. The dark colours and the foreboding size did not upset or send a shiver of fear into or through the colonel, as he stared at the general. Even though he was outsized by quite a considerable amount, those extra feet in height and the added width did nothing to scare Samiaraita.

It seem like the shards of time had frozen. Their hands upon hilts, sliding down to grip their chosen weapons. Not the clatter of plates or the hustle and bustle of those coming in and out of the hotel made them flinch. They were solely focused on each other. The world around them was beginning to notice the tension. It was like a voice had called the start and they set upon each other in seconds. Those that were between them were soon barged to the side, and the swords of the two fighters clanged against each other. The long sword was so much bigger than the Gaian katana. Yet the colonel was solid and steady in its craftsmanship. No words were spoken by either. Nortedes swung his sword down, his attempt parried, a kick reached his leg, and he almost lost balance, before blocking Samiaraita's lunge.

Samiaraita made up for his lack of reach against the huge build of Nortedes with a determined velocity in his counterattacking, his sword movements were the fastest the general had ever seen. Nortedes' long sword's length was the only reason the fight remained even; he parried and countered because his sword had less time to get to each move.

Chairs were flung aside as the two crashed through them. Samiaraita was fully aware of the general's strengths; he couldn't let up, and thrust and cut at every slight opportunity.

Nortedes couldn't believe his opponent could be this quick. He would have to apply himself more, he had been too distracted. He smashed his sword into Samiaraita's, the strength of his strike pushed the colonel backwards to tumble over a fallen chair. Ignoring the bruise from the wood, the colonel got to his feet within the tumble, putting all his effort into a another parry. Nortede's sword came crashing down on to the katana.

Nortedes could see from the colonel's eyes that he hadn't drank or eaten, and would tire sooner. The general kept up his thrusts and the swinging of his sword, the reverberations of each strike going through the katana and into the wrists of Samiaraita.

The militia looked on. Uncertain whether to engage the fighters, they watched from a distance. No one went close, instead, watched the battle drift to the staircase while the two battlers continued to try and run each other through. Nortedes lunged into a swinging strike at the colonel, who ducked beneath the longsword and reeled backwards through the staircase door.

Samiaraita moved quickly up the stairs, stumbling as hunger and thirst gripped him; he tried to catch his breath while the general came up the steps toward him.

Nortedes breathed steady, unfazed by the speed of the fight, his breathing controlled.

The colonel looked on, wondering if Nortedes was able to control his outward look. He knew Nortedes would be able to tell how fatigued he was, knew of the general's abilities.

The general, on the lower stairs, swung around from the right, up into Samiaraita, who in turn smashed down his katana on to Nortedes own, the clash of steel resounded around the staircase.

Samiaraita ran upwards, he wanted open ground, where his agility had more use. He knew Nortedes could block most of his strikes and could certainly finish him with shock, and he was in trouble, starving and with fatigue already setting in.

He smashed through the final door, out on to the roof. Nortedes chased out after him. Colonel Samiaraita was ready, his sword in his right hand, his left behind his back. He lunged forward into Nortedes as he left the doorway. Most of the strength Samiaraita had was put into his right arm, forcing his blade into Nortedes. His left hand revealed a dagger, and he plunged it through Nortedes' side. The general was able to move just enough to avoid major arteries. With the strength of the colonel's strike being transferred into his dagger thrust, Nortedes crushed down on the weapon, collapsing Samiaraita, and pushing his longsword on to the colonel's shoulder. Samiaraita fell down, the blood poured out from his shoulder, his sword drop to the roof's floor, clinking and scrapping to a halt. The colonel gripped tightly to his shoulder, trying to stop the flow of blood leaving his wound.

Nortedes, holding the grip and cross guard in his hands, stood towering over Samiaraita, lifting the sword above the Gaian, who lay back, his breathing heavy and pained, he laid quiet, accepting his ultimate death.

'... I can't do this... Not for Bushia.. Not for anyone.' He stepped away, and dropped his sword. The colonel was left staring after him, his life to be kept.

Σ

"Samiaraita has failed," one of the Traicans said, his ears flicking to and fro, "Emperor won't be happy."

"Furious, yes! We deal with them?"

"Send them in. Kill them, we must."

"Mercenaries, yes. Plattered heads."

"Yes! Idea good. Fetch them we must."

The Traicans had watched what they could of the fight through what they considered extremely bizarre telescopes, from high up in the haze of cloud. Now they ordered the ship to settle down. Mercenaries would be called and the orders for Samiaraita's and Nortedes' death issued.

32

LULSAN EMPIRE. LUSA

The thought of shopping had been too much for the boys and they had split from Isis and Valkesies. Hecate had gone on with the boys, the desire for shopping not within him either. They were at the harbour's edge, where the most of the shops and bars were located.

Several ships lay at anchor and the area was packed with mostly humans, who dotted about everywhere, some hanging at the sea wall or trying to buy fresh fish from the stalls, or just lolling around with people they knew, while they waited for the ships to bring on or off more cargo. Very few Gaians were around in Lusa and even old Hecate felt alone; his red eyes didn't exist in the human race. He began to long for the extra company of Isis and Valkesies. But they had just disappeared through a thong of people trying to see a play that was being held at the harbour's edge.

The roads through Lusa were often incomplete, the paving ending at dirt tracks at the crossroads. The city of Lusa outside the harbour area was a beautiful city, well kept and finished; a contrast to the poorly kept docks of strewn papyrus papers, and bones, void of the chicken they once had held, for the tame wolves to scavenge across the harbour area. People of differing ages were scattered about the place, buying or selling wares and a commotion of noise from those travelling lolling and chatting away.

Σ

Calum found himself having to push through people as it seemed a hindrance for the humans to let him through. He found it a good idea to barge them away, showing the same lack of manners they showed him.

The main plaza provided an array of pubs and basic supply shops, along with the ticket office for boarding the docked vessels. The main attraction along the sea front was the 'Creature Trap', a huge monster fighting arena in between two parallel streets that ended at the harbour's plaza. Its colonnaded front faced the sea. Its large entrance was centred between the two streets, and dozens of people were scattered before its open doors.

The plaza also held the 'Simpe Oaf', a place for those that dealt in the arts of the underground: assassins, spies, thieves, and any untrustworthy miscreant, or villainous vagabond. It was the kind of place that Hecate would clout both boys for even thinking of heading in. He was grateful to see they had already taken a keen interest in the Trap. They both scampered off into the building, while Hecate followed without any trace of excitement emanating from his red eyes.

Calum came to a slow dawdle as he looked over the lobby of huge canvases hanging from the ceiling along the circular wall; of creatures that were on offer. Above the single counter on its own at the back of the lobby was a dragon, it's name along a plate at the bottom; Kenemti, the fire dragon.

"Fantastic! Calum said, while craning his neck to stare up.

"Have you seen something you want to take on?" Hecate had seen Calum's eyes glow when he saw the Kenemti.

"That dragon! I can take it," Calum said, assured of his own abilities, smiling with awe as he looked upwards.

"I'm joining in!" Zidaini flexed his arms, desperate to get some action.

"Well, I could do with the training. Plus I need to give something a thorough beating," Hecate said.

The boys shook their heads, before leaving Hecate to

look at the painting.

Calum went up to the counter. An old lady going grey through age looked down at him. "I-We wanna fight the Kenemti."

Zidaini was leaning against the wall to the side, away from the woman's view. Calum knew he was up to something.

"Ok, hun. But we need to ask, how old are you? And where ya from?" Zidaini pointed, and pretended to laugh at him. Calum stood stunned as she continued. "And since you're new, I would ask you start with something smaller." She smiled down at him, while Zidaini bit his nails and grinned away.

"Would I be asking to fight a dragon, if I wasn't old enough," Calum said, lowering his brow on one eye.

She looked at him bizarrely. "Hun, age is irrelevant here at the Trap."

Calum sharply looked at Zidaini, and gave him a quick kick. "You tricked me!" Calum said as Zidaini blocked his boot, and giggled.

"Of course! The opportunity was there." The woman looked on confused, while Zidaini picked up a quill, dipping the quill within the ink, and writing his and their information on the parchment.

"You'll learn, one day," Hecate said. He had caught on within the very first second, and now grinned at Calum.

"Right! You'll face the Kenemti in an hour. That's ten thousand. Keep in mind, we haven't been able to save anyone yet."

Zidaini felt a knot grab his throat; the thought of facing the Kenemti just became unappealing. He looked at Calum and saw an unchanged and calm face.

"One hour. Doors around the hall. Toilets downstairs, on the left of the waiting room.

"Right, then. Shall we go down?" Hecate asked. He received an instant movement, but no reply. They went curiously wandering to the stairs downwards.

The tunnel that took them down revealed the large stone

slabs that were joined together by mortar, and acted as the Creature Trap's supporting infrastructure. The tunnel took them to the waiting room, where several competitors were preparing themselves mentally for their own match. A few injured lolled in the corner, murmuring at their wounds, of cuts and black bruises.

Calum and Zidaini sat down and waited. Hecate stood hovering.

Calum watched those around him; he saw their anxious faces but he didn't feel the same way. He had the desire within him and the fear was non-existent. Instead, he wondered on what the others had been fighting, or were going in to battle. He shuffled off to find a more comfortable spot to fit his bum onto. He failed to find a place on the hard bench, and decided to stand.

"No I'm not nervous, the bench sucks," he reasoned before Hecate opened his mouth.

Calum looked over at two men who responded to his questions; they were to fight a Drozan. He had absolutely no idea what a Drozan was.

Σ

Isis and Valkesies hung over the side of the harbour wall, looking out at the ships at dock. Caravels and old galleys sat anchored beside galleons of the Lulsan Empire, accompanied by several frigates that drifted in the open waters. The docks beside the galleons were filled with the many crews of the galleons, lolling about on the decking, waiting for orders from their officers.

A few merchant vessels laid at anchor at the end of the harbour, being loaded with wares for their next destination. Three of them were still taking passengers, and Isis had been convinced by Valkesies to take a look at the potential choices before making a mistake. Now they were at the wall, and Valkesies had already made his decision, based on the attitude of the crew he could see.

"I like the galleon," Valkesies said.

Isis could already see why. "Only because there is an Elseni aboard," she smiled. "We'll get the five tickets, and then will go look at the shops." Valkesies face dropped, and he sighed, while Isis led him away.

33

A TOUCH OF UNDERSTANDING

Samiaraita lay in bed, weak from the loss of blood. His shoulder was stabbing with pain as Nortedes sprinkled more of a yellow herb over the open wound that the sword had cut so deeply. Samiaraita winced with the stinging pain that shot down his upper chest, and gave him a feverish shiver. The general left the wound uncovered, to allow the air to reach the herbs.

"Don't move it too much," Nortedes quietly said.

The mood had become sombre between them. There was no hate in the room, just the feeling of depression lingering with the feeling of aching and writhing.

Looking down at the colonel, he asked, "Does it still hurt?" He was wondering if the Hacai tree's flowers were doing their job.

"It's better, pretty good for an open wound. Almost as good as magic."

"Never that good," Nortedes added. They looked at each other. Questions lay needing an answer. "I was sent to kill you," Nortedes said, ignoring the rules and regulations of missions.

"Really! And I thought you were an Amarian knight come to get me."

"I must have looked pretty bad, since I would be a thousand years dead," Nortedes said, and received a slight smile in return. The eyes of the colonel were looking heavy, sleepy and ready to drop.

"What was your reason?" Nortedes asked.

"Not to kill you, but to get the precious gems of the gods

for my lovely Emperor," Samiaraita answered with a touch of sarcasm. "They did say an Imperium officer would be here to kill me. Guess they sent the wrong one."

"How could your Emperor know of my mission?" Nortedes was shocked and came immediately to the conclusion he was being set up, and that they wanted to oust him from his army; it would explain their need to steer him away from his soldiers.

"How could your senate know of mine? It was kept between the First Royal, Emperor and myself; there was no one else present unless someone was hiding in the shadows," Samiaraita said.

Nortedes sat, equally confused: "Bushia, myself, and his puppet major."

"Strange," Samiaraita commented, looking up at the ceiling. He tucked his arms beneath the covers, the pain subsiding to leave just an ache. "How long will you stay?" He asked.

"I'll wait until you're ready to leave, then I'll go. We must be careful, something is going on behind are backs," He said, feeling uncertain about his future, and about his home, which was becoming a much more deceitful place.

"I'll be alright. I doubt they will bother me too much."

Nortedes doubted the assumption. Samiaraita sunk into his pillow, drifting off quickly to sleep, his eyes too heavy from the Kacai flower's scent.

"I'll get us some food." The general slouched into his hands, covering his head. He hated the feeling of not knowing, hated the sunken feeling of being overwhelmed, and without a way out.

He clutched his side where the dagger had pierced it, giving a groan of discomfort. He would put some herbs on his own side. He looked down to see Samiaraita's wound had closed a little. In a few hours, it should have healed, and eventually the scar would fade. With some help from magic it would have been instant. He got up and left the room.

34

THE CREATURE TRAP

A rumble reverberated through the concrete walls, the vibration of a hundred fans cheering for the blood that had been left behind. The sound that came through to the waiting room was followed by a large, grinning man, carrying a bewildered and bloodied human whose leg had been torn and battered so much so that he couldn't support himself and walk out from the arena. He was placed down, and medics rushed from the stairs to give him the aid he desperately needed.

The grinning man, with a comb-over, watched the human quite amusedly. "Well, weren't you something? That critter made mincemeat out of yer leg there." He barked a laugh at his own statement, then peered around the room. "So! Who be giving the Kenemti a try?" He asked looking around at the contestants.

Calum and Zidaini stood up from the hard benches.

"Gaians!? Well, we don't get too many tails at the Trap," he said, with a cheerful smile. "Ah, the old man's with yee?"

Hecate was not impressed and gave back a look of anger.

"Me name's Horatio. Me and my wife own the Trap," he said proudly, still giving them an unceasing smile. "If yee can beat.. Ha, ha! The Kenemti.. Ha, ha!" He calmed his laughter to finish. "Well, yee get a reward. But that ain't gonna happen. Of cause, miracles do happen." He mused over it.

"Can we go yet?" Calum asked, wondering if this was the sort of person who could speak forever.

The smile went, lost somewhere. Horatio was silent a

moment, as he pondered them. "This way," he said. He took them down the corridor of blood-stained concrete flooring. The sound of people reverberated louder as they neared the arena. The circular arena had metal bars giving some protection to watchers who sat high above, looking down on the action. A roof allowed pockets of air to pass through small holes across the ceiling and allow for the oxygen to get through for a mage's magic without letting flying creatures escape from the Trap.

The audience was blaring and ready, filled with a climax of anticipation, calling for the violence to begin, to give them the thrill their own lives lacked.

Horatio's wife was up in her own private box. She called for silence, and the air of the arena filled with it. The audience desperate for those next words: "Kenemti."

She had waved them to be silent, and now she broke it, shouting out so those the whole way around could hear.

"Welcome to the Creature Trap. Here tonight, in Lusa's best fighting arena, the greatest attraction in all of Gaia, brings to you two eighteen year olds, Calum and Zidaini Brutanii, with the legendary Grand Mage... Hecate!"

A roar of approval came from the excited crowd. The hero of the Adinan Empire was within their walls, and now they could tell their grandchildren and children they saw the greatest mage upon Gaia.

"Versus, the one and only, the undefeated."

The audience cheered and bellowed out calls for the dragon.

"The most deadly of all of the Creature Traps monsters, the... Kenemti!"

A bloodlust roar filled the arena, the fans of the Kenemti shouted out, for they would get to see the beast fight.

The gates to the arena were opposite each other, contestant and opponent behind solid steel before the match begins. Attached to the fronts of the gates, were long chains that would be winched from above, opening the gate without the danger of leaving the staff caught in the arena; instead they turned great ship's wheels to winched the gates open.

Behind the creature's gate, steam poured out from the bars, its hidden jaws revealing its presence with the steam of its fire.

Opposite the beast's gate, Calum, Zidaini and Hecate waited for the moment the gates opened. Calum watched the brief flicker of movement; the eyes of the Kenemti reflected the slightest of light from its eyes. The rest of its looks were disguised by the darkness.

Calum felt no fear as he watched it. He stood relaxed in mind, sound in his body, and he couldn't help but wonder why he didn't feel any sense of fear.

"Boys! Its scales are thick and I won't be able to do much damage without you two creating a wound for me to strike. Understood?" Hecate told them. He felt the usual touch of a bothering fear, something the battle had always eased.

"Oh, yeah!" Calum called. His eyes focused on the dragon.

"Let's kick some butt!" Zidaini called.

"Can you consider the hind of a dragon a butt?" Calum asked, drawing his sword.

"Will you two concentrate," Hecate ordered.

Calum came back from his distraction to the eyes of Kenemti. He could feel the rush forming within him, the rage of battle coming up from the shadows in his heart.

The chains pulled tight and tugged at the gate, pulling it slowly open. The chain was winched up while behind them a portcullis dropped down covering their exit, so creatures would not find their way to the waiting room. The three ran to the centre.

The Kenemti came from the gloom; indigo scales across its body gave it great protection against Hecate's, or anyone else's magic. Lava saliva trickled from its mouth, from the corners of its jaws to bubble and singe the sand below, turning touches of the sand to glass. Kenemti blared into the audience, deafening them with the loud roar, and charged towards the threesome, sending a fireball from its jaws at them while the gates slammed to a finish against the concrete walls. Hecate created an ice barrier ahead of them. The fireball smashed into the ice wall, melting through most of the block. A fall of water and a rise of hot steam fell and drifted. The block collapsed to the ground.

Calum and Zidaini split, running around with the shape of the circular walls, to attack the Kenemti. The dragon turned towards Zidaini, trying to snap its jaws into the quick Gaian. Hecate called ice to cover Zidaini, and the Kenemti chomp on to the ice block, steam piled from its mouth, from the melting ice. Another spear of ice went into the Kenemti, only just pricking the scales of the dragon's cheek bone.

Calum ducked a whipping tail as Zidaini slashed the dragon's neck and lunged away; then darted in to plunge his daggers into the Kenemti once again. The beast made no roar of pain, instead, became more tenacious, realizing they were more of a threat.

Calum leapt up onto the tail, gripping on and pulling himself up. Climbing up the graspable scales, he reached the nape of the dragon. It fired another ball of fire to cook Zidaini and Hecate alive; it yet again impacted the resistant blocks of ice that Hecate formed ahead of Zidaini and himself. In turn, the Kenemti was unable to get at the pestering Zidaini.

Calum got to the roof of the dragon's head. Gripping his sword, he turned it upside down and thrust downwards, again and again. Several times the blade ran through the tough skin, while the Kenemti violently swung its head side to side. Calum dove off, landing near the wall and rolling into it. Coming to a forceful halt, he got up to meet a swinging tail, dodged it neatly, and looked to Hecate.

"Ice his head!" he shouted. But Hecate had to dodge the massive jaws. Zidaini was still puncturing the creature, to no avail, trying to distract the beast so that Hecate could attack. The Kenemti had seen the obvious risk was the magic, and Zidaini stood a moment and looked at Calum.

"Keep trying!" He shouted at Zidaini. "Damn!" Calum ran at the Kenemti, and leapt high above it, reaching the height of the ceiling. The crowd gasped in awe as Calum formed ice around his arms, and his sword, and as he fell back down towards the Kenemti's head, he thrust his hands towards the bloodied head of the Kenemti, firing the ice in two long icicles into the gaping holes. The ice penetrated straight through. The Kenemti roared, feeling the searing pain of the icicles, and then it collapsed into a heap on the sand. There was pain on its writhing facial features as it crumbled.

Calum and Zidaini stood beside it, watching the smoke rise from the wound.

"End its suffering," Zidaini said.

Calum took up his sword, and ice formed around the blade.

"Aim here, at one of its lungs," Hecate said. He listened to the dragon breathing deeply. Defeated, it laid still.

Calum took a steady aim; the ice glinted and shined in the dark arena as if the sun shone on the ice. He thrust the sword deeply into the dragon, straight into the lung. The Kenemti was silent, its life gone.

"We kick butt!" Zidaini said, satisfied.

The audience broke their shocked silence and roared into appreciation.

"As always." They clasped hands.

"Looks like your daggers need new blades," Calum said, looking at the melted daggers turned black from the Kenemti's red hot lava, sitting hoisted in the sheaths, the silver hilts had survived intact.

"Hmm... Our winnings should deal with that," Zidaini replied.

Hecate walked behind, with a mixture of impressed, and disturbed by his lack of offence. Perhaps the isolation had weakened him; he was thinking back to his days when he could use multiple attacks and still defend himself. He vowed to himself to get back to his previous abilities.

They were greeted by both husband and wife. Horatio shook the hands of the three. "Very impressive; me and Helda made a killing, so many people bet against yee. Even me bet for yee."

"Yee just made us more money than yee could believe," Helda included, "now here ya are, yee winnings." She passed it over to Calum, who took it with a grinning delight.

Hecate grabbed it from him. "I'll look after that for you. You'll only waste it," Hecate said, while hiding a smile.

The two boys didn't bother to respond.

"Yee can also pick up some crafted weapons, if yee are interested. Two thirds off, of course," Horatio said. The two owners wandered off from the waiting room. The three left with everyone staring at them.

"Shouldn't the weapons be free?" Calum asked. The others hummed in agreement.

35

HABANA TOWN

She had made it across thistles that stung her, and through brambles that clung to her legs, then through the small alleys that led the way to the main street into the small town of a few thousand people. Allowing for plenty of space for trees and well kept grass paths along the dirt roads, all the houses were separated; with space between each for decent size gardens. At the eastside of the town center was a lake that the town surrounded. The waters filled with a bountiful supply of fish.

With her clothes dirty from the trek, and her red hair tangled and in a scruffy mess, she went looking for someone to take her, or steal from, to get to Lulsani. It was looking sparse until she saw the Carthian tavern come into view. The place had a few horses tethered up outside at a trough of water. This would be her chosen departure point.

She went towards it. A horse seemed so much more tempting to steal then risk a rejection, and the noise inside sounded of merriment, and she could see some travellers mingling with the everyday patrons through the windows.

She crept towards the tethered horses, keeping between two mares. She eyed the stirrups, not seeing the men that had come out from the tavern. They weren't intelligent enough to think about trapping her, instead went to confront her head-on.

She froze short of the stirrup of a light brown horse, never groomed by her owners, the horse's hairs were rough, and resembled her own. The red-haired girl recognized her opponents, men she had stolen from before. Her main fear was the mage that was with them. The rest of the drinkers carried a mixture of scimitars and rapier swords.

"You! You thieving little cow. The second time you've stolen from us," one of them said. His blood-shot eyes glared at her.

"Tried," she pointed out. "Well, um....!"

The quiet town was looking to erupt.

She backed away, knowing this was getting too hot for her. They followed her movements; they weren't about to let her go, and she knew it. She leaned away, and pushed off into a run. The group of nine gave chase. She stole away a few yards, getting a distance ahead, and knowing she wasn't going to be able to outrun them, she shot into 'Aunties Flowers', knocking over several pots as she tried to get in.

The lead chaser raced in, jumping up the small steps in one leap, and into the doorway. A knife thrust into his chest, directly piercing the heart. He fell backwards on to the grass path at the end of the steps. The rest faltered, and stopped short of the shop.

"Hey, Maridachi! You go first." The self-appointed leader ordered.

"Er! Left em, me beer, can't waste." Maridachi ran off.

The guy spoke again. Clearly he had long ago become the leader. "Fernando. What about your card debt. You go."

"So-sorry Durka. My wife. Em." He ran off. Gone from the fight. A few more quickly left without a word, leaving just the three of them.

Durka looked around him. "Fine. I'll go." He walked up to the door. The mage followed suit, with a man who was not able to comprehend the situation clearly, his mind was taking in the flowers scattered over the steps and the grass.

Durka laughed as he stepped into the four-aisle shop. "See! She's scared and hidden."

They each took an aisle. One was left spare, due to the lack of volunteers. Brushing aside the constant face-poking plants of ferns and leaves, and getting creeps at each creak of the floorboards, the dim-witted one crept slowly down the aisle.

"Ma-maybe we should go?" The mindless one asked, feeling disturbed by the creaking. Durka moaned in another aisle. Then the dim-witted one felt a tap on his shoulder. He turned around and looked downward, at the red-haired girl. "Hi! I'm Kimer," he said brightly.

"I'm Tika," she whispered. She leapt up with an upper-cut, whacking Kymer off his feet. His eyes shut, he fell to a crumpled mess, unconscious. "Night, night," she added.

"Kimer! Kimer! You ok?" Durka called with worry lines etching his forehead. He came to the end of the aisle to see the mage, whose dreary eyes showed no concern. He looked both ways and back up the aisle.

In the aisle Durka had just left, Tika was stealthily moving down, silent to everyone; she made no creaking noises, her position never given away.

"Damn it, Durka! The little brat's got Kimer," the mage said.

Durka growled his response, furious at being outsmarted. He walked to the mage, and went beyond him.

Tika came up the aisle behind him as the mage was checking over Kimer, crouching over the dumb human. She brought her knife to bear and came up right behind the mage; her body almost touching. Hovering just behind, she slit his throat across the artery. The blood poured out over the floorboards and the nearest shelves.

Durka turned in shock, staring helplessly on. The mage was struggling to live. Durka tried to hide his fear, he wanted revenge, but that fear had already gripped him. His shaking was obvious.

She stared at the fallen shaking mage. Durka's pants would have revealed more of his fear by the smell coming from him.

"We-ll," he stuttered, stumbling through his words, "I-I'll be off then. Er sorry t-o er bother you. I'm gonna get going." He walked trying not to let the urine-soaked trousers touch his skin.

She didn't smile, or even find it funny. "No one messes with me," she said, letting him go. She followed shortly after, heading for the open doorway.

"I don't think you are ready to leave yet," a white-bearded old man said, stepping into the shop and blocking her exit. She saw the shop owner coming out from hiding, walking out from the back closest, and to her place at the counter. The fright having been too much, she said nothing to Tika, but stared at her.

"Excuse me, old man, before I kick your butt." Tika ordered, her knife back out.

"My name is Dionysus."

She stood still, unable to make an immediate decision. Dionysus might be old, but even she knew of the old mage's strength. He was well-known throughout his life, his magic was that of a Grand mage, something he had been anointed as, long before Tika was born.

"I'm heading wherever my path leads. So if you clean up this mess, I'll give you a ride," he said.

She was silent, stumped by his offer. "You can start by getting the bodies buried." She found herself doing as he told her, it was better than walking.

36

YOU WHAT!? YOU'VE GOT
TO BE KIDDING!

Isis had spent the last ten minutes gloating how she had beaten the number three card master, who went by the name of Rinona. In truth, she had taken two defeats before she had finally won.   Now Zidaini was showing her his new tanzanite, blue and purple crystal hilts. His silver hilts stored away within Hecate's bag, who was sure Zidaini would be missing them sooner or later.

Hecate and Valkesies walked ahead leading the way, leaving the other three together. "Why doesn't he use a gladius, or even a spathanius for a longer reach, it would still suit his style," Valkesies said, without looking back, and instead was looking out at the obstacles of people and cargo that strewn along the pier to the anchored ships.

"He has, it's inside my coat. He needs to practice with it, before he goes jumping into a fight," Hecate answered, showing off the spartha short sword. Valkesies nodded his approval, noticing the silver hilt.

"We got that ship over there for a good price and the crew we spoke to seem quite friendly. The others looked quite unwise. The Saverii and Venetian just didn't quite match up to my desires for the journey. The food on this ship is quite the feast, and with my favourite stew," Valkesies said. While Hecate didn't recognize the new galleon, he accepted the choice without question.

Σ

"So which one did you get?" Calum asked.

"Oh it's really nice," Isis smiled, "you'll like it. It's a big galleon." She jogged up to Valkesies while Calum slowed down.

"Zidaini!?" Calum had slowed to a dawdle; the shock of one of the three last vessels was dawning on him. "That ship, Zidaini!"

"I know," Zidaini replied, looking incredulously over at the last galleon of the docked ships.

The two boys watched in horror as the other three climbed the gangway up on to the galleon. "Of all the rotten luck." Calum stopped in his tracks. Zidaini with him.

"Have the gods deserted us completely," Zidaini whined.

"She did, didn't she? She got us a ticket?" Calum moaned. Neither could move, frozen by embarrassment and fear.

Isis was talking with the first-mate as he regarded her with absolute politeness, and he listened to who the tickets belonged. She pointed the boys out from the deck of the ship. The four arms folded, and his face creased into a wide grin as he recognized them, he called out the crew to take a look. The boys went red-faced as they became the object of everyone's attention.

"I really can't believe it, Of all the turd-covered luck, we get the.." Zidaini paused, the horror too much.

"The Raiden..." Calum finished, and they began pondering another ship. "We are looking really sad just standing here." Calum nudged Zidaini into movement, albeit both were slow, they warily walked up the gangway to the first-mate. "Can we turn back?" Zidaini asked. Calum didn't respond.

On deck, the other three were confused and wondering what the problem was. They could see the embarrassment written on the boys' red faces. The crew of the Raiden gave a rapturous applause, and their captain came straight up to them, his face wide with happiness. "Well I'll be; our little helpers. I never thought you two would step foot on another boat again, let alone ride the Raiden."

The other three were still looking on, wondering why the boys looked so concerned. "Back to work!" The captain called, then walked the boys to one side. "It's good to see you two choosing the Raiden... You wouldn't mind helping Tifa again, would you?" He said smiling. They looked sternly and unimpressed at him. "Just kidding. We have another stowaway, oh they are such entertainment." He walked away, finished with mocking them.   Hecate   and Valkesies were grinning away at the two boys, and Isis gave a shy smile at them.

"You do realize Valkesies now has something to mock us with," Zidaini told Calum, who nodded. They watched their companions looking back at them.

"Have you noticed the way those two act around Isis?" Calum asked. They were still staring at each other. Hecate and Valkesies were obviously talking about them. "Valky is definitely the bodyguard. I have no idea why Hecate is so respecting to her"

"If he is her bodyguard and she's someone rich, that almost explains why he doesn't want us around her. So I think we should stay involved with her," Zidaini said.

"The thing is, Valky is protective of her. While Hecate has been very watchful of us," Calum said.

"Well, he is my grandpa."

"No, it's more than that; he's protecting us," Calum whispered. "Which will make Isis think we're important." They watched her briefly. "Come on! Let's go over to Isis, and annoy your friend," he said walking off.

"I'll be there in a minute, I wanna get us some munchies," Zidaini said, going off towards the kitchen. Once he opened the door to Tifa's kitchen, he was hit by the lush array of smells. The cherry pie's strong scent was drifting across to his nostrils. Tifa was merrily moving across his kitchen of pots and pans, singing away to himself. While his four hands sped through each of his dicing and stirring tasks. In the corner of his eyes he see the figure of a blond-tailed Gaian, and spun around to see Zidaini taking in the smells of his kitchen, immediately delighted to see someone sniffing at the air of his wonderful cooking. Once his eyes realized it was Zidaini, he rushed over to him, wrapping all four arms around Zidaini. "Well me boy, how ya been?" He looked past Zidaini. "Where's the other one?" He said, uncontrollably crushing Zidaini in his powerful arms.

"Ok, ok! Calum's outside, he's talking to our friends." Zidaini was released from the grip, and able to breathe. "Your stew's boiling over," he said.

"Oh, whoops!" Tifa rushed back and moved the pot from its place above the coals. He then looked over at his stowaway, sighing as he looked at the boy. "I think I'll give his gooladi in the morning. Pre-age Adinans tend not to handle their alcohol that well," he looked disappointed at the Adinan, who was slouched over half asleep, lost in his stupor. Tifa then just completely cheered up. "Would you like some cherry pie? For Calum and yourself?" He asked grinning, with that everlasting cheerfulness, that had even infected Zidaini, who couldn't help but smile.

"Of course!"

$$\Sigma$$

The Raiden's fore, main and mizzen masts' sails were stretched to their full tightness, the wind blowing them out and pushing the galleon along. The city of Lusa had long since gone, and the coast of Regonia appeared on the horizon. In the sky above, the demon soared, with its naginata in its long fingers, riding the dark grey and sleek beast. The clouds of grey which usually cover the sky of the southern continent were providing the perfect hiding place. Now it had seen its opportunity, and it swooped into a descent, dropping out from the clouds, and swiftly levelling out above the waters, its reflection that rolled with the sea as big as the real demon. Heading for larboard side of the Raiden, its targets in line on the starboard.

Calum and Isis stood leaning over the side at starboard, watching the tumbling sea, and full from the cherry pie.

Valkesies had seen the beast approaching; he took one

look at Isis and took in the situation quickly. He charged across the deck, as the demon soared up over larboard side. Valkesies crashed into both Calum and Isis, using each of his lower arms to throw both down. The beast tried to grab at them, its talons just missing the diving Valkesies, and crashing away the parapet wood of starboard side. It soared up and away, turning around in the air, it came back towards Calum and Isis.

Arquebusiers fired their inaccurate muskets, missing by wide margins, the lead ball coming out of the barrel at angles. Hecate had come on to the deck, and on seeing the arquebusiers, he felt the weapons useless, and the men and women had better chance with spear or sword, and frowned at them before turning his attention on the demon.

Wrath filled Valkesies as he readied for the beast and its demon rider. Calum stood ready, his emerald sword in both hands. Isis stood beside Valkesies, she was scared at her first battle. The beast charged towards them. Valkesies pushed them both away off their feet, and on to the floorboards. With his two top arms he grabbed the beast's legs, the talons missing his skin, and he turned the beast on its back, smashing it into the deck. The demon tried in vain to hold on, as he and the beast ploughed along the deck, the wood splitting and breaking up. The demon stood up and dodged Hecate's strike of lightning. Feeling the static in the air, the demon climbed back on to the beast as it lifted and ascended back into the air, and flew fast away. Although bloodied and sore, it came gliding back around to make its way down for another pass.

Hecate looked across at Calum who was in the middle of holding his head and insulting Valkesies. Valkesies looked across at Hecate. The mage knew the Elseni had enjoyed that. Isis had gone to the side of the bridges stairs. Once more arguebusiers blasted shot up at the beast.

The beast twisted and yawed to avoid Hecate's constant magic. It was hit nearing the deck; a ball of fire seared it skin. It screeched, and its rider called it on. It swirled to dodge the ever-firing Hecate. Over the deck it came with smoke trailing from its singed furs. Electric sparks formed in its jaws and it built up to lightning. As it swooped between the main and forward mast, avoiding the ropes and shrouds, it streaked out a beam of lightning that tore up the deck, shattering and setting fire to the wooden planks.

Valkesies picked up Calum in his left hand, and ran as the beast shot its lightning at him. The deck exploded behind them, and crew members were scalded and killed as the beast attacked, and planks of wood were melted and ripped to shreds. Valkesies got to Isis, dumping Calum back down. Calum was still angry at being rudely grabbed and thrown.

The arguebusiers had dropped the useless weapons that were nowhere near the modern muskets of the army, and had taken up buckets of water, frantically trying to put out the building fires. Bows had now come out from some of the passengers and one managed to wound the beast with an arrow that pierced its skin deeply. It flew out away from the smoking Raiden, taking another painful hit from Hecate's lightning. The demon sneered down at the deck of wounded people, and looked directly at Hecate, while the beast glided round.

"Target the one that calls the lightning, then we will take the other targets out," he snarled, clutching the naginata. His other hand held on to the folds of spiky skin at the nape of the beast. They came for another pass, and suddenly their faces turned to shock and creased with fear as the beast swooped back to the Raiden. Shiva, the god of ice, appeared as if from nowhere; she came into the world of Gaia, hovering with no wings.

The demon's beast broke the charge, pushing backwards with its wings, rearing at the sight of Shiva. She raised a hand and pointed a finger at the beast, shards of ice with dagger ends formed in front of her hand. The demon roared its beast on. The icicles shot rapidly through the air, more forming and following behind, shooting into the beast, piercing and ripping through its skin. The demon leapt from the doomed beast. The creature was riddled by the hail of ice, all its vital organs struck by the spears that Shiva created. The beast felled to the sea, dead before it begun to fall.

Shiva vanished from Gaia. The beast sunk beneath the surface.

The demon had landed at the aft of the Raiden, and it scanned its adversaries. Everyone was armed. The demon was going to fight, and would continue on. It had snatched up its other naginata as it leapt from the stricken beast, it now faced them, evil and ready to kill all in its path. "My Lethunius, my loyal servant, killed by a god, a worthy death." Its face twisted like the craters of the moon, it looked over them all. It stood as tall as the humans, but with more strength.

Zidaini had been unable to join the fight and now took up the task of taking on the demon. "You're an ugly fella, aren't ya... You are a guy, right?"

Calum had reached the larboard side aft stairs to the bridge. "Let's take it out!" He called, then went running up the stairs, while Valkesies took the starboard side.

The archers tried to loose their shafts at the demon, who ducked easily beneath the arrows. It leapt off before Calum and Valkesies got to it, bringing forth its naginatas, stabbing an archer and striking out at Hecate, who dove away. The demon went for another strike, and was blocked by the daggers of Zidaini. The demon parried again and smacked Zidaini down with the pole of his naginata. Zidaini rolled away, avoiding another swooping spear. The demon took a point-blank ball of fire, sending it writhing to the scorched and broken floor.

It got up quickly to meet Calum's emerald sword as Calum's quick arms wielded the sword, keeping the demon busy. Zidaini caught the spartha from Hecate and charged in taking up one of the demon's arms. The two boys gave it no time to attack, leaving it only with time to defend. Fear had come to its cratered face. Its face froze in horror and pain as purple blood splattered out from its abdomen and over the boys. They squirmed in disgust. Valkesies rusty axe was poking through the demon. It dropped to its knees. The purple blood continued to pour.

"No... Must get... Must kill... Boy with emeralds..."

Calum looked stunned. "Wh-why me?" He blurted.

The demon fell to the blacken floor. The blood running out into a large patch.

Swords were sheathed now the action had ceased. Zidaini took his new weapon's sheath from Hecate, and added it to his belt. They both stood with Calum, who was looking worried.

"Why would anyone want to kill me?" Calum queried.

"I would say that the Emperor has taken a liking to your sword, or maybe he is angry that you have taken the gem," Hecate said. "This likely is not the end." They stared down at the demon.

Σ

Isis looked over at the victorious three. "Why would it be after them? Do you think my father has sent it?"

Valkesies sat beside her on the shattered flooring. "I know you will want to continue to pursue heading where they go. But it is clear the Emperor is desperate to kill them." He said nothing more as they looked on at the dead demon.

Tifa came from the kitchen, his face hot and perspiring, he looked around at the carnage, not even losing his smile. "Let's eat ya," he shouted. He was beset by Calum and Zidaini, who had instantly put back the thoughts of being targeted, the cherry pie taking hold of their thoughts.

37

TIKA ON THE ROAD

Tika just didn't know what to make of Dionysus, who seemed quite happy to plod along, holding the reins of a single stallion. His cheery, wrinkled face was happy with the slow and relaxing pace that he had set for himself. She lolled in the cart, being pulled along behind, gently rocking to creaking and clonking wheels.

The scenery was of rolling plains of long, wavy grass. The odd tall deciduous tree towered lonely, dotted across the landscape.

Dionysus's smile stretched from ear to ear. The large lobes, like the rest of him, had the same wrinkles. Tika thought he was smiling for absolutely no reason at all. She had looked at his staff and wondered whether he even used the stick which had small writing down the length, or whether it was for commanding magic, or whether it was even a walking stick. She had also begun to wonder whether he was the legendary Dionysus.

"Hey, old man!" She called for his attention. "How much longer?" She was needing some speed to the lazy ride, as she was getting far too comfortable.

"A long while yet." She groaned at his answer. "What gods do you believe?" He shouted back, smile still upon his features.

She gave a look of wasting her time. "None!"

His head whipped around looking at her. "Another one? How can you not believe in the gods? It was Castelli who wiped out most of the Adinan army for the Liberian Empire to be able to subjugate Los Santos. Then there was Horus, who crushed the besieging forces of Lulsani. Even the ancient Amarians were attacked by a god called Eden, who killed thousands of civilians and soldiers.

Tika listened to the tutoring. She hadn't been taught much by anyone; thievery had been her most taught subject in life, and even that was often resulting in failure. "So where are they now?"

"How many summoners do you know?" The old man questioned. She sat up, the summoners were becoming a lesser breed over the centuries, and she was hearing more about the demise of the summoners from listening to conversations of others.

"None."

"Exactly! Most were killed by assassins in the Imperium's witch hunt in the Liberian Empire, with the deaths came less and less through birth. Books were destroyed by all sides fearing such a war of gods. Thankfully there were those that hid the books and documents."

"Isn't that a bad thing?" She asked.

"Of course not. Fear of the defeat is what keeps everyone in check. You wouldn't attack someone if you think you're going to get butchered without even getting a shot in," he said.

She smiled at his belief, and understood the concept.

"Did you know that a long time ago there was more land on Gaia then there is now?"

She mumbled "no" while folding her arms and leaning over the side of the cart.

"The Amarian Empire ruled the lands of the Imperium, Idona and right across to where San Adina is. The history books mostly blame Bahamant for the annihilation of the once powerful nation, and the rumours of their advance technology still exists today. Which is why Adina has been putting resources into excavation, hence those great flying airships. I can't see how even such a great god like Bahamant could have destroyed the Amarians alone, but no other word remains. Anyway! Explorers have even told of a large pyramid somewhere in the ocean, the home of Osiris."

She listened, dreaming of finding those gods, and their stones. "Has anyone tried finding whether these pyramids really exist?" she asked, moving a strand of red hair from her eyes.

"There are treasure hunters. But I don't think many people know very much about the pyramid's location. Maybe one day you can take a look. If you find them, make sure you show me," he smiled.

"Why would a god wipe out an empire?" She curiously asked.

"Could have been any number of reasons. Your own people would turn against you if you took away too many freedoms. There's also the culture conversion. Wouldn't surprise me if the humans derive from the Amarians, as there's so many of them. Maybe a crazed summoner went and called Bahamant. Maybe disgruntled Amarian diplomats called Bahamant. Maybe the god turned on the Amarians. Even civil war. We probably won't ever know," he said sadly, "I bet there's a lot of treasure in those seas of ours," he said, picking up his cheerful self. "So why you going to Lulsani?"

"It's the base of an airship belonging to my mother," She raised a smile. "Perhaps I'll even go hunt this treasure of yours," she said, dreaming of an improbable future adventure.

"Something tells me your path is not too far off," he murmured quietly so she couldn't hear.

The border wall that sat between the two empires of Adinan and Lulsan stretched from the ragged south coast up to the Troubled Pass, which was an unguarded mountain where few people survived. The border wall had two entrances: the north gate, with its walls of twelve feet high, and like the rest of the wall, was guarded by the Lulsan and left unguarded by the Adinans. The Adinan side was painted sapphire blue, the colours of the Lulsan Empire. The other side was covered with red and orange, so as to give the impression of entering the other nation's territory. In the south was the train's gate, larger and with new towers at intervals along a large section of the wall.

Dionysus looked over the guards at the gate, wondering if the girl knew she needed a pass. "Tika! Have you a pass?" He asked, wondering how he could have forgotten to ask her about it.

She sat up, still and unable to answer. She looked at the wall, deeming it not climbable. "Oh, bugger!" She moaned.

"Unless you take a boat, which includes a manifest of all travellers, you need a pass. Basically, they're trying to stop any smugglers from getting illegal goods into the country. Personally I think they just want to control the people easier, as this is a Lulsan thing. You might notice that there aren't any guards of the Adinans." He realized she wasn't even listening to him. Her eyes were fixated on the Troubled Pass, which sat over the other side of a lush meadow of tall golden grasses.

"Now, young lady. Do not risk the Troubled Pass. It's called that for a reason, and it's unguarded because it's dangerous. Nor can you climb the steep mountainside of sheer rock. The cave, my dear, is treacherous, to say the least. He had stopped the horse along the track, at a long distance away from the border wall. His concern for her was rising. She jumped off the cart and into the long golden grass.

"Thanks for the ride, old man. Perhaps you can give me a lesson on the gods one day." She sprinted off, leaving a trail through the grass that brushed the red of her hair.

Dionysus watched the red head dash away, and shook his head. "Good luck young'un"

38

HARBOUR OF REGONIA

The Raiden had reached the village harbour, and grey clouds signalled the vessel's arrival. The Raiden was the only carrack to drop anchor in the harbour of Regonia. Others had been and gone, and a single caravel sat at the dock. Trawlers that fished the seas around Regonia were quietly bobbing at their moors. The Raiden was sat against the sea wall, and it carried the stares of many locals. Its sails were scorched, and melted. Smoke still gently drifted up from the smouldering deck. She looked like the fallen, limping in to anchor; the dead carried off the vessel to be buried.

Valkesies escorted Isis off the damaged vessel, hoping it would make a full recovery, as he had heard the story of Calum and Zidaini's first visit aboard and applauded what they had done to the boys. Reaching solid ground and that welcome motionless and unwavering feeling of steady paving, he placed an arm over Isis. "Good work on the ship. I didn't know you could call Shiva, especially this far from her location in Adina," Valkesies said impressed with her.

"It wasn't me." She looked back at the others, as they begun their descent off from the Raiden.

"Not you? Then who? Not that little thief. Not even Hecate, he's a mage not a summoner." He was in disbelief.

"Calum!" Isis said. He seemed to hear her and he looked over and smiled at her. She smiled back, and wondered if indeed it was him.

"That must be what Hecate's hiding, but why is he protecting them both when they have such strength? Maybe there's something else," he mused.

Isis herself thought on the reason when both boys seem quite capable; she wished she had better ability. *'But Shiva. They must have the Sunstone.'*

The other three finally arrived at her side.

"We'll get some supplies. Maybe we'll buy Valky a new axe," Zidaini said at the forefront of the suggestions, "Calum and I will check out the food and weapons stores, all two of them. Come on, K!" The two boys went off quickly.

Valkesies looked at Hecate. "Joining us?" He asked hopeful.

"Um, no. I want to keep an eye on them," he said, marching off to find the mage's den that only a very few knew about.

Σ

Valkesies looked down at a smiling Isis. "What?"

"Time for the tour, of course."

"Fine. First, its history," he said, and she frowned at him.

"I know its history. It was once the capital of the Regonia Union. They had a civil war. Three cities were wiped out, due to a hurricane, which basically ended the war. The cities now are separated and chaotic."

"No, no, no," he interrupted. He shook his head at her, and wanted to whine about her teaching, but thought better of it. "Once, long ago, the people worshipped a god called Siren, a seductress of souls. She was worshipped by most of the continent's people." He began to walk her along, passing the many fishermen heading for the single inn. "It wasn't civil war that destroyed three out of six original cities; it was a god's hurricane, by the name of Thor. The former capital of the nation was devastated to a few houses. Thousand died, and eventually Londinium rose and became the economic centre for the continent, and subsequently the capital city. Of course that city has fallen to the slime pit it is now. Regonia has become the most pleasant of the four current cities, and has a 'no weapon' policy in the inn. Also the temple to Thor was built over there; you can just see its steeple. It has a painted ceiling of Siren being defeated by Thor. The town has kept a more thatch-cottage look to the place and refuses to allow much in the way of city growth. Now the town has, several years ago, severed ties with Londinium and is now just a place for trading with the Lulsan Empire. Obviously they had enough of the corruption within the other continent cities."

She allowed him to guide her along the streets of flower verges and wooden fences.

"Apart from its boring history as a capital, with records destroyed, the town does have its present history kept away from the town just in case it befalls another disaster. This place has a lovely beach not too far away, and quite secluded, and plenty of fish in the sea." He finished with not much more to say, except to show what was around.

"You've finally accepted we're going with them?" She placed an arm through his. He tried not to smile. Although she saw it, she said nothing more.

"It's unfortunate," he replied.

$$\Sigma$$

Calum and Zidaini ventured into the cluttered weapons store, with two rows of shelves and walls adorned with longswords, broadswords, sabres, scimitars, rapiers, arming swords, gladius and spathanius. Every type of halberd, spear and lance, this shop had, as well as every dagger and knife. The clutter was furthered by bows, and sheathes and arrows strewed the floor.

Zidaini had taken an interest in, although Calum couldn't see why, were the different axes. The new thorns and spikes on the back of the axe heads glimmered, even with the lack of light, and he went searching through the clutter that left little room to move along.

Calum walked over to the selection of swords, most of which had traditional snake-skin grips and carmine rapier handles, each with patterned guard. "The Thor's Ruby," he said reading aloud the name.

A short female human came to him, smiling broadly. She greeted the armed potential customers.

Calum stared at her, before moving his eyes away. Her smile seem fake to him, and he thought nothing of it, as she was trying to sell, after all.

"Can I hold the Thor's Ruby?" He asked.

"Of course you can my dear. Try them all. This one looks just right for a Gaian's small....hands." She held a smile as she spoke. She seemed to Calum to be intrigued with him.

A crash of blades resounded in the small store as Zidaini knocked them over at his feet.

"Sorry!" he said, overcoming a little embarrassment. "Don't bother, Calum, rapiers are for thrust, and lack any strength in the blade," he said, scanning over the axes and trying not to knock over any more weapons along the floor. He wanted to rid Valkesies of one of the ugly lumps of rusty metal.

Calum played with the rapier, trying not to hit anything in the small confines.

"Do you like it?" Her eyes bulged briefly.

Calum stared at her, he couldn't help but stare; those eyes bulged, definitely bulged. Her smile was still there, and it made the eyes even weirder.

"Er, no! The blade would snap in the first strike against my own," he said, still staring at her.

"I like this axe, a nice big war axe," Zidaini called from across the room; he was holding it in his hands. The axe was as long as him, perfect for Valkesies.

"Well, how about the attachments for it?" she asked. Going back behind the counter, she began hunting.

Calum watched her search; something in her manner confused him. "I would've figured you of all people would know where you keep things hidden."

She said nothing.

"Hey, lady! How much will it cost? I ain't paying too much," Zidaini said.

She said nothing.
Calum waved Zidaini back to the door as even he had moved nearer to the doorway.
"Are you ok in your cupboards?" Calum asked.
Zidaini was clutching the giant double-headed axe.
Again she said nothing.
They looked at each other with raised brows. Then she began convulsing, rattling and shaking, her head still stuck inside the cupboard. Her back became a lump; something was trying to get out.
It pushed up, failing to rip through the clothes on her back. It tried again, her arms flailing, turning to fluid. Everything caving in, then the clothes began to plop through blue jelly; a neck formed at the top of the now liquidized thing. The creature redeveloped into a limbless mass, its flan squished and flapped over the counter, and wobbled about, as the neck climbed up into a head of the former shop assistant.
The boys looked on with surreal impressions upon their faces. Zidaini gripped the axe, not really thinking it will help. Calum had already dropped the rapier. The flan lashed an arm of jelly at Calum, forcing him to dive backwards to the floor. Zidaini, with a heave, threw the axe at the flan, it went straight inside the flan, slowly dropping to the floor.
The previous arm returned and another talon struck out at Zidaini who dove out of the way.
Calum grabbed him up, and pushed him out through the doorway. Another arm smashed through the wall, and another accompanying talon shot through the doorway after them.
Both Gaians ran out to the other side of the street. The flan was slow, in its slimy exit through the doorway of the store. Its gelatine body flopped over each step, and rolled out onto the street. The boys kept a stance ready to leap out of the way. As onlookers stood at a distance, no one dared to help, nor were any soldiers present to help in the situation, while villagers that were too scared, or simply unable to help, watched from afar

"So what do we do?" Zidaini asked. "My daggers are a waste, can't even use my spartha," he sulked.

The flan struck out at Zidaini, its entire body following. Zidaini dove out of its way, as it landed behind him, and he ran back across the street, crying out in a scream at the annoying flan.

"Magic!" Calum said rolling away from the flan's arm. "Ice? Fire?"

Zidaini's question was answered with a lightning strike which lit up and sizzled the flan's mid-drift. Smoke rose up from the blue being, and the creature looked down at the evaporated section of its jelly body.

Calum looked down the street to see Hecate standing at a distant, his hands clasped behind his back.

"Why is he just standing there?" Zidaini moaned.

Calum smiled and shook his head.

"What?" Zidaini ducked an arm that had shot out at him, then he leapt out of the way as the irate flan's body came with it.

"She likes you, Zidaini. I tell ya what, have a present." He pulled his sword from its sheath, aiming it at the flan. The sword flashed with lightning that surrounded the blade.

"Calum, hurry up!" Zidaini called, with the flan still after him.

"Hey, flan, meet lightning." A constant bolt of lightning broke the air with multiple cracking noises. It came from his hands along the blade, and shot out at the flan. The flan writhed, as it frizzled and popped in bubbles, its body evaporating into the air. Calum did not let up, until there was nothing but the scorch marks against the street paving. The flan had boiled away.

"Bye, bye!" Zidaini and Calum stood over where it had once been. "Do you think we should take the axe, as payment for our services?"

Calum shrugged. "Where did Hecate go?"

Zidaini looked to where they had seen him last. "Yeah! Why didn't he help?"

"He called the first lightning strike."

Zidaini sighed. "He was using the fight to make us train."

"..It tried to kill us!" Calum moaned.

"Yeah! But it didn't."

39

A VISCIOUS PATH OF TROUBLES

Tika had come to a breach in the rock of the Troubled Pass. The pass formed a canyon, dusty red, mixed with golden browns and amber along the walls of the canyons cliffs. A sprinkle of dust drifted across the pass, hanging in the air. Squawks from vultures echoed off the rock, searching for more carnage, and to pick off scraps from the dead.

The pass was a dot on the planet, an obscene world amongst a beautiful one. Where beast ate monster and monster ate beast, and critters were among it all, right down to the life forms that the eye could not see.

Tika could feel the heat rising up from the hot sand; the calls of pack animals coming with the heat. A bead of perspiration ran down her cheek and then off the end of her chin. All she had was a knife, and it scared her.

She glimpsed something coming from the corner; she ducked behind a rock, as a reptilian with hairy paws, and long sharp claws came near. The pass created bizarre sights, of creatures that had gone away from normal evolution. This twenty-foot long reptile could smell her, could smell the scent coming from her Adinan body. A growl came from behind her, sending a shiver up her spine, causing her to turn sharply around to see a pack maroon-coloured fur wolves, their eyes taking in her flesh, their tails completely hairless, and drooping along the sand.

Now surrounded by reptile and wolves, she had to choose quickly; she chose to run at the reptile. It was alone, and she preferred to take the lesser number, which scared her less.

It braced itself to snatch her up, and as she neared in her run, it went to crush her within its jaws. She felt the wind of the jaws snapping shut by the skin of her back, as she ducked and dove beneath it. The screech came from a wolf, crushed between the jaws of the reptile as it went for the target of wolves. Quickly tossing the torn body into the rocks, it turned its attention on the rest.

With the first wolf dead, the other wolves warily stood their ground, their teeth bared at the reptile. Bodies rigid with blood lust, the wolves attacked. One was taken straight into the jaws of the reptile, two other maroon wolves bit into the hind legs, trying to wound the beast in the pack's need to weaken the reptile.

Tika was the last wolf's target. It went for her, racing between the legs of the reptile in its chase after her, with jaws drooling.

The reptile crushed another wolf, snapping it up in its teeth. The other wolf ran, heading down the pass in the direction of her own desperate getaway, the reptile following closely behind.

She could feel the jaws close at her spine. Even without the wolf's teeth catching her, she could feel it too close for comfort, and at the same time, thankful she didn't have a tail. As the sandy trail turned, with adrenaline rushing through her veins and the fear gripping her, and making tears brim at her eyes, she leapt up, and flipped in the air. The wolf snapped its jaws out, missing her again. She came down on the wolf, her knife in her hand. She plunged the weapon into the snarling wolf, into the nape of its neck; its four legs collapsed. She pulled back her knife and stabbed it again in the open fear. She breathed deeply, turning sharply around as she looked with fright for the wolves.

The reptile was chomping on a wolf. It was ignoring her, leaving her be, eating up the flesh of the dead wolf.

She breathed a sigh of relief.

Vultures settled down for their dining, ripping out flesh from the carcasses, tearing off the pieces, and defending their part of the flesh from the rest of the vultures.

224

The ground rumbled. Her heart stopped. She stumbled with the shaking, and groaned at the never-ending problems. The rumbling stopped and she searched the area with just her eyes for anything else. Nothing but the dusty air and the insects that buzzed in her ears; insects that numbered more than grains of corn in a field. And the reptile with the vultures, tearing up the dead.

She moved a few steps on, and the ground beside the reptile exploded. The sand lifted into the air, and a rock came up from the ground, and smashed two arms of rock down onto the crying reptile. Blood splashed the path.

The sight was enough to tell Tika to run, and she did. As she rounded the bend in the trail, she glanced back. The ground had become a headless body of rock that remained a part of the trail, scrapping its arms and body along the ground as it moved; not in a run, but like water, it moved as if falling sideways.

A cave was ahead and she ran with all her might, the rock after her. The cave that she ran for was not covered with the same red sandy rock, but with grey stone. She ran leaping over a group of skeletons, and glancing back to see the rock creature catching up with her. The cave opening got bigger and bigger, her legs pumped harder, and she got nearer and nearer, the hope rising, and the rock monster was upon her. She dove through the gap, and the golem smashed into the cliff face, and shattered to the sand below.

She stared back, and dried the tears from her eyes; she breathed heavily and the perspiration drenched her. She was no longer on the sand of the trail, but the stone of the cave, the solid grey stone. Small bugs wriggled over her hand, scurrying to no place in particular. She turned her nose up, shaking off the critters, and climbing to her feet, squirming. "Great! More disgusting things. What next? The mountain will turn into a giant golem, or maybe it'll fly away." She tried to calm her breathing, watching a snake crawl out from the cave, onto the now quiet red and amber sand. "Ironic!"

She turned to the dark cave, reaching into her pocket for the pack of matches and a small candle that the old man

Dionysus had given her on leaving Habana. It made her wonder whether he knew she would need them. She didn't light the end of the candle until the darkness overwhelmed her. She had her knife held down-facing as she walked along, gripping tightly in fear, and her continuous panting echoed out into the air.

Inside, it was cool, and a breeze brushed past her hair, lifting it gently from its scruffy place. She went into a jog, going deeper into the cave. But the light of her candle was not diminishing, as the little fluorescent critters that were clinging to the wall reflected the light, multiplying the lucent light through the passageway, each critter reflecting it to the next in a wave of glittering lights.

She ran past a line of red fungus, of dull red fur. Her breathing was quick, and the fear still clung to her throat as her steps echoed along the tunnel.

All around her became a wall of mirrors, her reflection in a dozen mirrors, every detail a perfect replicate. The critters no longer inhabited the passageway; they massed at the entrance of red fungus, never crossing the line of fur. Her breathing stopped. The mirrors changed to an image of ruins, a world lost to some devastation, decayed further with time. Windowless towers, with just the framework left. The sky was only a mixture of dark greys and black above a charred and blackened ground. The lifeless city changed to a boy in a waterfall, allowing the water to fall upon him.

"You! I've seen you. One of them from the train," she cried. Her words bounced off the mirrors. The picture changed again. A war was raging in front of her. Gaians and Adinans fought side by side.

"Mirrors, mirrors everywhere. See your world's past, here and there," a voice said, sending a jolt of fright through her.

She looked around to where it came from. The mirrors changed again. Castelli, el Dios del fuego, took up the wall of mirrors on both sides of her. She found it difficult not to tremble, she held her candle in front of her, her knife ready. She knew there was more to the pictures.

"Yes! Come and play. Die! Stay with me, my world you will see." Castelli changed to a single tree, short and leafless. She could see the end of the passageway of mirrors, lined with the fungus. She could see what looked like a way deeper into the cave. She bolted.

"Where you go? Away from me? Leave you be? Nooo!" The voice cried.

She went shooting past the line of red fungus, trampling the squelching insects and other critters that crawled on the ground, coming out to a cavern, standing on a platform above a pool of flax yellow liquid. Three pillars provided a stepping-stone path, levelled at her height across the coloured liquid. She stood before it as the voice ran out.

"My pets, do not leave her be."

From the cliff top which dropped into the pool of liquid, she could see the path continuing on over the other side.

She gasped in disbelief as zombified people emerged from the passageway that she had come from. Her previous path was now festered with the walking dead. They were fast, and in the moment of seeing her, they reached out to grab for her. She leapt on to the first of the pillars, balancing in the small landing area.

Behind her, walking corpses were piling out of entrances behind and below her. Their faces were torn and mangled, mutilated at their deaths. Hundreds of souls, left with mind and thought missing, by everyone who knows them. Their minds no longer possessing their born intelligence, they simply walked off the edge of the cliff after Tika, falling to the pool below. They were coming from both top and bottom pathways.

She jumped over to the next wider pillar, keeping an eye on to the zombies which waded through the pool, still with their eyes focused on her.

"Tika! Keep moving!" Dionysus voice ran through her head. She leapt to the next pillar, and jumped to the ledge, where her exit lay.

"Where you go? Stay with me." The voice was near, she was sure of it. As the zombies surged into the ledge below and squashed each other in their vain attempt to reach her in the swarm, she looked at the floor in front of the gap to her exit. She waited just a moment, listening to the cries and moans of the lost souls. The tunnel that led away had moving, rustling sand.

"What now?" As she said it, sand was thrown up and over her, followed by huge, ten-foot circumference snake, its mouth hissed with two long fangs that she knew had her name on them.

"There you are!" It called and struck out to sink fangs into her. It was halted in mid flight, sieving with pain. Valkyie, an ancient god, stood beside her, the claws of one paw around the snake. Valkyie threw the hissing snake into the wall. It slivered and sidled up to the god.

"What is you? Protect the child, you will? Die, you will!" The snake hissed, and launched itself at the god. Valkyie caught the viper and threw it down to the zombies.

The undead were still moving through the tunnels, their only way to her; they moved with their acquired thirst for blood and flesh.

Tika ran for the tunnel, while Valkyie dropped down onto the zombies, releasing them from their stricken curse through death by its claws. Valkyie killed several as Tika flew through the cavern pass without looking back.

She ran the tunnel path, crunching less critters along the way, their numbers less in the area, her footsteps gave her position away with loud echoes, and she knew she couldn't stop. The walking dead had found the connecting tunnels, and she skewered one with her knife at an intersecting tunnel, racing on without a pause as fast as her tiring legs would carry her.

The trail went into a slight incline, gradually taking her upwards. She passed more fungus, stopping at a skeleton, and a dead end. She turned around, her candle flickered a faint light, to reveal the entrance gone.

"Hello, my child." She felt panicked, and shocked by the development. "Thought you got me? Dead you thought?" The voice called sarcastically. She went to the skeleton, which lay with decomposing skin still on its frame. The stench filled the air. She took out the dagger, then sheathed her knife to pick up the loaded crossbow. She looked at her surroundings. A red fungus ran in a line around where she was sure she had come from. She stared at the fungus, her eyes widening as a finger protruded from the wall. The hand twisted and mutated, came with it, an arm followed in much the same wretched look. A second hand rose from the wall.

She brought the crossbow to bear, aiming at the spot where she believed the head would appear.

An eyeless and half torn-off head upon a shredded neck came from the fake wall.

"Yes, my beast! Bring a new pet for me," the snake called.

Tika released the arrow, It pierced the head of the zombie, through the bone of the skull, and out the other side. It fell backwards, the arrow snapping at the ground. More followed through. She slashed at them with her dagger, dropping two zombies, who fell awkwardly. She turned and ran, closing her eyes briefly as she went through the fake wall, opening them again to see the passageway. The wall had been a hologram, maybe a hallucination.

"Noo! Girl, stay with me. You be happy and mindless. Please stay in my world!"

She didn't stop, she didn't take the words in, she charged on. The walls closed behind her, crushing the zombies in her wake. The ground and wall shook violently. She kept her balance, using her hands to push herself steady off the walls. A light was up ahead, the light of the sun, and she knew it. She ran to it with a pulsing heart, the slamming passageway echoing behind her. She could feel the tunnel almost closing in on her behind. Once again she thanked herself for not being Gaian, and threw away the candle.

She leapt out from the tunnel entrance, to blue sky surrounding her, and the sun shining down at her. The cave closed shut at her back, and she put her efforts into stopping, her arms and legs scrapping along the rock, the cliff's edge in her path. She scrapped a little further, her body at the cliff edge, she stopped, and pushed fearfully away from the edge, and laid upon her back in the gravel. Trying to catch her breath, she stayed there for a while, letting the pain of the grazing and the tiredness in her legs and backside subside enough for her to get back up. She stared up at the sky, squinting at its strength.

$$\Sigma$$

Tika rolled over and sat up. She looked out over the cliff. Directly below were scattered Lucyi trees, short trees that had oval shaped leaves, and dried out seed pods, and earlier in the year would have had fruit across its spurs. For several kilometres the trees were surpassed by wild golden grass that covered most of the land, until the yellow walls of Lulsan's capital Lulsani. She could see the epic walls that surrounded the city]s border. The sea rolled and glittered with the sun's reflections, which made her desire for water, or at least food.

She looked for a way down to the Lucyi trees, and found a sharp decline. She began her descent, allowing herself a controlled slide down the first part of the decline. She checked each foothold, and every joint she touch with her hands. Stones and gravel trickled down the cliff, where she disturbed it with her careful movements. She refused to rush herself, she knew not to. If she fell here, it meant dead or broken limbs. She wouldn't survive for long and the vultures would have someone else to feed on.

It took her almost an hour to get down to the bottom. The sun had sapped her considerably, and she perspired and baked under the heat of the sun. She needed water, or food to keep her going just long enough. She heard the sliver of a snake, and she went behind it, licking her lips at the thought of stuffing mouthfuls of the dull brown snake. She pounced on to it, gripping the hissing mouth shut, she pulled it out from the straggly long grass, and swung it hard against the rocks, then thought of the large snake she had encounter inside the cave. She killed the creature in the one hit.

She left the carcass on a smooth rock, and went to pick up some wood. First, she picked up the pods of the Lucyi tree, and then took up some broken branches. Eventually she had a well-aired pile for her fire. Taking out a match, she lit the pods, which set alight quickly and spread fast through the rest of the stack. The flames licked the sky, and she added wood when needed. She cooked the snake over the flames, ethe heat cooking it with crackles sounding out into the air.

Dionysus ran through her head "You know some survival skills, that's good, it will help with your future. As I'm sure you will require them." She looked around her, to nothing but the trees that were motionless in the still air. "The boys on the train. Find the Gaians, and join them."

"How on Gaia do you know about them?" She asked the air. No answer returned. She looked at the snake, and with a smile, tucked into the cooked creature, grateful for the replenishment, which had enough of a taste to cause her to eat happily.

40

MUSCOSA ROAD

Calum kicked his feet back and forth, as he sat on someone's garden wall, waiting at the very edge of Regonia. On either side of the leaving road were tall trees covered in acorns, and touched off with violet flowers among the foliage. The trunks at the bottom were as wide as horse-drawn carriages.

Zidaini was sitting in a low L-shaped section where a branch came from the main trunk. Several feet above the ground, his tail swayed over his back, and he moved swaying on his palms, pushing against the branch on which he sat.

The axe they had gotten for Valkesies now rested against the crumbled, decayed white wall on which Calum kicked his feet.

Hecate stood silently and patiently, watching the sun dropping behind the horizon.

An old woman, with hair that showed her old age and wearing a dress that fell to her ankles, came from the cottage behind Calum, looking at Zidaini fidgeting and staring down the road. She then saw Calum kicking his feet. "Hello, there. Who might you be, sitting upon my white wall?" She asked.

Calum hopped off as she looked at him. "Sorry! Just waiting."

She realized Hecate was standing near them. He was now staring down the road. "Yours, are they? That must be little Zidaini. Am I right, Hecate?" She said, with a smile.

Hecate stared at her, trying to put a name to her face.

Calum and Zidaini had stopped fidgeting, and watched them curiously.

"Aren't you......?"

"Your old teacher," she chuckled. He went to her, and hugged her with a tight embrace. "You two can go inside and have some tea and cake."

They didn't hesitate, and came up to her quickly walking.

"Inside on the table," she watched them head in, "I thought they might want something," she said, as they vanished inside.

"It's been a long time, Teresa Avila," Hecate said, looking down to her. He towered over almost everyone but the Elseni.

"You've kept Zidaini strong, like his father," She said, and walked Hecate to an old bench within her garden.

"No, he kept himself strong, and quicker than the wind." They sat down together, his teacher held on to his arm.

"His friend looks like Saborio," she said, and Hecate's eyes brimmed against his will.

"Yes he does, except with a tail," he smiled thinking about the similarity. "His hair was more like Zidaini's." He went teary-eyed, remembering.

"Do you still live in the Liberian Empire?" she asked, wondering if he had healed from the loss of his son so many years ago.

"In its territory."

"You should never have tried to replace him with Gaians," she told him.

"It gave me comfort."

"It stopped you finding another woman. Although you still have some time," she said frankly. "Now, tell me what you three are up to."

Σ

Inside the cottage, the boys had taken places at the table. Sitting beside each other, they munched on the biscuits from

233

the tray that Avila usually kept around.

Calum was thinking about the way Isis was treated by Hecate and Valkesies, and the way she herself acted. "Answer me honestly. Do you think Isis is more than just some girl?"

Zidaini raised his eye brow. "What are you on about?" he asked, confused.

"Isis! She is treated like a princess, and protected like one, too." Calum said.

"There isn't a real princess of the Empire, just rumours of one. She's probably got lots of money."

"Come on, think about it. Valkesies stood to protect her, without regard to himself; he would have died for her. And look at Hecate, he talks to her as if she is a queen, and even Valkesies does what she wants. Anndd! When that weird demon thing attacked, Valky flattened me just to save her."

"Ok, so you might be almost right. Although maybe Valky wanted to save you, too," he joked. "We'll keep an eye on her. You never know, she might slip up."

Σ

"Valkesies and Hecate, together again," Teresa said, "protecting another royal." She had listened through Hecate's story so far, and was intrigued by it all.

"We failed last time," he said. She looked at him with a frown. "I know, it wasn't our fault. What more could we really have done?"

"You really think that Gaia is in trouble?"

Hecate nodded. He had seen the chauffer at the reins of a hay cart and Isis lolling amongst the hay, with Valkesies sitting against the frame.

"Oh my! I haven't seen Isis since she was just a baby," she clutched her chest, overwhelm withed emotion.

Calum and Zidaini peered out from the cottage window, watching Avila and Hecate. "I can't hear them. Can you?" Calum asked.

"You two can come out now," Hecate shouted over his

shoulder. He leaned to Teresa. "They don't know about Isis being a princess." Teresa nodded understanding.

"Did he know we were watching?" Calum asked Zidaini.

"Can't have. Surely!"

The horse and hay cart pulled up to the low open gate of the cottage. Isis peered out over the side. Teresa tried to keep her feelings in check, while Calum and Zidaini climbed aboard, and Hecate sat next to their chauffer.

Valkesies watched Zidaini spread himself out in the hay at the end of the cart, keeping his thoughts of how nice the axe was, yet he couldn't find it within himself to ask about it, instead he stared at the intricate design and the double head. He could see just looking at it that it was extremely sharp and well balanced.

Σ

They left Regonia behind, heading south to Londinium. The night sky had drifted over them, and they moved steadily under the cloudy night. The surrounding scenery was serenity: still, with no wind pestering the fields of grass and bundles of forest that were static, and lifeless, but with the beauty and strength of a picture.

Hecate remained ever watchful of the area around them. Meanwhile, Valkesies kept an eye on both Isis and Zidaini, who were curled up, sound asleep.

Calum listened to the air. Music drifted over him. A harp was playing notes through the air, enticing those on their way along Muscosa road. He got to his knees to see where the music was emanating from, watchful and listening. Something was out there, and he could hear and feel it, her, he was sure of it.

Valkesies looked at him. "You always seem to be looking for the first time," he said. Calum said nothing in return. "It is the music of Siren. A lost god. Except for her harp, her voice and her entity have gone. So has the stone." Calum looked at him, then looked back out to the side of the road, just listening.

Groups of travellers mingled together, around a fire, praying with the music. A few other tents had been set up for the night. The travellers feeling safe under the music of Siren.

A temple, small and circular came into view, tucked behind the trees and rocks. A statue of Siren was on the roof. The seductress played the harp which stood as tall as her.

Hecate would have had the chauffer go on past, but Calum jumped off the moving cart, the music luring him in. Hecate ordered the cart to stop, and he sat watching, wondering what the boy was up to.

Calum was surrounded by the music, drawn to its origin. He walked slowly to the open temple, he could hear something else in the music, a voice singing, he was sure it was just for him.

"Wait for me!" The voice almost went unheard, just breaking through to Calum. He didn't respond at first to Isis, but took a look at her when she came to his side. "Let's take a look together," she said. She took his hand, and walked him through the doorway. The walls were built solidly, a foot by two feet stone blocks, creating a permanent structure. There were paintings of Siren around the wall, with her harp in each of the pictures, and a main painting above the altar, of her sitting on a rock, a ship off in the distance. There were several benches in the room, and a single walkway through the middle.

Both of them stood in the temple in silence, the music still hovering in the air. Isis took Calum over to a book which sat on the altar. "The book of Siren." Calum didn't feel alone with Isis, he felt there was a third person watching them.

Isis scanned through the book of the rise and fall; her deeds and honours that were accredited to her.

Calum, though, stared at the painting or a sign, a reason, an explanation for the endless music.

The painting seemed alive, yet it did not move. He could hear the waves crashing against a shore of rocks. He could hear a ship creaking with the waves, and the screams of sailors, and their subsequent deaths upon the rocks. He could hear her, her voice singing in his head.

Isis turned to him. "Ok. This place has now been seen. It's quaint. But her stone was lost many decades ago. Her music must still yearn for her return. Let's go, Calum," she said, leaving.

"I'll be just a minute. I'll meet you outside."

She smiled and went out of the temple, leaving Calum to the paintings.

He looked into the eyes of Siren in the main painting. "Want to come?" He asked

"Yes!" She answered.

41

CLOSER

"Feel better?" Nortedes quietly asked, on sighting Samiaraita's eyes opening.

"Hmm!" Samiaraita turned over to his side, squinting his eyes at the morning light.

"Looks like the Hacai flowers have done their job. Does it hurt?"

Samiaraita had removed the covers from his top. His wound had healed considerably, just a small and light red mark where the cut had been. "Not really," he replied, while straightening the hairs of his tail.

"We'll get something to eat," Nortedes said. The hunger was at his throat as well as the pit of his stomach.

Once Samiaraita had finished slowly getting ready, they left the room behind and would not be returning. They went into the cafe and were greeted by a bored waitress.

"Two teas, please!" Nortedes asked. She went off without a word to get their drinks, her face continued on blank, a featureless wreck.

Samiaraita sat down at a window table, and with Nortedes, they watched the people go by. Their own respective cultures would be out and about, packing the cities on such a day where the sun actually broke through the normal grey clouds of Londinium's continent. Here, though, it was just another beggar's day, for harassing people who themselves could barely afford to live.

Samiaraita leaned forward on to his elbows, placing his cheeks into his palms. "You sure you should go back to the Imperium?" He asked, "I'm sure the guys on the roof are for us. Most likely for you."

Nortedes looked out and up to a building's roof. Two men quickly darted away from being seen. "They are not for me. My failure wouldn't warrant my death. They will wait until I reached the shores of home. I have the impression they wanted me gone. Sending assassins after me would be a waste. They will wait for me before unleashing whatever plan they have. Anyway those men loitering around are not assassins, they are mercenaries; most look like they've never held a weapon before." He noticed the employees of the hotel watching them, wondering if it would all go off again. "Is your mission that important? The stones of gods and no one to use them?"

Samiaraita took a gulp of tea, and sat back in his chair. "I've seen the power of the gods wielded, they can be devastating. Your Imperium is preparing an invasion, so my Emperor says. That means they are hugely important."

Nortedes rubbed his face with his hands. "Senator Bushia says the Liberian army is at Caracoa, preparing their invasion."

"Perhaps both sides play for war. I'm not sure whether the gods should be in either hands," the colonel said.

"There are more people skulking about." The two knew they were the intended targets. "Bushia will use any he gets, if he is looking to gain any. I will have to continue the mission, just for that reason alone. We must find out if anything is being kept from us. Like soldiers at Caracoa. I do not believe there are any there. I would have found out if there was, or will be. But the Emperor, if he wishes, can always find away to bypass the generals."

Nortedes took a sip of the tea, and slammed the tea back down. "Awful!" He moaned looking down into the brown liquid.

"I guess are leaders are looking for another page in the history books. They're certainly on another page to their people, they wanted war here today. Yet the people have such ideas far from their thoughts," Samiaraita said, counting the mercenaries that were amassing on every street corner and at every wall.

"How many?" Nortedes questioned, and received a smile.

"Quite a lot. I would keep counting, but more keep coming around the corner. Should be fun," he said, grinning.

"Think they'll mind if we fought together?" Nortedes asked. Any answer was distracted by a rising commotion, as people started racing away towards their homes. The city became restless in moments, and screams of scared people came from the streets outside. In the hotel, guests and employees became worried as the outside turned to fear.

"What's happening now?" Colonel Samiaraita asked.

"I would think something violent, by the looks of those running away."

42

LULSANI

Tika had crept along the ocean's edge and began wading through the moat river that run across the plains and was diverted around the city walls to provide a stronger defence against the enemies of Lulsani. She was an ant against the background of the epic walls of the city. They were the biggest on Gaia, although they lack the battlements of bastions, embrasures and turrets, only relying on loop holes for the archers and an abatis at the moats edge to give extra annoyance to those trying to get to the walls. Guards patrolled the parapet, night and day, watching out for any possible intruder or monster that came near the fields of the outlying farms.

She waded in the water, keeping close to the side of the wall. Hoping they would not lean over the edge to find her. *'There must be a way in. Surely?'* She questioned herself, hoping for something along the lines of a waterway that would lead into the city. Instead, all she could see were the farmers and workers hurrying with panic to get back into the city through the gate. Shouts from the guards called the warning of a incoming carnivore, which was not a problem for the city itself, but the many hard labourers that tended the fields. The beast would take up any chase for stragglers that were too slow to get away.

With the gate open, she seized her chance and moved up from the moat towards the throng of scared people who were being pushed aside to allow the Lulsan Lancers to get out from the city. And once they had forced a path through the throng, the lancers flew out, lances longer than the horse, held in their arm, and horses covered in thick heavy armour. Tika came up behind the watching crowd, taking her place within them.

The thunder of hooves shook the bridge, and echoed throughout the gatehouse. The riders' polished helmets glinted past, and the mass of people went on in, giving up work for the day. She followed close behind a farmer in animal skins, and a few women covered in the perspiration of work gave her some reasonable cover. She felt the throng of people was enough to hide her. But a guard who had pushed aside some of the people and ended up at the end of the draw bridge had seen her enter through the workers who were surrendering to the demoralization due to the carnivore. Normally he would have just checked a foreigner for a pass, but she looked like a wreck, with a mess for hair and dirty clothes, she probably couldn't afford to get a pass for the north gate. Therefore, she couldn't be someone on vacation, nor a merchant, as she didn't have any wares. She was, in his mind, clearly a scoundrel.

He crept up behind her. Even his other colleagues turned away, so as not to reveal his presence. He squeezed between some women, etching up to Tika. The throng stopped moving, and Tika felt someone close beside her. Putting it aside as another member of the crowd, she didn't turn.

The guard lifted up a wood baton. Raising it above her head, he whacked it down upon her. Tika's eyes went black, and she fell to the ground, completely unconscious.

The guards surrounded the fallen Tika and onlookers watched on. The youngest guard stared down at her with the others, he had never been out from the city, and was new to guarding.

"Is she one of those Gaians?"

The guards sighed and looked at him with crooked faces.

The guard who had knocked Tika out spoke up at his idiocy. "You grow up in an asylum? She's an Adinan, you know, red hair and no tail." The young guard looked down at the floor. "Right, take her to a cell. While you're at it, make sure she hasn't a pass, and if she does, you know what you should do," he said impassionedly.

Σ

Tika woke to a throbbing ache pressing at her head, accompanied by bruising, and grazed legs. She could barely open her eyes, as the tiredness of the Troubled Pass, and the lack of sleep had severely weakened her. What she could see did not fill her with confidence. A single beam of light came from a ceiling, peering down vertically at her where she lay on the unbending concrete floor. A small squat toilet was an unbearable sight, and unforgiving in the smell. The world blackened around her, as unconsciousness took over her eyes, the injuries she had obtained took over her body.

43

THE CITY OF NIGUARGA.

Horizontal rain lashed across the faces of the black army that had surrounded the city, and now, under the night, they formed their lines for their assault. Lines of infantry held their shields tight against their chests, the rain somehow making it through the slits of their helmets, and forcing them to squint with the wetness. Scores of archers stood in the sludge of rain-swept snow, turned from the clear white to a mixture of brown and black. The call sounded and the archers launching a rain of arrows lit with flame over the walls of Niguarga, to pierce the huts and light them with licking flames. The rain continued to douse out most of the thousands of arrows that flew over the walls, and more often than not, the archers hit civilians in their spray of fire. The civilians, falling with yelps and screams, sent quivers of fear into those around them.

Upon a man-made hill, the cannons with trebuchets behind them that threw up rotten cows fired their round shot. The Niguargans were covered in the guts of dead carcasses, and the round shot blew holes into the towers, the bodies of Niguargans torn apart from the shots. The guts-covered men cowered in fear as the blood of the dead covered them with thick sangria, and body parts along with it, sent at them by the trebuchets, the dreadful weapons slinging the rotten guts far over the wall.

On a distant hill overlooking the battlefield, General

Aros Narsisis stood with his runners, and the not-needed cavalry that waited for orders to engage any routing enemy trying to flee the city. Aros looked over the army of halberds, swordsmen and spearmen. All poised to assault the city, once the orders were given, and the general was satisfied the archers and cannons had done enough. He had already given the orders to kill every single Niguargan, and to not leave any alive. He was standing unfazed by the constant hail of rain, watching the cannons boom over the round shot. He marvelled in the powerful shot smashing chunks of the city's wall into pieces, that covered the occupants in shards of shrapnel, flints of stone and pieces of wood from nearby houses; the stone falling into rubble on to the sludgy ground.

"Send in the siege!" He called. Runners took off towards the waiting siege towers. "Change to stone," he ordered. More runners went off to the trebuchets. More arrows were sent like a stinging swarm of wasps, striking into the defenders, and leaving their numbers on the walls to dwindle further.

The cannons fired into the same area of wall, some flew over missing, and crashing down into the homes of the citizens, the rest ploughed into the city wall, leaving large holes and destroying the structure. The stone crumbled, and soldiers on the wall fell with it to death or broken bones. The arrows finished them off.

The siege towers begun to move forward, pulled by horses and pushed by the strongest men. The wooden towers had been covered in the slop of animal and human dung, to stop flaming arrows from setting the rolling towers alight. The approach was supported by numerous shots from the cannons, and the less-than-accurate trebuchets that sent up rocks that crushed the houses of the city.

Colonel Rika Liarta led his regiment from the side of the siege tower. His eyes followed a haze of arrows over his head as his men and women heaved the tower to the wall. The arrows struck into the Niguargan soldiers, some of which fell like falling stars, alight with fire, their bodies flapping with the searing pain. He was fascinated by the flames that climbed the sky, to falling rain. The pulling armoured horses were cut loose, and the soldiers put more effort into pushing the tower. Under several arrows that struck his soldiers, the tower touched against the stone wall, and he ordered his soldiers to take the ladders to the top of the tower. As he climbed, he could hear the thuds of arrows digging into the wood, unable to light with the dung spread across the structure and the constant lashing rain that continued to soak the planks that held the structure in form. Climbing the ladder with his swordsmen, he listened to the sounds of death coming from the parapet. He gripped each rung of the ladder, to a shout or scream from the Niguargans dying on the parapet. The sounds of death rattled the nerves of those that climbed with him. He got to the top of the roofed tower, and waited for the section of tower to fill with soldiers, clutching their shields and swords, ready to charge from the tower's drawbridge, and assault the enemy on the parapet.

Rika Liarta listened to the noises outside as he waited. He knew the war was wrong, not for thirty years had the two worlds collided in conflict, but he was here now, and there was no going back. Instead of the contemplation of why he was there, he shouted an order. "Specialli, ready, lower the bridge!" The siege towers ropes were cut, and the drawbridge dropped down on to the parapet. "CHARGE!" He roared.

His third infantry Specialli ran onto the parapet, into a thin wall of Niguargans, cutting through the poorly armoured enemy, Rika himself chopping through an arm with one strike, before turning on another with a stab through the neck. The blood came out fast and went over his breast plate. He did not cringe. Uninterested in the blood, he continued on, and his soldiers fought with him. The third marched through the Niguargans as if they were nothing. The siege tower was one of three that reached the city wall, and where the cannons had collapsed a section of the stone, the halberds were walking through, hacking and stabbing the Niguargans like they were carving up a defenceless lump of meat. Even archers were being sent on behind the infantry to add to the carnage. Aros Narsisis was sending every single soldier into the city to kill all its occupants, and the cavalry weren't to be left behind, they were also heading for the gate that would be opened by the men at arms.

Aros was grinning at the progress; the walls were being taken by his soldiers that had taken almost the entire length of the city's parapet. Aros was enjoying the massacre, and his face gave a smirk at the events enfolding.

Σ

Colonel Liarta sat on the ramparts, overlooking the city. His sword was stained with blood, but he was unable to continue; he didn't want to kill anymore. The enemy were pleading for mercy, surrendering to his men, but the cries were ignored. His soldiers were grateful for the orders of Narsisis, and they killed without remorse in their bloodlust, happy to fulfil and embrace the general's policy, they were free to be completely and sickly out of control, and they went about on their complete mass destruction of the Niguargan people.

Colonel Rika Liarta only had a few of his loyal soldiers with him. They watched on in shock at what their fellows were capable of doing. Across the ramparts, bloodied Imperium soldiers looked on as the people were slaughtered. The city was burning in the chaos. Whether injured or not, young or old, they were slaughtered, unless they see a reason for them to be a slave. Every house was raided and every shop left ransack and gutted.

The city belonged to the victors, and they accepted it with open arms.

An old enemy vanquished.

44

THE TRUE LONDINIUM

Nortedes finished his coffee. "They're been waiting a long time," he said, watching the frustrated and impatient thugs outside amongst the sounds of a city gone wild. Samiaraita said nothing to the statement.

"Shall we go?" Nortedes said standing up.

Samiaraita calmly stood up, and pulled his sword from the sheath. Around them people cowered in the back of the hotel, the security quiet beside them.

Nortedes briefly took in the scared eyes that watched them leave; he could see they expected the chaos to begin again.

Outside it already had, and both the two commanders, and the hotel guests and staff knew the only reason the hotel hadn't been sack by rioters was because of the mercenaries that waited outside.

General Nortedes stopped at the door of the Rossiya. "I don't see any archers, for the most part we should be fine," he said, the confidence echoing from him and even the colonel's features.

Within the first steps of leaving the hotel, the thugs ran in, their weapons swinging at the general who quickly impaled the untrained men. Even Samiaraita felt left out momentarily as he hadn't even left the door when Nortedes killed a third.

Those first deaths, and the agony of a man writhing with the pain in his gut, had scared the mercenaries, and they halted the attack. Instead of charging in, they surrounded the two soldiers. As Samiaraita took them in, he knew most had never held a weapon in battle, he could see that, in the way they gripped their chosen weapons. He would not, though, underestimate the situation they were in, as more mercenaries came down an alley. He looked over the heads of the aggressors. Smoke bellowed into the sky, from dozens of burning buildings. Down the road he could see guards attacking guards. The city had turned to riot, and people were being butchered because they were there. Along the other end of the street, cocktails of alcohol were set alight, and thrown through the nearest house to explode and send more fire into the sky, and screams of fear at death approaching followed the violence.

"What the hell is going on?" he asked. The mercenaries begun to inch forward.

"Civil war! We need to kill these and get out of the city," Nortedes said, and noticed the increase in tension among the mercenaries. He even caught a gulp being taken down by a man covered in perspiration, definitely someone who desperately needed money, otherwise he would've stayed clear.

"Kill them you must!" A Traican shouted from a roof top, desperate to see the targets assassinated.

The mercenaries came at them. Nortedes swung his longsword with ease, his muscled arms wielding the sword with lightness, and he sliced through several attackers in quick succession, ripping long gaping wounds through their bodies to those crumpling with the strikes. These wounds they did not survive.

Samiaraita was more nimble on his feet, weaving and cutting and stabbing his way through the mercenaries. He was fast to turn and attack each person, seemingly able to sense their presence before they had even gone to thrust at him or Nortedes. His sword was sharpened to such perfection it went through their skin and bones as if they were jelly; the bones of the humans gave no resistance to the strikes. Yet still more mercenaries came into the fight. As the bodies and blood covered the road and they fought on, the two Traicans looked at the melee in despair.

"They not do well."

"No! We must send more."

"Everything!"

"But we need archers!"

"Yes, archers!"

They quickly sent what few runners they had up on the roof top, to find people to serve their needs, with promises to fulfil every desire of those that accept the task. Left alone they watched on, cringing as Nortedes longsword went through an old decrepit chest plate of a man.

Hades stood over them, his dragon clutching the roof's parapet wall. They trembled, and stumbled backwards on realizing he was there. The dragon screeched over them, as it smelt the scent of carnage, beautiful to its nostrils.

They had no idea to why he was there, no clue to why he was by their side.

Hades walked to the edge, leering down at the two fighters. His twisted and evil face, an arrogant darkness in his presence, he summed up the two allies. "Honourable, aren't they." It wasn't a question directed at anyone, and received no answer. He climbed back on to his dragon. "Drexaria, let us fly." The dragon leapt from the wall, the concrete fell in its lift, and they went disappearing into the foggy sky.

Σ

Nortedes and Samiaraita fought valiantly, but their previous injuries that they had sustained against each other were beginning to plague them.

"We're gonna have problems if we don't get any help," Samiaraita stated while he ran his blade into another mercenary, he pulled it out, with blood covering the blade.

"We need to get to an alley, somewhere we can funnel them in," Nortedes said, grabbing the hilt of an opponent's sword, and crushing the wrist with his own hilt, and slew another attacker. With wrist broken, the other mercenary fled from the battle, clutching his agonizing wrist.

"With me!" Colonel Samiaraita called; he led Nortedes away from the front of the hotel, via the death of two more.

They ran to a narrow alley, wide enough for two people to move down, but only wide enough for one to wield their sword. Nortedes took up the fight, allowing Samiaraita to rest his shoulder. While he leaned against a wall of a house, the smell of fire drifted throughout the air, the buildings around them had been set alight, and were burning through. It wouldn't be long till they would need to move again. The smoke was already covering the air.

Σ

"She burns!" Isis said, watching the plumes of smoke, rising up from the city, and melding with the night sky.

"We have come at a bad time," Hecate said; he worried for the safety of those with him, and for Samiaraita. With the city burning, no doubt through riot, they might not even find the colonel.

Scared people were fleeing Londinium. Those who had the ability to leave were already trekking as far as they could, their scared faces telling the story of the fallen city. The surprise at seeing people heading for the city, was a shock that they revealed with stares at the group.

Calum kicked Zidaini awake from where he lay. "Expect some violence," he said to his sleepy friend, who found his way over the side of the cart to look out at the city in flames.

"Bugger! Hope you're up for some fighting, Valky?" Zidaini received a scornful face from Valkesies.

"Boy, you better not be a problem," he moaned, then quietly spoke to Isis who sat up beside him, "Stay with me inside the city, you don't leave my side, unless I say," he told her. This was his territory, and she would do as he told her, not as she wanted.

The city grew larger as they came nearer, and Calum stared out past Hecate, watching the plumes of smoke rising while the cart etched closer to the city gate. Already they could see guards fighting, and what Calum could make out, they were all in the same uniform, with the only difference between them, a single arm band, white or black, one colour for one side. He watched people trying to get pass the barricade of fighting. They ducked and scurried, trying not to get caught up in the violence. Calum watched, shocked by one man being caught between two swords. His body went limp and dropped almost lifeless, the blood running from the wound. The two guards continued unabated, until at last one had a sword pierce his back from another guard. His face turned creased in agony, and his opponent finished him, cutting off the bloodied head.

The cart stopped, shaking everyone out from their trance. "This is as far as I will go," the driver said, desperate to leave the stricken city before he ended up as just another victim. He shuddered as an arrow was loosed from a single archer up on the city wall and killed a guard on the ground.

The group leapt from the cart, quickly stretching and assessing. Valkesies sneaked off the back, taking the new axe up but trying not to let Zidaini see him take the axe; an axe that was as long as a Gaian.

Calum see only one current way in, he wanted to cut his way through, and one side was dominant. The white arm bands were more in number, and Calum was sure there was more inside.

"This might not take too long. I see more white bands," Hecate said, thinking about waiting. Zidaini grumbled at the words.

Calum unsheathed his sword. "This Samiaraita might be good, but he won't stand a chance in there." He went straight towards the gate, leaving the cart and horse behind that was quick to go on its way back, leaving them stranded. He heard the unsheathing of two weapons behind him, knowing it was Zidaini. Calum looked up as he neared the fight, at the black-armed archer who was sizing them up, peering down at them along the shaft of his arrow. Calum wasn't sure whether to move faster, or be ready to dodge an attack. The archer convulsed, shaking violently, as lightning struck him from above. The guard fell backwards off the wall, into the smoke that climbed behind the parapet.

Hecate stayed at a distance behind. Although he carried a dagger now, he felt it useless, and remained ready to give support of his powerful magic.

Calum went straight to the nearest black-armed guard, thrusting his emerald sword into the chest, alleviating the worries of the white arm-band guards, only to have them instantly dashed, as Calum sliced the next nearest guard, a black arm-banded. Zidaini came in and joined the attack upon the guards. Hecate's hand was forced, but the fact he needn't worry about hitting the wrong persons, was a bonus. He moved in with the boys leading. They crossed the threshold of the small gateway. Hecate was enjoying sending balls of fire over the heads of the short Gaians, and thankful they were Gaians, so he could. Ahead of Calum and Zidaini guards were set ablaze, to screams of searing pain and melting skin.

With twenty guards of both sides looking confused, and having two enemies to fight, and causing an already fear-driven perspiration to soak their skins, some ran through fear, some ran because Calum and Zidaini were untouchable in their fast movements which had left seven guards dead; the rest ran because fear is infectious.

They stood alone; the three had made the battle end through violence. After seconds had passed, the civilians begun rushing out through the city gate. Valkesies and Hecate came up behind the boys, and Isis watched them slap the boys' heads. They cried out with the shock of the slaps, confused with the action, until Hecate explained he wasn't happy with them attacking everyone.

Isis went in with Valkesies. "Why do the guards of the city fight each other?"

He turned his face to her. "You're either a Royalist or a Nationalist. When it comes to the soldiers, you're employed by either. The Londinium Royalists have a black flag. Nationalists, white. Londinium has a king, and a falsely elected parliament." He carried the new axe, as his own was still sheathed.

"Falsely?" She asked, following the other three as they

went into the city.

"The parliament wasn't elected. It was the disgruntled rich who formed an organization, then begun calling themselves elected by the people. People, being stupid, accepted that others had wanted them to rule the country, and thus joined in with the debacle, even though no one had wanted the rich to rule them. If you take each member of this parliament, each one was rich before they were given, not elected, given a position in the new parliament. In other words it's just the rich gaining power, on top of their wealth." Calum listened in on Valkesies, recognizing it from a distant shadow, a dream from a past overshadowed by another.

Zidaini walked beside him, and was smiling. He had seen Valkesies holding the double-headed axe, and was keeping his thoughts to himself.

They walked through smoke drifting streets and smells of carnage. The odd house was covered or grazed by scorch marks, charred with burning fires. Overturned carts had been used as cover from arrows, and fire bombs. Some were smouldered with smoke, others had their wooden frames riddled with shafts. Even as they walked the sewage lined roads, they constantly passed dead bodies and people looting and fighting, even the dead were pilfered of whatever they had. It was all happening down every street. Every now and then, they spotted a probing archer, which was sniped by Hecate. A few managed to scramble away, thankful they weren't burnt alive.

All around them, the voices, cries, calls, screams and shouts of the victims and aggressors, the people of the city sounded out above the buildings of Londinium; throughout the nearby streets and alleys, people were dying. They could all feel it in the air around them, and could see it on the ground they walked. Death was in the smoke that drifted past them.

At a crossroad, the living begun to drown out the dead. Calum could hear them around a corner, their voices were that of the poorly educated, and it wasn't a few, it sounded like a hundred. He was sure it was, and moved along a wall, trying not to step in the sewage that ran along the gutter.

He moved close to the corner, trying not to be seen. Zidaini had sneaked up behind him. The others were following. "We need to get down that way," Zidaini said, listening to the shouts and barbarism coming from the voices of the rioters.

"Not unless you feel like dying," Hecate said, "we'll try to find a way around. There was a previous turning just down there, it'll do."

They listened to his advice, and walked back the way they had come, with glances back to see if anyone was in pursuit. They expected to use their weapons; people of evil always struck those not prepared.

A rioter, carrying someone else's bags cuddled in his arms, walked into the crossroads. He stopped and stared at the foreigners, his eyes gauged them with interest.

Calum stopped in his tracks, and looked back at the young man who was smiling with glee at the new targets. He took hold of his sword in both hands as the rioter called over his temporary allies.

"Look foreners! They always ave money. Let's get some." Their voices ran out, and the rioters advanced on the group. Their numbers, well over a hundred covered the width of the street, while more filed in at the back.

"This is not good. How are we going to take on this mob. With just five?" Valkesies grumbled.

"Valky, this is nothing!" Zidaini answered hiding his own nervousness at the closing horde.

The advancement of the horde was quick, and was almost on them. Then, from nothing, flames ripped across the road and covered the surface between the rioters and the group. The rioters stopped in their tracks, their eyes staring with fright at the floor of fire. A beast with hairless skin climbed from the breaking ground, appearing from the flames.

The group watched in awe while Castelli, with its claws, pulled himself up from his realm through the concrete. It came on to solid ground, its red skin ablaze, its horns black and steaming.

The horde stood in fear, not believing a Gaian god would come to defend its people in their city.

Castelli's claws gripped the floor of flames, and picked up a wall of fire, a wall with no base, a wall of pure fire. Castelli threw the wall of fire at the horde. The heat shockwave went backwards into the group, knocking all but Valkesies off their feet; he stood like a rock, watching the firewall smother all in its path, burning them to a cinder, the rioters were engulfed with the flames, that burned them to their deaths, their faces scream in fear and agony. The wall shot through them, killing them all. The wall of fire collapsed as it reached the other side of the crossroad, dissipating into nothing.

Castelli turned around and looked directly at Calum, then dropped through the blazing ground at its feet, vanishing from the road.

$$\Sigma$$

Calum and Zidaini pushed themselves up on to their backsides, looking at the carnage that Castelli had created.

"I see the way he looked at you, he thought you were hot."

Calum punched Zidaini in the arm. "Argh! That actually hurt."

Isis stared out at the devastation and the charred corpses. She felt horrified by the way they had died, and uncertain by the lack of remorse shown by the others. Even Valkesies and Hecate seem uninterested in the persons who died, or the deaths of so many. They were more intrigued by the fact that Castelli had come.

"Did you call him.?" Valkesies asked Calum.

Calum got up, and lifted both palms open to the air. "Nothing to do with me."

"Well, who did? Old man can't do it. Valky only knows axes, that leaves..." He couldn't help but smile at Isis.

Valkesies shuffled his feet, realizing Isis must have stolen the Sapphire of Castelli.

"I don't just cure people. I can summon," she said.

"Good move, Isis. You just saved two scoundrels from getting their butts kicked," Hecate said, stepping off along the scorched road. The two boys looked at him unimpressed.

They were heading to hotel Rossiya, and knew now that nothing would surprise them in the dirty city. As they walked they see two Royalists engaging Nationalists on a street corner, some comrades laid dead around where they fought. The group left them behind to fight each other. The guards only seem interested in fighting other guards. What Calum had noticed was that both sides were beginning to barricade themselves in buildings, rather then go on the offensive.

Calum was snapped out of his assessment of the rioting city, as a man was chased out of a home by an axe-wielding woman who was screaming insults at him, her face filled with rage at the intrusion. They watched her chase after him until she no longer could. He raced off into the distance. She hurled more abuse after him, before she turned angrily away.

"I can't believe a place would go this way," Isis said, "it's just so horrible," she said, in disbelief.

"You should see it when it doesn't riot. It's a crowded hole of despair," Zidaini explained. "Londinium is called the dirty city, not for the piss and crapt that lines the streets, but because the people are the crapt and piss of the city."

"The people have nothing here. They fight and loot because that's the way out of the hole they are in," Hecate said.

Moments later, they began to see armed men and women, clearly not the looters and rioters of before, or even the guards that had declared war against each other. They were armed with a variety of sabres, jians and backswords. They were clearly not military, just people in rags, being given the swords, and sent down a nearby alley. The man sending them was covered in a long bushy beard, shifty in his appearance. He carried a schia cona sword at his waist, a wider blade than the rapier. His brown rags made him look like a peasant, and no doubt was. He had a pouch of gold in his hand, filled with foreign gold. He waved them over, his face with false smiling.

"You there! You look like you could handle a couple pesky soldiers." He beamed a smile at them, which annoyed Calum. The man's beard frizzed as he spoke. "There be two gold pieces for starters, and a further one hundred if you kill them."

"We want cash," Zidaini told him. The others looked on angrily at Zidaini.

"I believe that can be arranged. Now, how about it?"

"Who are we supposed to kill?" Hecate asked, knowing he wouldn't be letting Zidaini do anything of the sort.

The man gave a wide smile. "It be a general from the Imperium, and colonel of the Liberian Empir-" The emerald sword almost pierced his skin. The man was quick to dodge, his schia out in his hand, to protect his body. "Come on! You don't have to be nasty, You don't have to do what I ask. You can leave, it's not a problem," he said, not realizing what he had asked of them.

Calum held his sword in his hands, ready to strike into the bearded man. "I'm gonna kill you."

Hecate and Valkesies couldn't wait, they went off with Isis and Zidaini following.

The man's face turned sour. "Look, Gaian, this blade is the finest metal in all of Gaia. Will snap yours, you see, even on your wider edge. So if you don't want me to cut off your furry tail, get lost!"

Calum smiled. "Really, you see!" He mocked. "Why don't you try?"

The man jolted a thrust at Calum, who stepped neatly aside, and pushed his palm towards the man. A spike of ice, blasted out from his hand, smashing into the not so serious face of the mercenary employer. His face was frozen in shock, and Calum sliced through the neck. He quickly caught the pouch of gold as it dropped from the release of the criminal's hand. Then he was gone, racing down the alley to get to the others.

Calum immediately saw Samiaraita's blue uniform, stained crimson red with the blood of his enemies. His shoulder was clearly causing him to struggle through each swing. Yet neither he nor Nortedes looked like they had a match on their hands. They were chopping down enemies with relative ease. Calum could see the Traicans barking out the same orders time and again, furious with the ineffectiveness of their mercenaries, shouting out kill them multiple times.

Calum charged straight into the fray. Hecate's magic flew pass his head, into his intended target, while Valkesies was chopping away at each opponent and Zidaini competed beside his rusty and new daggers, slashing and slicing his way through the weak mercenaries. Calum slipped beneath a swinging sword, and shoved an elbow into the stomach of the attacker, ripping his sword around and slicing across the chest. The man fell backwards, trying to hold in the blood coming from his ribcage.

Around the group, the attackers fell, until none were left to be felled. Isis felt left out as she stood at the side, near Hecate. She may be able to call gods, but in a melee, where gods would be unable to wield effectively, she was only a healer; she wanted to be able to use a sword. Once the fight was over, and there was no more attackers coming for them, just the bodies of dozens upon the ground, she raced to Samiaraita, who reeled with shock, until she quickly settled his surprise at seeing the princess in the dirty city. She healed his shoulder with a simple raise of her hand.

$$\Sigma$$

"You see that?"
"Yes! Help they did."
"Bad move! Kill them?"
"Oh, yes! Must prepare."

"No archers. Very bad city. But very dead."
"Yes, very good."
"No, very bad."
"You're confusing!"
"Really!"
"Yes! Think Emperor want stones. Colonel failed. We get them?"
"Yes, I think so. Yes!" The two Traicans marched off back down the stairs of the building, setting off to hatch a new offensive.

Σ

Calum looked around him. His sword, scarlet stained, matched the spaces in between the bodies. He looked at Nortedes, curious as to who he was, he walked over to the general "Who are you?" He questioned.
"Who are you?" Nortedes reversed the question.
Calum looked bemused. "Cheeky bloody.."
Nortedes smiled at him. He looked down at the emerald sword, the Sparda del Dios.
"My name is General Antonio Nortedes. You will call me Nortedes," he ordered, towering over Calum.
"Oh, really!" Calum said.
"We might want to call you Ant," Zidaini said.
Nortedes pondered the two standing together."Are these yours?" The general asked Hecate.
"It seems that way. They still haven't learned. I apologize, General." He looked over to Samiaraita. "Colonel, this blond-tailed brat, and his brown-tailed friend are Zidaini and Calum, the beginning of our team. They were sent by the Emperor to meet with you."
Samiaraita nodded and stepped over the bodies of the dead. "Nortedes. Accompany us?" He asked, knowing the general was heading to certain death.
Calum and Zidaini groaned. "Not another bor-"
"Will you two be quiet? General Nortedes is a renowned and tremendous fighter," he said, looking sternly at them.

260

"It is ok, Hecate."

Calum and Zidaini wondered on Nortedes knowledge of Hecate. "I'm honoured to meet you in person. I'm afraid I must return." There was sadness on his face. They could all see it, and he did not hide it from them. "A word of advice, Gaians, there are fighters as good as you out there. So watch what you say," Nortedes told them.

Neither replied.

Certain the Traicans wouldn't be a problem,

Nortedes headed back to the Viracocha, and to go home to Centrali.

Σ

Zidaini sneaked off as everyone came together; he had seen a glinting stone upon the road between two bodies. He crouched down and picked up a ruby off the road. Wiping the blood off the gem, grinning as he looked over it, he quickly pocketed the gem, reminding himself to mention it to Calum. He hopped across the fallen mercenaries to the others, and realized Calum had seen it all. Their eyes connected, and they smiled at their prize.

"Once we're finished here, we are to head to Idona. Then to search the islands that are supposed to be in the sea of ire," Samiaraita explained.

"Those islands are supposed to be extremely dangerous," Valkesies said, of the islands close to his home.

Samiaraita nodded. "Of course. But that's where we're going. The Emperor said something about the stepping stones, but it was nothing more than what I just said," he paused as one woman stabbed another down the street from them. Her face twisted with tears of malice, and the fear and mud of Londinium. "There was also the Thor ruby. That was with Nortedes; not my orders, so I didn't bother with it." He looked over as Zidaini laughed and Calum grinned.

Zidaini pulled out the ruby. "Do you think this is Thor, the thunder god?"

"You stole from him?" Hecate fumed.

261

"He found it on the ground. Nortedes must have dropped it," Calum told him.

Hecate nodded his head, actually believing them. "Pointing out the obvious, why are we here?"

"There was a god called the Phoenix. We are going to its only temple. Since people no longer believe it exists," he said looking on north, "it'll be quieter there, away from the fighting."

"Well, whatever. How are we going to get around? Especially to the lugarta final." Zidaini asked, his mind switching to playing lugarta.

Samiaraita shook his head. "Lugarta? At a time like this?.. Thankfully! I have an airship waiting for us, nothing great, just a merchant vessel. We will head to the lugarta, then get on with the mission."

"You don't sound like you want to be here?" Isis asked. She knew him well enough to know how he felt, and could see the lack of desire in the mission.

"Isis, I am a colonel in the Liberian Empire. On a mission suitable for a captain, or even a major, at the most. I am sure I'm being kept away," he said, and changed the subject. "Someone has set the two factions against each other. The riot would have created the perfect opportunity for a strike against me, or even Nortedes. Those creatures were Traicans, a lost species. They must have been a part of it. But what I want to know is who sent them? The Imperium, or Liberian, maybe a third party. We may need to watch our backs," he said, thinking about their possible future. He led them away from the blood and sewage laden road.

Σ

With the city riot dying down, those that had been too scared to venture out into the chaos before, now took to the streets, like the street children who began raiding the shops for bread, and other food to nourish them. They even raided the dead for whatever had been left; their little eyes searching in their scavenger needs, hands pithering through pockets. Giving wild looks at the group as it went past, the children were scarpering as they came near them, their dirty faces and bright white eyes flashing away, back into the shadows.

They reached the quieter suburbs, going into a church area where trees of proud stature enveloped the small church, one place that remained untouched by the destruction of the city. If it wasn't for the deciduous trees covering the church and giving it a serene look, the church alone would have looked a dilapidated wreck.

Samiaraita led them up to the oak door, stepping through onto decorated stone paving. Light filtered in through the patterned stained glass and a single window that sat high above an altar platform. The multiple colours of the windows were redirected by the outside lanterns, placed to give the effect of the array of colours that spread rays of the rainbow over the pews where visitors would sit to receive a sermon to give them sustained belief that their chosen deity existed.

A single human man, in his fifties, stood motionless, watching those that entered.

Hecate passed the crimson-stained Samiaraita and went up to the lonesome priest. His black robes covered him from shoulders to ankles. He stood with bare feet, and his eyes told of a wilderness.

"Excuse me, priest. Is this the temple to Phoenix?" Hecate asked. The priest's eyes burned him furiously. "This is the church of a real god. Not some beast," he thundered. He listened to his voice echo round the church, his eyes closed as he took it in.

The group watched him nervously. Hecate tried another question, unsure whether he should. He went to speak, and as he opened his mouth, he was waved silent by the priest.

"This is the church of Hades!" He bellowed.

"You what!?" Calum cried. Zidaini and Hecate went silent in their surprise, shocked by the mention of the Mary Rose's nemesis. Isis and Samiaraita knew the name from the palace, knew the twisted face of Hades.

"He's the nob who killed several of my crew mates!" Zidaini shouted, infuriated at the prospect of someone calling the vile being a god.

The priest was taken aback. "Go! Leave this church. Do not leave such blasphemous remarks here. Go to the Phoenix temple and make such disregarding remarks to the beast." He pointed to the corner where a door went outside. The group rushed to it, wanting to ask more questions of Hades, but feeling the fanatic would waste their time.

He shouted out to them. "Hades foretold the coming end, he knows your destinies, knows your weaknesses. You must repent your sins before me," he cried, following them to the door.

"Yeh! Next year, old man," Zidaini called, pushing Calum out faster.

Σ

The door crashed closed behind them. They stood outside, in a garden of well-kept reds and yellows, of tulips and magnolia roses, which climbed the walls at the garden's width. Small stepping stones led around the multiple patches of garden flowers and well- trimmed grass between.

The temple itself was just as dilapidated as the church. The door in was painted with orange and yellow flames. A short path connected the door to the garden under the large chestnut trees. Only a small gap through the trees allowed for the sight of the changing clouds.

An old lady in her fifties and dressed in a white robe weeded the ground around some fuchsia, She looked up smiling, as she saw them. It gave the group a relaxed feeling, they hoped she was sane. "Hello there. Welcome to the Phoenix temple. May I be your guide?"

"Please!" Hecate said, happy for some kindness in a lost city.

She walked over to a small table, and took off a draping cloth. The boys' eyes lit up, as they set their eyes on a team of trays with the delights of peculiar cakes and biscuits, and even a pot of tea. Even Valkesies muttered approval, relieved at the chance to end his hunger. They each grabbed a slice of a meat pie and went to go inside. Isis went straight through with Hecate following, anxious to see the temple.

The woman took one look across the blood stains and Valkesies' new axe. "Oh, no! You four are too dirty. You won't get blood over the floor in here. Outside you will wait." She closed the door for good measure.

The four sat down on the paths edge, food in hand. Valkesies slumped with them, and they listened to the chirping of the birds in the trees. Samiaraita wondered on how the flowers survive under the shade of the chestnuts without any sunlight. The four of them were tired, and wanted to fall into the cascade of sleep.

Valkesies, though, was more interested in those around him. Originally he had no desire to travel with the boys, and yet as he sat there, he was finding the idea pleased him, although their manners were lacking. He was on a journey that would take a warrior's path, even giving Isis the experience she needed to become more extrovert, and more in charge of her self esteem. This he felt was the right path to travel, with a legend in Hecate, an old friend, but now incredibly, the colonel; a soldier who was famous throughout the kingdoms. Most of all, he had a new axe, which he promised himself he would thank Zidaini for....Someday.

Calum slowly ate a cake, admiring the comfortable silence between them, and the butterflies that flitted across the garden to descend on to the flowers that were all around them. With white and pink wings, they flapped over the group, to gently land on their chosen perch.

Zidaini had fed himself well, and rose from the verge, holding his flat belly with satisfaction. "Come on, Calum, let's look at the graves." They walked through the gardens to the small gravesite. "These are so old," he said.

The graves through time had succumbed to erosion over the years. Names and messages had faded away. Each had a bird of prey, surrounded in the stone carving of fire.

"I guess they thought the god would bring them back,"

Zidaini said.

"Stupid people, that's how religion works best, plays on your hope, dragging you in with brainwashing when you're at your weakest, or when you're young and know no better," Calum said. Zidaini stared at him.

"Calum, what are you on about? Our people don't worship gods that are given scripture with, or named by us."

Calum shook his head. "I don't know where that came from."

"I'm sure it's right somewhere," Zidaini said. "You could be wrong about Isis, Samiaraita hasn't called her princess," Zidaini mentioned, "you could be completely wrong," he said smiling.

"She got to him while we were distracted. She could've convinced him to stay quiet." Calum was looking down at a grave. "Valky likes your axe."

"Yeah! I'm waiting for him to get the guts to thank me."

There was a silence between them as they looked through the graves. "It's not here," Calum broke the silence.

Zidaini looked strangely at him. "What's not here?"

"Phoenix!"

"How do you know?" Zidaini asked curiously.

"I can feel all the gods we get close to. Just wasn't always sure. Anyway, the Phoenix is gone, dead or just flown away, it ain't coming back," Calum said.

"Ok! I'll get everyone going," Zidaini said, believing without doubt. He had already accepted Calum's ability with the gods. Zidaini left him alone, and Calum just stood listening to make sure, he heard nothing but the birds and rustling leaves.

45

A FAMILY OF SORTS

Tika gripped hold of the cell bars, leaning against the door in boredom, staring down the narrow corridor of white-washed walls. The skirting was stained brown and dirty, over a concrete floor, unwashed and dotted with grime and blood.

She could see down the corridor of twenty-two cells, split halfway by a passageway out. At the end was an office. Her vision was perfect, and could read the 'Block Chief' engraved on to the wood. She could hear someone repeating the same words over and over again; it made her think of someone rocking back and forth in their insanity.

"Mousy! Mousy! Mousy!"

She groaned at her predicament.

The chief's door threw open. Tika fell to the concrete, cringing in false agony. The chief passed each cell to a heckle of abuse, and pleas which followed her footsteps. She did not look into any of the cells, her eyes fixated on the newcomer.

Tika took glances at the chief as the big-built woman came to her cell.

"What's with you, child?" asked an angry face.

Tika groaned and moaned as she spoke. "I don't know, must have been bitten by a rat."

The chief stared down at her "You shouldn't pretend to be sick, for when you are, no one will help you," the chief said, her face in front of the bars.

"Stupid bitch!" Tika cried, she crawled up the bars still acting as if she had been stricken by the plague. She reached level with the woman's breasts.

"Be careful what you say, Adinan. You're to spend a week in gaol, plus one for pretending to be sick."

"What!?" Tika slammed her hand at the bars in front of her, and at the chief's spotted face. The chief involuntarily shot back from the bars, and immediately went from startled to angered.

"Three! You shouldn't be so frustrated, it's only a few weeks of no food." The chief was laughing as she went away.

Tika smirked, she had distracted the chief long enough with her tantrum that she was able to get the lump of keys from the chief's waist. She searched through the keys quickly, trying each one in the lock, until the echoing clang of the lock was turned. She pushed it slowly open, believing it wouldn't be making the creaking noise, and alerting her presence, if it wasn't for the fact she was trying to escape.

The first cell she went past, a man whose beard had overtaken his face sat motionless, staring at nothing. *'Don't want to end up like that,'* she thought to herself. Most of the cells watched her go by, whispering to let them out. She tried to tell them she was getting her weapons first. She had no plans to help them. She surreptitiously moved along the corridor, listening out for any incoming guards, and especially the chief. She got to the last cell before the passageway, when the lunatic, sitting and rocking how she had imagined him doing, piped up on his sighting of her.

"Escapee, escapee, escapee!" He repeated over, while clapping his hands at her escape. She tried in vain to get him to be silent, tried to shut him up, even banging on the bars didn't help. He just didn't take it into his head. She gave up on the waving and whispering, as he continued repeating words. Though the words had changed. "Gaian, Gaian, Gaian!" She knew the guards were now getting suspicious, and no doubt already on their way towards her. Tika scrambled through the keys, trying to unlock the crazed middle-aged man's cell. She got it open and grabbed the lunatic, and swung him round into the passageway. Tika ran down the corridor, to the chief's office, hoping desperately that her weapons were there.

The chief shoved pass the lunatic who provided barely an obstacle for the large chief. Two other guards wrestled with the lunatic who gave an all-out resistance, fighting and slamming them into the walls. At the first hits that gave warning to them, they backed off each time he lashed out at them.

Inside the office, papers piled up from the floor, creating gingerly towers that looked set to fall. Tika bolted the door, and went to the chief's desk where papers of new prisoners were still unfinished. She scanned through them until she found hers. "Two months, the fat cow!" The chief banged on the door. Tika picked up her weapons. They had been left on a pile of others. In the corner was a grate, which she snapped open. She looked down it, and at the very end was light. She turned back around, and took the papers, burning them in the chief's own wax candle. Tika left the papers to turn to ash with someone else's, and crawled through the grate. She squeezed through the wet tunnel, and the sound of the office door being smashed open behind her echoed up the small air tunnel, and vibrated throughout the office.

The chief searched the room. "Wher-!" She looked down at the open grate. "Escape, two year sentence." She stormed out from her office with her chair in hand. She went straight up behind the lunatic and smashed the chair, which shattered into pieces, over the crazed man's head. "Put him into his cell!" She blasted. "You! Call out the guard. We have an escapee."

Σ

Tika crawled out to the roadside to stares from some old people. She smiled at her escape, taking in the fresher air. She ran down the road, taking the first left which she was sure would take her to the airstation.

"Tika!" Tika stopped in her tracks, and looked to the familiar voice. She couldn't help but smile at who she saw, and jogged over to the woman, who carried at her waist some leather bottles of various potions. More likely to have some molotovs on her person than healing remedies. "I take you just escaped?" She had a double round-headed hammer on her back, the handle as long as her, the head bigger then any part of her width. She was going to smash through the cells until she had found Tika, and now was thankful she didn't have to.

"I'm an artist, and they don't have any file of me," Tika said proudly.

"I'm sure it isn't too difficult to find a red-haired girl in dirty, unwashed clothes, and is an Adinan in Lulsani. Hmmm?" The woman told her.

Tika turned her face in embarrassment.

"Now, let's get going. We head for the airstation."

They made their way down a street, stopping at the doorway of a tavern that had chairs and tables sitting outside, where people drank, and ate, and enjoyed the nicer part of Lulsani. This was an area where several restaurants and small shops sat, a quieter part than the airstations hub, where many shops filled the streets surrounding the station. Here was a piece in the most polite human city on Gaia.

They looked from the doorway, down the street they had come. Police and prison guards were racing down the street towards them. The old people had told the chief the direction that Tika had fled.

"We have to take to the alleyways," the woman told her. Tika obeyed without remark, following the woman as she led the way, running down the nearest alley.

The chief saw the faintest touch of Tika's red hair, she roared her chasers on, desperate to regain her prisoner.

The woman grabbed a prepared leather bottle from her waist, stuffing a rag into the bottle. She made her hand set ablaze with fire which took to the rag straight away. She dropped the bottle to the ground at an intersection, stopping on the other side. The bottle exploded as the fire touched the liquid inside. Smoke plumed and smothered the entire intersection. The woman dragged Tika into the corner store, and took her through the shop and up the back stairs to the second floor. The shopkeeper, made no acknowledgment of them, and continued to read from a brown paperbook. Tika was led to a room, with basic food supplies, grains of coffee, and a few loaves of bread that the woman didn't think they would be using.

"This is my store, bought it last month. It's quaint, and serves this purpose," the woman told her, listening to the police and guards running off in different directions as the smoke begun to clear, and reveal nothing that could threaten them.

Σ

The chief did not bother to continue the chase. She grabbed one policewoman and sent her off to get more reinforcements and to send them off to the airstation and port. She herself walked to the airstation; she was certain that would be where the criminals would head.

Σ

"Did you come for me?" Tika asked, hoping for a positive answer.

"My troubled child, of course I did." Tika tried to hide her happiness, but couldn't help to smile. "We'll have to go to my airship. I'll cut short my trip here, and get us out of the city."

"You have an airship! How did you get that Aurelia?"

"That, my young'un, is a secret," she answered. "Just remember the name of the airship is the Ravanov. You know you're quite lucky. If we hadn't seen you sneaking to the city gatehouse, you may never have got help from us. You should think things through a little bit more. It doesn't cost much to get a pass for the border crossing." Aurelia leaned against the wall, thinking the place needs a few touches of furniture.

Tika just hid the smile on her face.

Σ

The airstation of Lulsani loomed over the city, with four portals for receiving airships. The four portals swamped the incoming airships. All down the airstation's tall, narrow structure were turrets that projected out from the walls, with windows that looked out across the width of the airstation, and gave persons a view of the entire landscape beyond the city walls. The roof of the airstation had its own restaurant, up in the clouds. On a clear day, a person could see for kilometres over the city walls, while lunching or dining on the finest cuisine in Lulsan. Draped down the airstation was yellow, white and the dark blue of Lulsani, distracting the attention of Tika as they headed for the port.

The very highest of the portals was for the military of any country allied to Lulsan. The other three were allocated for freighters and passengers. The airships were powered by the newest of steam engines, and massive rotary blades lifted the airships.

As Aurelia and Tika walked on, they could see the Royal Losonia slowly entering the very top of the station, its cannon port holes closed across its hull. Tika stared upwards falling behind. Aurelia stopped, and begun shaking her head. "Tika! Tika, move!"

"Hey, Aurelia!" Three men and a Gaian waved them over.

They came together before a plaza while Tika looked over the crowded park. A waterfall was in its center, with benches circling out from the water until they reached the two streets running parallel with the curved plaza. In front of the entrance to the airstation were the Lulsani police, and they were checking any Adinan that came near the port's entrance.

"My nemesis is here," she moaned as she finally caught up with Aurelia.

The chief looked over the people, regarding each person, with a searching stare.

"Oh don't worry about them. Take it you upset a hornet's nest?" The scruffy-haired and yellow-eyed Gaian boy said. He was wearing a brown jacket over a blue shirt that had black hide arms, and black scruffy trousers.

"Yes Jorgejia," Aurelia answered, looking out at the police, and wondering about a way in that didn't involve confrontation, "I hope you lot have hatched a plan, John?" She asked looking at a young man wearing a cap.

"We have hatched a plan; take a look," John said. Tika and Aurelia peered into the bag, one of three.

"Urgh! That's disgusting!" Tika stepped away, with a sickly look. The bags were filled with gooladi, and alive. Most of the people on Gaia can't handle Gooladi's slime and smell.

"I get the idea, John. I take it you and Chekov are on this detail?" Aurelia asked.

"And you, ma'am. I think she will be too squeamish." The blond-haired human, Chekov, handed over a third pack.

"While me and Tank will annoy the guards," Jorgejia added, standing beside his muscle-bound friend who towered far above him. The Adinan was a natural powerhouse and had become Jorgejia's friend from their first meeting, a bonding that had drove them to always team together.

"That shouldn't be too difficult for you," Aurelia said, giving him a pat on the head.

He twisted his face at her gesture.

"Let's do this," Aurelia ordered.

They had all moved into position. Jorgejia and Tank drifted closer and closer to the chief and her few guards, waiting for their moment to strike.

Tika hid behind Aurelia, as they moved with the crowd. "Remember, people will panic. As the gooladi start hopping, we start running." Tika wasn't listening, her eyes were staring at the bag filled with wriggling gooladi, she despised them above all else.

The bags were opened near the throng that were entering the airstation. With the bags dumped, the gooladi bounced free, burping and dropping their excrement over the floor.

273

The crowd ran wild, screaming as the creatures leapt over them. Even the guards of the prison and the police couldn't help but run away. The few that stayed had their swords out in their hands, hacking at the Gooladi that frightened most of the crowd.

Jorgejia and Tank pretended to be scared witless, and ran screaming into the chief who had been standing unafraid. She was bowled over by them. "Oh, sorry! Pardon," Jorgejia blurted falling over her. Tank's weight on top added to squashing her. She grunted at the infuriating two, as they flattened her.

Aurelia pushed Tika through the entrance, and Tika was screaming and squirming as gooladi ran at her feet. The others ran in behind, even Jorgejia and Tank had left the chief to get up from her trampled grounding. They charged through the barely-guarded airstation gate, and into the foyer; the shopping centre of the airstation. The inter kingdom airport was a jurisdiction of the airstation's own guard. A safe haven.

"Shall we get something to eat?" Tika asked. She hadn't eaten much, just some bread to take away some of the starvation. Jorgejia and Tank ran straight past her, their eyes already on the food bar; ordering as soon as they caught the attention of the waitress. Tika and Aurelia went and sat at a table in the fairly quiet bar. Aurelia told Jorgejia to get them something, then she turned her eyes to Tika.

"What have you been doing?" Aurelia asked. The frantic screams were still echoing out from the entrance, the gooladi had not been dealt with just yet.

"Oh not much. Just a few deals to keep me going. Everything has gone pear-shaped since I saw those two Gaian boys," she moaned. Aurelia laughed at her.

"You stole from them?"

"Their girlfriend that was with them had precious stones, I'm sure of it, especially the way they chased me."

Aurelia mouthed the word stone, thinking of precious gems, it burned in her mind. "Stones of gods? Or everyday stone?" She questioned.

"The gods, I'm certain of it. I was this close." She put her finger to thumb with a slight gap between. "But he pinched it back just as I leapt off the train."

Aurelia let out a hush in awe. "You leapt off a train. While moving?"

"Yeh!" Tika's gaze went distant.

"Why are you thinking about them?"

"I'm not!"

Jorgejia and Tank came over with their food, plonking it on to the table, and shoving it over to them. Four plates, piled high with chips and burger each, a beef in bread, with relish.

"Thanks guys!" She turned her attention back to Aurelia. "The stones would be worth a fortune. What I saw convinced me they had a Castra stone, the sapphire. I'm positive on it." She took a bite out of her burger, losing half the relish inside to her plate.

"They must have been pretty good, the sapphire is suppose to be in the hands of the royal family," Aurelia said, as Chekov went straight past with a single wave to acknowledge them, he was off to start the Ravanov. John went to the bar in his own need for food; he pulled up a chair beside them, once he had ordered.

"You should have seen that fat woman's face. She looked so mean at me. She wasn't happy with us flattening her," Jorgejia beamed, his light brown tail waving behind his back.

"I think she was scared of me," Tank added, his massive body made the chair vanish behind him.

"I think she needs love," Jorgejia said, smiling at Tank, who wasn't sure whether he was grinning at him or at what Jorgejia had just said.

"Do I?"

The five of them shot a look at the agitated chief. Staunch in her job, she was making it clear she would get them one day. She stood clutching her knuckles, needing to bash some heads.

They knew she couldn't arrest them, but that didn't stop

them from getting scared.

The bar called for John, and he rushed away to get his food, grateful for the release.

"Right, got to go. Sorry!" Jorgejia said, grabbing as much of his chips as he could, and stuffing the burger down his throat.

"Yep, me too!" Tank kept pace, already filled with food.

"You won't get far. When you mess up, I'll get you," the chief shouted after them.

"Ok.. I'm off," Tika said, "nice to have met you, and escaped. Bye!" She scarpered quickly.

Aurelia couldn't help but grin, she had none of the fear that had made everyone scamper. She smiled at the chief. "John, we're leaving," she ordered. She left the chief to stare after them.

John watched them go. "That's so unfair."

The chief looked scornfully at him.

"Em!.. Bye!"

Σ

They all ran to the dock where the Ravanov was stationed. It was the newest of the new, with flight controls in the bridge at the front instead of the back. The top deck had become just space for the rotary blades, the passengers having plenty of red carpeted hallways and the finest crafted cabins. The engine rooms were the only exception to the sleek look of the Ravanov's exterior, the engines were bulky and noisy, and smoke drifted along the ceiling. The Ravanov even had a quality eating area, and a fine kitchen.

The biggest feature of the Ravanov was not its polished finish, or its well designed layout, or the fact it was one of the fastest airships on Gaia. It was the fact it had five demi culverins either side of its bulk, the only non military vessel to do so.

Chekov had already got the Ravanov moving, and the ship shook and rumbled the dock around it. The horn bellowed to let the airstation know it was on its way out. In the lower levels, the engines were kept in pristine order. Kane and Ricky were in a constant, never-ending check whenever the vessel moved, while Lyasa and Eyasa ran checks on the rotors, and propellers; never were the latter two found easily aboard the Ravanov.

Outside, John had only just reached the Ravanov. "Wait for meeee!" He cried. His burger uneaten, he carried it running up to the side door of the Ravanov. He ran and ran, his heart trying to keep up with his desperation. The side door was drifting away. The Ravanov was moving forward. John chased with takeaway in hand, tears straining his eyes. "Pleease!" John was at the side door, his body already giving in to his weak muscles.

It opened, and Tank reached an arm out, and grabbed John, while still holding on to the doorway, and pulled him in. The burger fell from John's hands, splatting to the floor. John began crying in relief.

45

PERPIOUS, THE CAPITAL
OF THE IMPERIUM

Bushia stood beside a large map of the world with a face of frustration and a stern euphoria. Grand general Bortedes and several majors, who were General Hastatia, and Narsisis chosen voices, were with the senator. Major Niratan waited at the back, watching the man he so worshipped. Not present was anyone from the Nortedes Specialli.

Hades entered with papers in his claws. Bushia greeted him with a smile. The rest gave looks filled with disdain.

"Hades, welcome to the war room." Bushia waved Hades over. The twisted figure couldn't tell for sure whether the smile was genuine, or just a false face for him. But at least those around him showed their true feelings of disdain on their faces for him to clearly see. He preferred their distaste, it made him feel proud.

The room was far smaller than what Hades had seen of the normal halls and rooms of the Imperium hierarchy. This one had maps of each empire upon the walls around the map of the world in the centre.

"My reports on Liberian and Adinan fleet and army movements, sire." Hades passed the papers over to Bushia.

Bortedes was standing typically ceremoniously. "Your honour, runners report Niguarga has fallen, and the Arosian Specialli are enroute to Little Cravi." The senator observed the map, as Bortedes pushed chess-like pieces around on it. "The Hastati Specialli are waiting on confirmation."

Bushia became displeased, clearly showing it upon his face. "Why does he need confirmation?" He fumed.

"Sire. Hastatia is just making sure he has received the orders from the senate, and not false orders from someone pretending to be acting as the senate, sire." Bortedes explained.

Bushia creased his face in frustration. "Order him in. We both will," Bushia ordered.

"Certainly, sire," he paused and played with the Nortedes Specialli pieces. "Sire, the Nortedes wait for their general at Eastania. Apart from that, reports of very little casualties, sire. Almost as if we haven't invaded anyone."

Bushia smiled. The results were satisfying.

"Sire, at Caracoa, the Emperor's son, Julious Lousous, has built up an attacking army. Warships of the Armada guards are docked at the town, and the Royal first airfleet of twenty airships are also based outside Caracoa. They will attack." Hades gave the information as if he had been standing among the army of the Liberian Empire and had been watching their every movement.

Bushia stared down at the pieces that were to represent the Liberians. "In that case, Grand General Bortedes, you will lead the eastern front. Take control of the Nortedes, and take the Eastania regiments in a counter-strike."

Bortedes hesitated "...Sire, the Nortedes cannot be led by anyone but Nortedes himself, even his colonels will get more say then any other general."

Bushia slammed his palms on to the table. "You will lead them in any way you can," he raged, annoyed with the general's reluctance.

"Do you still plan to attack Bamtam, sire?" Hades asked, hoping the senator has had a change of heart.

"Yes," he simply said.

"If you do, you'll be facing the entire eastern continent. The Adinans woul-"

"Shut up!" Bushia shouted, his veins seething, he leaned on to the table upon his elbows. "How much of a fleet does the Dracian territories have?" He asked, calming down. He didn't notice the officers giving looks to each other, asking questions of the man.

"One hundred and thirty ships in two armadas, Tripoli and Scipio. It may be best if you leave them for another day in the future. Perhaps after the eastern wars." Hades grew angry as Bushia laughed at him. "They also have at least a hundred thousand soldiers, plus armed plebeians." Bushia's laughing was annoying him far too much. "Why do you laugh?"

"The Dracians are irrelevant. The Stranie people have informed me of their wares, and they have asked us to take Port La Harve. The alliance was born today," Bushia grinned, much to the shock of those few around him. Only Niratan seem not to care on the huge task being placed on the military. "The Hastati Specialli will invade the Dracians, and wiped out all that stand in their way. We will wipe out the filthy creatures."

Hades looked horrified. "Sire, you are taking on far too much."

"Hades, shut up!" He blanked the cold figure out. "I, the voice of the Imperium, have found something that has the potential to win the war on its own. Should the war not be over, by the time the Liberian Empire is finished, our new finding will destroy all in our path."

The hall accepted Bushia's words. Hades found it infuriating. Even though they had been angered at the senator's plans, they accepted the orders with loyalty, and Hades just didn't understand their obedience.

"The Stralayans have conceded us El Gare and Flurnia city as our own. This deal includes the Forbidden Mountains, that means we will have a natural fortress, while at the same time give us access to the city of the lost people."

"If it exists," Hades interrupted.

Bushia ignored Hades again. "Now, go conquer." They rushed away, accepting the papers of their orders.

Hades left quickly, angered with the senator. Once the clatter of feet left the room, Major Niratan took his place beside Bushia.

"Soon, Niratan, soon Gaia will be mine. Just think what fun you'll have with the Lulsan Empire as your own." He grinned, thinking about all the wealth and riches that will be his.

Niratan thought nothing of the territory given to him, his thoughts were that of standing beside the fat bald man of Bushia.

46

OVER SAN ADINA'S HORIZON

Calum hung his head over the side of the starboard rail, staring out over the horizon, at the mountain city of San Adina, which sat upon mount Adina, proud and pristine. The sea below glistened with waves in a never-ending movement sparkling in the light of the sun.

He was glad to be heading back to the Liberian Empire, where he had found a home, and a deep liking for the place. As he looked across at the yellow, red and gold city of San Adina, he knew now he was almost home, albeit he knew there was something missing, it was still his home.

"She's beautiful!" Zidaini said, joining Calum's side. "You can't make it out from here, but the palacio is the center building, with an obelisk made of glass at its center. The palace is on three tiers. The obelisk starts from the bottom, and its tip is higher than the palacio roof. You can also see the airstation, it's massive, and the tallest in all of Gaia. It's right beside the palacio, joined by a bridge of brick and mortar. On the other side are the huge steps from the bottom to the top of the mountain. We can see the tram for taking people up and down now from the train. Adina is getting too advanced, too quickly."

Calum listened to his voice, and the clunking of the ship. The propellers forever spinning, keeping them airborne. "Is that forest?" He asked as the city came nearer, as the airship flew towards Libernian.

"The Enchanted Woods, some wildlife, but nothing like Foresta Nero; it's pretty surreal there. So they say. For some reason most people don't trek into the actual woods, they just skirt around it instead... It'll give us something to do whenever we get there."

Valkesies was on the bridge looking out at a bearing airship. It had been getting closer for a while, following their every move, but now it seem to be picking up speed. "Is that military?" He asked the captain of the merchant vessel. Valkesies was becoming concerned as the ship bore closer. "Captain?"

The captain came from his watching the crew, looking at the nearing ship. He grabbed a telescope from his second, and peered down the scope. "Well, that's Liberian military. A lot faster than ours," the captain said. "Getting awful close, mind you. Perhaps they mean to scare us, have a laugh, you know, Gaians in all," the captain smiled. Valkesies frowned at the excuse.

"Or perhaps they mean to blow us out of the sky," The Elseni grabbed the taffrail in his frustration, then rushed below deck.

"Pilot, I think we have a problem."

Calum and Zidaini watched Valkesies race down to passengers quarters; with the expressions of anger mixed with concern written upon his face. The Elseni clearly had his axes on his mind. The boys already had theirs on.

"You wanna go stern?" Zidaini asked. Calum ran up the stairs with him, and they stared out at the airship. The captain issued the call to arms, as the Liberian vessel came corner bow to corner aft.

"They wanna board us!" Zidaini called. Passengers had crowded the bridge, taking fearful looks at the manoeuvring military airship.

Valkesies returned with Hecate, Isis and Samiaraita in tow. The wind rushed through them as the merchant vessel's crew spread over port side. Fear of an expecting doom stabbing at their hearts and minds.

"They wouldn't attack a merchant ship, surely?" Calum asked Zidaini.

The Liberian vessel crept up to broadside, keeping with the merchant airship's manoeuvres. The broadside cannons were opened, and primed.

"They will fire! Get away from larboard side. Pilot, get us away!" He shouted. The pilot listened rather than stick around to face the cannons. The warship dropped and matched them as they tried to get away from the broadside of cannons.

"Where are the Gaians?" Zidaini queried. He could see the humans and Adinans upon the deck, waiting to board, but Gaians seemed non existent.

Calum looked at the lack of movement from the passengers. "Get away from her cannons!" he blasted.

Grapples shot from the deck of Liberian airship, ripping into the side, shards of the wood that held her together, splintered and shattered. The merchant vessel was stuck in the military airship's grasp. The cannons roared, exploding with a loud boom. The round shots smashed through the decks of the vessel, sending every defender off their feet, amongst the shredding wood. Two unfortunate souls went careering off the side of the airship, from the impact of the cannon balls. Two rotors were torn apart, one fell over the side, the other buckled and fell to the deck, digging in through the planks of wood. More shards went tearing through people, as the crash sent shrapnel flying across the ship.

Calum was laid out on the deck, his sword out, gripped in his hand. "Get up, get up now, they come for us!" He shouted, rousing the defenders to action.

A roar went up on the warships side, as the privateers leapt over from the Liberian ship, with cutlass and sabre in hand, they charged through the dazed merchants who could barely resist the prepared attackers that ploughed through them, killing several within the first rush on the ship.

Hecate ran into the privateers, sending them to their deaths with his fast magic. Lightning and fire shot out in multiple shots, of which only a few missed, the rest wounded, or killed the enemy to agonizing deaths. Valkesies went to work, with his axes wielding, the new axe slicing through, instead of tearing through two privateers in his first assault. His other axe chopped through like he was hacking at a raw and tough lump of meat with a blunt knife. It torn through the bone and skin without ease. The blood of his work caused two other privateers to slip and fall, they were easy prey for Zidaini, who leapt over the bannister of the bridge and thrust both his dagger and spartha into the pair, his hands moved quickly, striking several in each of his attempts at killing the enemy.

Calum wielded his emerald sword with finesse, each parabola resulted in a clean cut, or slice through a privateer. He slashed his sword through one enemy, and ignoring the blood coming from the chopped open arm, he severed the legs of another man who was trying to get at Isis. She picked up the man's fallen cutlass, and as Calum turned to intercept a woman's strike against him, Isis thrust the blade through a man swinging his sabre at Calum. He would've thanked her but found himself dealing with another privateer. He kept where Isis was in his thoughts as he fought, not allowing anyone near her. For some reason he felt he should protect her and was sure she couldn't handle a fight.

$$\Sigma$$

Samiaraita woke grabbing his sore head, at the bottom of the stairs leading to amidships cargo hold. He brushed off the bits of kinderling and broken wood that covered him, and in a strain got himself corrected. He pulled out his katana, and ran up the stairs, smashing the hilt of his sword into the face of a running privateer, and turning the point towards the chest of the woman, he ran the blade clean through her to stick out the other side, bits of her back ripped off on to the deck. He went straight into the chaos of the fighting.

Aboard the Liberian warship, the few Gaians that were on the vessel, had sighted their fellow Gaians aboard, and on sighting Colonel Samiaraita, they began to disobey their orders, and drew their katanas and went chopping through the grapple's ropes, ethe sharpened blades only needing the single chop through the thick cable.

The Traicans stood watching.

"Annoying Gaians!"

"Pestering Gaians!"

"Can not stop them."

"Doesn't matter, mercenaries useless."

"Fire the cannons!"

Valkesies and Hecate fought side to side, against the remaining privateers

"Not very good, are they," Valkesies called, skewering a man with the axe, an impossible feat by most persons' ability.

"Reminds me of the good old days," Hecate said with a laugh, as he unleashed a ball of fire which burrowed through a man's chest, his face cringing still, dropping to the shattered planks dead.

The ship dropped as the ropes were cut. Another round of round shot blasted the airship. The cannon balls shot out and crashed against the masts that held the propellers, the splitters of wood scattered across the ship, ricocheting off the bodies and flooring. Many of the masts fell to the ground below, others crashed through the decking, taking both privateers, and passengers with the falling propellers.

The merchant vessel was fast losing altitude, without the propellers it would drop to the sea.

Colonel Samiaraita and Zidaini kept their impeccable balance among the fallen, and went gliding through the unstable deck, and the fallen bodies, and ran their blades through the remaining privateers.

The captain and one surviving crewman went crawling over to the bow where Calum and Isis held on, as the ship veered towards a mountain with a flat grey stone top, and sheer dropping sides. They stared at the nearing peak.

"We have to brace for impact. There's no way we can turn the ship," the crewman shouted.

"How the hell are we going to brace? Does it look like it'll be worth it?" The captain groaned, staring at the wall of the mountain. They held on tight, watching the wall, trying to keep their balance.

A possibility, an idea, a way out formed in Calum's mind. "Isis, what god flies?" He shouted over the wind. She thought only for a moment.

"Quetzalcoatl!" She exclaimed, with pleased remembrance.

"Call him to the stern," he shouted to her. He saw her face look confused. "Even without the diamond in your hand, he will hear you." Calum ran across the swaying ship. He stood at the stern, behind the ship's wheel which had been ripped in half by a cannon ball.

With the mountain getting nearer, its cliff face was looming closer. The ship rattled and creaked, and bits of loose timber left the deck for the open sky. Some rotors barely turned. While Isis raised her hands to her chest, and whispered to the god. The last of her words, "help us!"

Calum, in awe, watched Quetzalcoatl appear into the sky. The great white hawk, with a body the size of the airship's width, wings that spanned countless feet in a magnificent beauty, its claws ripped into the aft, gripping at the airship. It flapped its great wings, and the airship jolted as it slowed. Everyone looked for somewhere to hold on to. The massive hawk, Quetzalcoatl lifted the airship. With all its strength it would not stop the eventual crash, but Quetzalcoatl could slow and lift the ship, at least from impacting the face of the mountain. The merchant vessel was now heading for the peak of the mountain. The god flapped and spread it wings to slow the descent.

"Get to the sides of ship, and prepare to jump," Calum roared. He knew the vessel would crumble in on itself as it struck the peak of the mountain. They wouldn't survive no matter how slow the impact was.

Calum held on at the larboard side, he would jump just before impact, at one of Quetzalcoatl's thrusts. It was the only way he could survive the fall without breaking bones. "One last big beat of your wings," he whispered. The god heeded.

The ship smashed into the mountain peak. Quetzalcoatl

leapt from the stern, and into the air. The bow crumbled as the vessel ploughed through the grey stone, scraping across, the vessel turned in on itself, parts of the airship flew out in different directions, as the structure became a mass of shattered wood piled together. After the long scrapping across the peak, everything came to a halt. No more bits of wood flew through the air; it stopped cracking on to the stone. The ship gave one final collapse. The makeshift runway was strewed with parts of the ship, and bodies of the dead. A light haze of smoke drifted across the peak.

$$\Sigma$$

The Liberian warship continued on its way, their commanders pleased with their effort.

And so concludes Book One of the GAIA series. Book Two will be at your favorite book store in the fall of 2010.

12004372R00156

Made in the USA
Charleston, SC
04 April 2012